KARID
SVESTI FATED MATES BOOK 5
WAVY MARTIN

OTHER BOOKS BY
Wavy Martin

SVESTI FATED MATES SERIES
Vared

Devik

Ash'n

Ronan

Table of Contents

Prologue

ALL DATES MENTIONED are using Earth's calendar.

Unbeknownst to humans, since the early 1900s an alien warrior race called the Svesti have guarded Earth's region of space, as well as others, from another warrior race called the Zuvgran. Not because they see great potential in humans, but because the Zuvgran are that bad.

How bad you ask? Well, the Zuvgran invade worlds, kill the elderly, the very young, and some of the males. They take the rest as slaves or subjects for their experiments. Ruled by an Emperor, they strip conquered worlds of natural resources and move on. They attack anyone they feel is weaker, so ships or colonies are unsafe as well. As a whole, the species doesn't engender affectionate feelings.

A king and council representing their twelve Houses rule the Svesti home world, Costonia. They worship a deity they refer to as the Goddess and would look at home in gladiator pits with their toned bodies, tight black pants, and leather. But their technology is much more advanced than anything on Earth.

The Svesti also call each other by their last names. Only family or close friends use first names. If there is more than one present with the same last name, they use titles as well. Titles are also used in formal situations or when the situation calls for additional respect or gravitas. Females are called by their first name preceded by Lady.

In the early 2000s, the Zuvgran released a virus on Costonia killing eighty percent of the Svesti females, including all female young, and rendering the remainder infertile. It's now 2037 and for thirty years Svesti scientists have been searching for ways to keep their race from dying out. No other race has been biologically compatible, until—you guessed it—humans.

Like all large groups of beings, they're not all bad or all good, although as a whole, the Svesti check mostly boxes in the good column. The Svesti Council remains divided. Some want to invade Earth and abduct females to impregnate, while others believe any young born of a Svesti-human couple would no longer be Svesti. The current ruler, King Traxen Sovex wants to open up negotiations with Earth to procure willing human females for breeding or troth contracts.

A troth contract is similar to a short-term marriage. A breeding contract, now called a birthing contract, is specifically for the bearing of Svesti young. The Svesti also have true mates, where they have the biological urge to bite the other and mate for life. True mating supersedes both contracts. The Svesti used to have fated mate bonds where it was believed the Goddess blessed a couple by gifting them the one being in the universe who is their other half. However, there hasn't been a fated mate bond recorded on Costonia in over a century.

King Sovex sent Commander Vared Durek of the *Invictus*, a space cruiser holding 3,000 warriors, to Earth to initiate first contact. Durek's long-time best friends serve on the *Invictus* as well—Lieutenant Karid Wurvez, head tactical officer; Lieutenant Devik Tolvex, head security officer; and Healer Ash'n Rivezt, head healer.

After their research of Earth, Durek initiated first contact with six countries based on the size of their territory or influence—as humans haven't figured out how to become one planetary entity. Each country convinced or ordered one woman to take the two-month trip to Costonia, live there, gather information for fourteen months, then return to Earth. Of course being human, Earth's leaders wanted information about Svesti military capabilities, weaponry, and technology.

Unbeknownst to the six women, Earth's leaders allowed the Svesti to believe the women volunteered to be part of a Choosing at the King's Court, where they would choose a male for a breeding or troth contract. Needless to say, when this information became known to the women, they didn't take it well.

The American, Talia Sullivan, was appointed as an Ambassador by the President and worked with the Svesti on a fair treaty. About a month and a half into the trip, Durek received word from the *Defiant*, the ship they left to protect the space near Earth, that Earth's leaders publicly proclaimed the Svesti kidnapped the six women. Earth's leaders called for increased military funding and gave the appearance of gearing up for war.

Talia developed a plan to get the correct information to Earth. King Sovex approved and allocated resources. When all was said and done, King Sovex named Durek and Talia Co-Ambassadors to Earth.

During their travel to Costonia, Commander Durek, his trusted friends, and the women became aware of at least one Svesti traitor onboard the *Invictus* who was communicating with a Svesti noble on the home world. In a temporary alliance with the Zuvgran, these traitors were attempting to kill human fertility via another virus. What the traitors didn't know was the virus also killed Svesti male fertility. Fortunately, the Svesti, with the help of the human physician and the botanist/biochemist, Natasha Petrov and Lin Chang respectively, developed a vaccine to protect humans and Svesti before the virus spread.

So far, the loyal Svesti have not been able to identify the traitors. Based on information they do know, Durek sent Wurvez and another warrior, Grulen Jevax, on a secret mission. However, they missed four daily check-ins so Durek sent another team of five warriors to find them.

As this is Karid's story, the tale begins just prior to Wurvez and Jevax leaving the *Invictus* on their mission.

For those faithful readers who have read the previous books, all I can say is—*I know, I know. The characters made me do it.*

- Wavy

Chapter 1

LIEUTENANT KARID WURVEZ shook his head as he left the on-call room of the *Invictus*, leaving behind two of his three best friends—Commander Vared Durek and Lieutenant Devik Tolvex. Vared had shown them news footage of Earth's leaders accusing the Svesti of kidnapping human females. *I don't know why I'm surprised. Those same leaders lied to the human females less than two months ago by not telling them they were meant for breeding or troth contracts. At least Lady Talia, the American Ambassador, had a plan for informing humans of the truth.*

During the meeting, Devik received an alert showing the missing Frezzian freighter on recent scans. They knew the ship had been making regular runs to XB9428B to a hidden Zuvgran lab. *Well, at least until we blew the lab up.*

Karid strode quickly to his quarters to pack for his mission. They suspected the freighter was making supply drops to other Zuvgran labs. If they could follow it, or even better, infiltrate its database, they might increase their chances of finding more labs. It had been over thirty years and the Svesti still hadn't found the one that held information on the virus that killed most Svesti females or rendered them infertile.

As head tactical officer and second in command of the *Invictus*, it was becoming increasingly rare for Karid to be slated for missions like this one. It was not widely known that a traitor worked onboard with a noble on Costonia. These traitors attempted to sabotage the king's efforts to create a treaty with the humans. The need for secrecy while they searched for the traitors made for a short list of available warriors to send after the freighter. Fortunately, he was on that list.

In his quarters, Karid checked his go bag—something most warriors kept ready. A couple changes of clothes, a weapons harness, favorite weapons, credits, some survival gear, and rations encompassed the majority of the contents. He tossed in a couple water pouches, a container of cookies, and debated whether or not to take his personal project along to pass the time. Stroking the oblong chunk of black stone, he imagined the finished item once he sculpted it. He wrapped it in a soft cloth and carefully placed it in an inner pocket of his bag with the leather pouch that held his smaller sculpting tools. Glancing around one last time, he nodded in satisfaction. *That should be everything.*

His comm chimed. He smiled when he saw the message from Devik, the head security officer, telling him to meet in Hangar Bay Alpha. *Good. I still have time to stop by the kitchen before I leave.*

Picking up his bag, he headed to the dining hall. His tail swayed as he drew closer to his destination. Sniffing, he realized a new edible scent mixed with his favorite one. He dropped his belongings just inside the door and observed.

"These don't look like cookies," said Talen Previv, the head cook.

"They're bar cookies. When they cool, we cut them into smaller pieces." Ava Taylor slapped Previv's hand with a grin on her human face. "Don't touch them."

Karid crossed his arms and leaned against a wall. "How many times have I told you—no sparring in the kitchen."

Previv wiped his hands on his apron. "Lieutenant, let me guess. You are hoping to be the first to try these bar cookies. It's amazing how often you just happen to stop by when there's something new on the menu."

"Guilty. However, this time I was hoping to speak with Lady Ava privately."

Ava smiled at him, her green eyes filled with mirth. "I have no doubt some of the toffee bars will somehow leave with you when we're done." She glanced at Previv.

"Go. Talk with Wurvez. I'll guard the toffee bars." Previv's fangs flashed white against his caramel bronze skin.

Ava squeezed his forearm. "Thanks, Talen. I'll be back in a bit." She hung up her apron.

Karid straightened as she approached, admiring her curvy figure and the bounce of her red curls. He gestured for her to precede him out the door. As he picked up his bag, his eyes roved over her plump ass outlined in pants she called jeans.

"Walk with me, please," he said as they entered the brightly lit corridor. He guided them to a room.

"Where are we?" Ava looked around the room filled with cleaning bots and two tables and chairs.

Karid dropped his bag on a table and lifted her to sit on the other.

"Maintenance room." He stepped forward and inhaled her citrusy sweet scent. *Like wimma and sugar—my favorite scent.*

"What's with the bag?" Fortunately, sitting on the taller table, her height was close to his own and he didn't need to bend far.

"I'm leaving on a secret mission soon. I wanted to let you know." Extending his claws, he combed through her curls.

"Is it dangerous?"

"I laugh in the face of danger." He frowned when she didn't smile. "Wasn't that a line from one of the Earth movies we watched?"

"Yes, but I need you to answer me honestly, not with humor. Is the mission dangerous?" Her concerned eyes stared into his.

"Doubtful." He stroked her cheek with his thumb.

"Are you going alone?"

"No, there will be another warrior with me."

"Good. You'll have backup." She bit her lip and tilted her head sideways. "For how long?"

"I don't know. I hope to be back before the *Invictus* reaches Costonia. I want to see your first impression of my home world." He paused, then continued quietly, "I didn't wish to go without telling you."

"I appreciate your thoughtfulness. I would hate to think you ghosted me." Her hands caressed his forearms. *I like how her lighter skin contrasts with mine.*

"Ghosted?"

"Disappeared with no word."

"I would never willingly do that to you."

"Good."

"I'll miss you."

"You'll miss my cooking," she teased.

"That, too, but I'll miss talking with you more." He leaned closer and nuzzled her hair. "You've become important to me." His tail rubbed against her lower back.

Her eyes widened over her pert freckled nose. "You've become a big part of my life, too. I'll miss you and your antics."

"I only have a few more minutes before I have to go."

She stroked his furrowed brow with a gentle forefinger.

"Then stop wasting time and kiss me."

"As you command." His lips met hers and their tongues played with each other. Their breathing quickened as their hands roamed over each other. Long moments later, he lifted his head and smiled at her passion-glazed expression. His cock bulged in his pants. *The things she does to me.*

"You do that very well, Karid," she breathed.

"We do that well together." He rested his forehead on hers drawing her scent into him. "I really do have to leave, *raralumia.*"

"I know." Ava pouted, then hugged him. "Stay safe, warrior."

"Of course." His hands clasped her waist and he lifted her down from the table.

"Did you want me to get some toffee bars for you to take with you?"

"I don't have time. Besides, I have the leftover cookies from yesterday in my bag."

Laughing, she said, "It surprises me they lasted this long."

Grinning, he grabbed his bag and they left the room.

"Be well, Ava. I'll see you soon."

"Go. The faster you leave, the quicker you'll return." She made a shooing motion, then turned to walk back to the kitchen.

Karid strode to the lift, then looked back at her retreating figure. *When I return, raralumia, we need to talk about a future together.*

Leaving the lift, he met up with Grulen Jevax, the other warrior on the mission. They walked to Hangar Bay Alpha in silence where Devik was waiting for them.

"Here's a list of what I put onboard the *Tenacity* in addition to the normally stocked items," Devik said as he forwarded the info to their comms. "The commander also ordered emergency trackers for each of you." He held up two syringes.

Karid frowned. "We can inject them when we're on our way."

Devik's braids swooshed as he shook his head. "No, not taking the chance you'll disobey orders."

Karid grunted in annoyance. He opened his mouth wide and Devik injected the tracker underneath his tongue. Karid moved his jaw in exaggerated circular motions.

"I hate these things. They make me feel like I've got a pebble in my mouth."

Devik and Jevax laughed. Jevax opened his mouth for his.

Devik explained, "These are the upgraded trackers. We received a lot of complaints about the heat from the old ones as well as the fact that it was too easy to inadvertently activate them with the shorter codes. Clicking your teeth in a three-two-two pattern or tapping it directly with a claw in the same pattern will activate these. You should feel a minute of cold under your tongue to let you know the activation was successful. Inactivated, they should pass any frequency scan for trackers."

"With the Goddess' favor, we won't need them," said Jevax.

Devik nodded and stepped back. "Let me know when you finish your preflight checks and I'll open the bay doors. I already loaded the engine signature you're following in the *Tenacity's* computer. Stay safe and good hunting."

Karid and Jevax boarded the shuttle, stowed their bags, and headed to the cockpit. He motioned for Jevax to take the pilot's seat. Once Jevax ran his preflight checks, he requested clearance to depart. Devik opened the bay doors and the *Tenacity* left the *Invictus*. Jevax entered a course to the last known location of the Frezzian freighter and sat back.

"Lieutenant Tolvex said you would brief me on our mission."

Karid looked at the male whose skin was a reddish bronze similar to his own and gathered his thoughts.

"There is at least one traitor onboard the *Invictus* working with a noble from the home world to sabotage the king's efforts of a treaty with the humans. Healer Rivezt needed to put Lady Talia into an induced coma when someone switched out one of the uploads for the females. You know about Lady Talia and Lady Emmy being poisoned and Lady Emmy's experience with the trip-wire. When they kidnapped Lady Talia on Theron, they injected her with a virus that kills human female and Svesti male fertility."

"So that's why she and the Commander sequestered themselves on the *Intrepid*. Not PTSD like we were told." Jevax's brown eyes hardened.

"Yes. While they were there, the traitor attempted to port Lady Talia to the *Invictus*, then the other human females to the *Intrepid*, as well as used mind control on Mantoor to have him attack Commander Durek. We believe the traitor wanted to infect the other human females. Fortunately, Rivezt developed a vaccine with the aid of Ladies Natasha and Lin and inoculated everyone onboard."

"The one we were told was for a flu virus." Jevax's forehead furrowed. "But why would the traitors work to kill Svesti male fertility?"

"We believe the traitors are unaware of that aspect of the virus. It seems the noble made some sort of deal with the Zuvgran for the virus."

"Have there been other incidents?"

"Yes. Lady Lin almost fell from a sabotaged ladder in aquiponics and was also gassed in her lab. We suspect the oven explosion was meant for Lady Ava. Fortunately, she wasn't in the kitchen at the time."

"How can any Svesti try to harm females?" Jevax growled and his tail whipped furiously behind him. "Or work with the Zuvgran?"

"I don't know, Jevax." Karid sighed. "The engine signature is for a Frezzian freighter we believe has been visiting Zuvgran labs with supplies."

"Do we think the Frezzians are working with the traitors?"

Karid's ponytail brushed his shoulders as he shook his head. "It's possible, but I doubt it. It's more likely the Frezzians are just dropping off food for the Zuvgran."

Forehead wrinkling, Jevax said, "I'm not sure I see the connection between the freighter and the traitors."

"We suspected these Frezzians supplied the lab on XB9428B before the Durelians delivered Lady Talia to the Zuvgran lab there. The scientists who injected her made comments about a Svesti noble working with them. The freighter may only lead us to other labs, but we can't discount the possibility we may find additional information about the traitors. Either way, we increase our knowledge."

"What are our orders when we find the Frezzians?"

"Follow them discretely and attempt to get into their computers. If we aren't able to gather sufficient intel that way, then we can always capture one of them and interrogate them."

Jevax nodded, then tapped the console. "We're automatically scanning for the engine signature, and I've set it to alert us throughout the ship if we find it before we reach its last known position."

"How long until we get there?"

"Seven hours."

Karid released his safety restraints and stood. "Let's go check where Devik stowed everything."

"As you command."

Chapter 2

AIR SAWED IN and out of Ava's lungs as she looked up at the high ceiling of the training area of the *Invictus*. The exposed parts of her sweaty body stuck to the mat under her. Male grunts, groans, trash-talk, and flesh hitting flesh made for interesting background noise when the blood rushing through her ears subsided. Squinting, she realized the overhead lights were wide strips traversing the entire length of the area and covered by panels of something that looked like metal with circular holes in it. *I never noticed that before. Wonder why it's like that? I bet Lin would know.*

Her ruminations ended as Rachel Llewellyn blocked her view, grinning down at her, blue eyes sparkling.

"Taking a nap, Ava?" Rachel's faint British accent suits her. *Even when she's kicking ass, she's got this unflappable way about her.*

"Just lying here reviewing my life choices. Like why I voluntarily allow you to put bruises upon bruises on my weak body." Ava finally had enough breath to sigh heavily. *I'm glad I learned to pull my hair up into a high ponytail early on. At least*

I didn't get a divot in the back of my skull when I hit the mat this session.

Amusement grew on Rachel's face, framed by short blonde hair, and she held out a hand to help Ava stand.

"You're such a wimp. The Svesti have healing wands. You don't have to suffer long."

Once upright, Ava leaned forward to rest her hands on her bent knees. Damp curls stuck to her forehead and her neck.

"Shit, Rachel. I don't like to suffer at all." Ava glanced up to look at the other women—Talia rubbing her hip, Natasha stretching her back, Lin looking miserable, and Emmy tapping her foot.

"We're done for today," Rachel said. "Everybody hydrate and walk it off. You did well."

"Bullshit," muttered Ava under her breath. "The only thing I did well was fall down...repeatedly."

Lin Chang, a petite Chinese botanist with short dark hair and brown eyes, hooked her arm through Ava's elbow.

"Come on. Let's grab some water pouches and limp back to our quarters."

Ava straightened and allowed Lin to lead her to one of the cooling units in the wall. She took a water pouch from Natasha Petrov, a Russian physician, and nodded tiredly at Emmy Norton, an Australian hacker with darker skin and hair, when she handed her a towel.

"Rachel worked us hard today," said Natasha, her long blonde braid looking disheveled.

"Honestly, it was easier when she was teaching us to get out of chokeholds from behind yesterday. We hit the mats occasionally, but not over and over like today," said Talia. She brushed her auburn hair from her flushed face with a towel.

"At least you have someone to rub your hurting body," Ava groaned.

Emmy got a faraway look in her eyes. "I wonder where Devik is now."

Ava pinned Talia with a glare. "You want to add your two cents, too? All of you getting some can be irritating at times."

Lin's face grew concerned. "Are you alright, Ava? You seem cranky today."

Blowing out a breath, Ava said, "I'm sorry, guys. I really am happy for you. I think I'm hormonal or something." *No, I'm worrying about Karid and it's only been a few hours since he left.*

"I still have some chocolate left from when we left Earth. Do you think it would help?"

"That's sweet of you to offer, Lin, but I'm not sure what I need other than a long, hot bath and some quiet."

Emmy said, "Rachel looks busy schooling some of the warriors, so let's head back to our rooms and recuperate." Her curly brown ponytail swung as she continued, "I'm worried that she'll come up with something even more painful tomorrow."

They all groaned at the thought.

Leaning back in the hot, steamy water, Ava felt the tension seep out of her muscles. Closing her eyes, she reflected back on her shock when she first learned aliens existed in the Canadian Prime

Minister's office. Suddenly being faced with seven-foot-tall muscular beings with fangs, claws, and tails felt scary as hell. *The fact that they were all wore weapons harnesses didn't help calm me either.*

The Commander, Tolvex, and Karid ported out in the whitish-blue light after telling the story about their female population being decimated and Svesti scientists discovered human female compatibility. The Prime Minister and the Governor General told her they wanted her to go to the Svesti planet, Costonia, to determine what it might take for human women to adjust to the differences in cultures, especially food since she was a chef. *Honestly, they didn't give me much of a choice, even though I argued. She now knew something top secret which made her a security risk unable to walk around free until they informed the general population about the Svesti. The threat compelled her to agree or be sequestered alone for an indeterminate amount of time.*

Small waves caressed her breasts and shoulders as her legs shifted in agitation. She recalled waking up in the *Invictus* med bay with five other women and finding out the Svesti had implanted translators and trackers as well as messed with their DNA. They performed other medical procedures—nothing life-threatening or bad, but having her body changed without her consent infuriated her.

When the women discovered their Earth leaders outright lied to them and offered them to the Svesti for Choosings for troth or breeding contracts, all hell broke loose for a bit. Ava smiled at the memory of Talia facing off with the Commander on their first day. *And now they're living together in the same quarters. Who would've guessed?*

Fortunately, the Svesti backpedaled and, as a whole, treated the women with respect. *Well, with the exception of the traitor who keeps messing with us. Hopefully, with Talia back onboard the Invictus after her quarantine, we won't keep getting ported unexpectedly.*

Now she was learning Svesti cuisine as well as introducing them to Earth recipes. Her creative side loved trying to replicate Earth favorites with Svesti ingredients. *I can't believe they didn't have cookies or bread.*

Talen had become like an older brother to her. All those long days cooking together—sharing stories and recipes—and laughing at the same things made her feel like she knew him better than anyone else onboard other than Karid. The other males working in the kitchen were nice but didn't engender the same sense of camaraderie in her. *But then, Talen doesn't make my insides quiver in excitement like Karid either.*

She leisurely washed herself. Water streamed down her body as she stood in the huge bathtub. She stepped into the drying tube and closed her eyes as the warm air removed the droplets. *Gotta love Svesti technology.*

Ava tapped a wall and the surface shimmered before reflecting her naked image back at her. Running her fingers lightly over her abdomen, she traced the few scars Healer Ash'n Rivezt couldn't remove on that first day. Although the other scars no longer showed on her pale skin, she remembered all of them with a grimace. *I'm in a much better place now, but I can't erase the memories as easily.*

She turned and looked at her backside in the mirror, again noting the missing disfigurements. Even with Rachel teaching them self-defense techniques daily, she still carried more padding on her hips and ass than she'd like. Her mood lightened when she saw the toilet in the reflection. *I'm so glad Lin discovered a height adjustment on the toilet. I was tired of having to hop up to relieve myself.*

Brushing her hair and pulling it up into a ponytail, she decided she would head to the kitchen after she dressed to see if Talen needed any help with evening meal. *Making meals for three thousand warriors daily is a lot of work. Maybe I'll get an early start on tomorrow's cookies since I won't be spending time with Karid tonight.*

In her bedroom, Ava frowned as she pulled some clothes out of a hidden drawer. For the past month, she and Karid had been spending most evenings together. They watched movies, talked about their respective days, and shared stories of their pasts. They walked about the ship—sometimes stopping in the aquiponics or observation areas. He was a prankster and they laughed a lot. She introduced him to Earth music and discovered he liked the twentieth century music more than the more current songs. Somewhere along the line, their time started including kisses and heavy petting. *I'm not sure how he snuck past my defenses, but now I feel adrift knowing he's not onboard.*

Slipping her feet into black sneakers, she straightened her shoulders. *Maybe this time apart is a good thing. It gives me *time to decide if I'm willing to go further with him. Do I trust him enough to really let him in and know my ugly secrets? Even when I was with Stefan, I never told him the entire truth. Damn, I really wish I could talk to my therapist right about now.*

After evening meal in the dining area, Ava sat with the other women enjoying *leringa* pie.

Talia said, "I have bad news, ladies."

"What?" asked Lin.

"Earlier today our governments have accused the Svesti of kidnapping us and are calling for military funding."

"So people on Earth know about aliens," said Emmy in between bites. "Bet there's some interesting shit making the rounds of social media."

"All of our countries?" Ava asked.

"Yes."

Rachel's blue eyes glittered with anger. "Are they bloody nuts? It wasn't bad enough to lie to us, so now they're lying to the entire planet?"

"So it seems." Talia opened a notebook. "I have a plan which King Sovex approved, but I need your help."

"What do you want us to do?" Natasha leaned forward with her elbows on the table.

"I'd like you to make videos explaining how you got here and how we've been treated. We'll pair them with the videos the Svesti have of our leaders agreeing to the Choosings. I could also use help finding contact information for credible news organizations and journalists in your respective countries.. I figure each of you has a much better idea of who we can trust to be impartial in their reporting than I would. I made a secret video before I left Earth, just in case, that I'll also include with a copy of the draft treaty and information about the virus and vaccine."

"I can help get the medical information ready," said Natasha.

"I was hoping you'd say that."

Ava looked at the serious faces surrounding her, the background noise of silverware clinking and warriors' low voices fading. *Shit. The videos will go worldwide. What if someone recognizes me? But it was so long ago, and I should do my part to make sure the truth about the Svesti is known.*

"I'm in," said Emmy. "I'll help with the tech stuff."

"Count me in," said Rachel.

Lin and Natasha nodded. Ava shrugged.

"Let's do this."

Talia smiled. "Thanks, everyone. I still need to finish my list of everything that needs done to make this happen. How about we meet in the War Room tomorrow after breakfast?"

Ava picked up her tray and stood. "I'll be there."

Chapter 3

KARID PICKED UP a valadium point chisel and carefully placed it against the black stone. He gently tapped the end with his hammer. Moving the chisel in tiny increments, he repeated his movements, marking a thin line in the stone. Blowing off the dust, he picked up his project and turned it in the light to check for flaws. Noting an uneven spot, he corrected it, then sat back and stretched. While he enjoyed the detail work, it could take a toll on his spine. He cleaned and packed his tools and wrapped the stone in its protective cloth before stowing it all away. *I'm glad I brought it with me. There's too much downtime on this mission.*

He and Jevax had settled into twelve-hour shifts, with an overlap of four hours together. It was almost time for him to join the male. Standing, he cracked his neck and did some training forms to loosen up his muscles. Then he went to the dining area to pick up some snacks and water pouches.

In the cockpit, Karid dropped his bounty on the console. Jevax grabbed a water pouch and some green crackers.

"Thanks. I can always count on you to have food." Jevax grinned.

"We're growing males. Need to keep us fueled." Karid waggled his eyebrows. "Anything new?"

"It's taken us five days, but we are finally receiving a constant signal from the freighter's engine signature." Jevax tapped the console and a holographic image appeared above it. "See?"

Karid perused the map and the location of the freighter. "It appears it's going to Praxis. How long until we catch up?"

"I'd say less than a day and we'll be in a good position to follow it cloaked."

"Excellent. I was afraid I'd have an eternity with only you for company."

"That would've been a fate worse than death." Jevax's fangs gleamed against his skin.

"Not quite that bad." Karid sat back and nibbled on a cracker. "Why have you never moved up in the ranks? You're more than capable of leading your own team, Jevax."

"I'm happy as I am."

Karid side-eyed the male. "Perhaps a change to security would suit you. You have an excellent cross-section of skills that would work to your advantage. Devik mentioned he may need to form additional teams to protect the females."

"Why the interest in my career?"

"You're a good male with a great deal of the competence and experience preferred in the higher ranks." Karid laughed. "Besides, I'm bored and you're the only one here to annoy."

"Perhaps I should channel the Commander and spar with you to make my case."

Karid slapped Jevax's shoulder. "See? That's what I mean. If Durek can become commander of our flagship, you certainly can aspire higher."

"Respectfully, sir, you are a *naroon*." Jevax laughed and tossed a water pouch at Karid.

"Honesty—another admirable trait for an officer to have. You just keep proving me right."

Hours later, after Jevax left to rest, Karid sat back in his chair and closed his eyes. He made a mental note to talk to Vared and Devik about moving the male to a different specialty. *I'm not sure what Jevax's issue is, but in security, he would occasionally have to lead a team. The experience would be good for him.*

His stomach growled. He reached for some crackers and chewed. *I should've been late for the mission and taken a bunch of those toffee bars. The leftover cookies only lasted a day.*

The thoughts of cookies led Karid to think about Ava who was never far from his mind. Unlike Vared, Devik, and Ash'n, who jumped right into sexual relationships with their females, he courted her slowly. When Vared had told them his fangs elongated with Talia indicating a potential true mate bond, Karid knew he wanted that rather than a troth or breeding contract. He knew many believed he didn't take much seriously except protecting others from the Zuvgran, but he held his true desires close to his heart.

With so few Svesti females left close to his age, he believed he was destined to be alone for the entirety of his life. He felt fortunate that he had enduring friendships, but he longed for a lasting bond with a female. Watching all those Earth movies with Ava, he realized he was what humans called a romantic at heart.

He wished for a true partner for the remainder of his life—one who understood him, excited him, and made him laugh. *I want someone who will love me enough to support me even if they don't agree with all of my choices and not try to control me. Unlike my father.*

Karid was self-aware enough to know Ava initially piqued his interest because of her talent with food. But it was her humor, compassion, and her loyalty to the other human females that kept him coming back for more. *Her wonderful scent, soft flesh, and bountiful curves only increased my attraction.*

When they kissed, he felt her passion, but he sensed she kept it on a tight leash. Not like an untouched female would but something held her back. He wanted that passion unbridled with him and only him. His pants tightened as he imagined it. Shifting uncomfortably on his chair, he willed his cock to soften.

I wonder if she misses me as much as I miss her.

The next day, the *Tenacity* entered a cloaked high orbit over the Zuvgran-controlled planet Praxis. Their scans indicated the freighter, the *Sept Reserve*, kept loading supply crates of some sort. Karid used some of the skills Devik taught him to try to hack into the freighter's computers.

Growling in frustration, Karid sat back and huffed. His tail flicked in short, fast movements.

"We could use Lady Emmy right about now. According to Tolvex, her skills would have that database wide open for us already."

Jevax said, "I apologize that I am unable to assist. I can't even code a synthesizer. I usually ask Volax to do it."

"We'll add some computer courses to your training."

"Please don't do me any favors." Jevax shuddered.

Karid chuckled. "I'll keep trying, but for now, let's just follow them and see where they lead us."

"As you command. I'm trying to determine the number of beings on the ship, but even on the ground, they are using a dampening field."

"Of course they are. Well, we wouldn't want it to be too easy, would we?"

"Easy would work for me. We could get back to the *Invictus* sooner. Synthesizer food and rations are poor imitations for Previv and Lady Ava's cooking." Jevax pouted.

With a grin, Karid slapped Jevax's shoulder. "A male whose stomach agrees with mine."

"Opening an encrypted comm to the *Invictus*." Karid tapped the console and waited.

Vared and Devik appeared holographically.

"Report," said Vared.

"We found the freighter and should be close enough in another hour or so to begin following it. We believe they will be landing on Praxis to take on more supplies."

Vared's fangs gleamed against his golden bronze skin. "Excellent. You may be able to determine the sites of numerous labs."

"From your lips to the Goddess' ears." Karid paused. "Anything new about the traitor onboard?"

"He appears to be taking a break from harassing the females. They've been spending most of their days in the War Room while we deal with Earth's nonsense," Devik answered.

"Yesterday, the *Defiant* broadcast Talia's videos and released the proposed draft treaty as well as the medical information about the virus." Vared's smile widened. "The initial responses on Earth's social media have been voluminous and show no signs of ending soon."

"Well, that's one way to open up discussions." Karid's lips turned up.

Devik's braids brushed his shoulder as he shook his head. "Already there are groups gathering with signs asking us to 'beam them up.' Emmy said we might have to consider psychological testing before allowing any of them on a ship." He shrugged. "I'm not entirely certain she was joking."

Jevax snorted. "My interactions with Lady Emmy would suggest she probably meant exactly what she said."

"I concur," said Devik. He looked at Karid. "We're still working to pare down our list of suspects to identify the traitor. It's going slowly."

"How is Nerid Mantoor?" Karid asked.

"Ash'n has been keeping him sedated. The traitor using an implant to brainwash Mantoor made his mind delicate. He has no recollection of attacking me." Vared's growl rumbled low. "We hope the mind healers on Costonia will be able to help him recover."

"Brainwash?" Jevax said.

"I'll explain later," said Karid. Jevax nodded.

"Anything else?" Vared said.

"No. Only that we may not check in when we're close to Praxis, depending on how long the freighter remains there. I'm not sure what capabilities the Zuvgran have to catch transmissions near one of their worlds." Karid's eyes hardened. "We're too close to potential answers, and I don't want to inadvertently give away our position."

Vared's facial scar whitened. "I don't like you going dark."

"It probably won't be for long."

"Report no later than three days from now, even if you have to break off from your surveillance temporarily."

Karid sighed. "As you command."

Chapter 4

AVA LOADED THE last batch of frozen sugar cookie balls from the pan to containers and stored them in the secondary freezer. The huge shelves mostly filled with frozen bread dough wrapped in some sort of plasfilm that self-sealed without sticking everywhere pleased her. She was glad she took the time last month to speak with Leriv Volax, the supply master, and ask for his help synthesizing strapped bread pans so multiple loaves could bake evenly. He also made her bread dough attachments for the kitchen mixers usually used for making the pastry for pies and *brellia*. It took them a number of tries before he could synthesize a baker's yeast that worked with the Svesti grain used to make their pastries, but now she had something she could work with and she was happy with the results.

Spending the past week in the War Room with Tolvex and the other women readying everything for Talia's plan, then dealing with the subsequent media barrage from Earth, left her little time for stress baking. But she worked on the bread dough most of the week, and now the snacks took priority. *And that's why I'm here alone in the kitchen at midnight.*

Cleaning up after herself, she thought of how most of Earth's leaders started saying there had been a huge misunderstanding between them and the Svesti. *Not sure how they plan on manipulating the truth—again, but if nothing else, I've had less time to worry about Karid with all the extra work.*

Earlier, she gave instructions to Talen about how to bake the frozen cookie dough since she knew she wouldn't be helping him in the kitchen again for a few more days. The Svesti warriors certainly liked cookies and their introduction to sandwiches amused her. *It's difficult to have sandwiches when you don't have bread.*

Turning off the lights, she took her time walking the darkened corridors to her quarters. *I like how the corridor walls change based on the time of day. We don't have sunlight on a space cruiser, but mimicking natural planetary rhythms makes it easier on the body.*

Inside her living area, she toed off her sneakers and padded in the dark to the bedroom. Stripping down to her underwear, she tossed her clothing in the vicinity of the refresher. She placed her comm on the bedside table and crawled into bed, pulling a sheet over her. Clutching a pillow to her chest, she willed her mind to shut down. *Where are you Karid and are you okay?*

A couple days later, Ava sat in the War Room with the other women and Tolvex going through Earth's reactions to the knowledge of the Svesti, the leaders' obfuscations, the draft treaty, the virus, and the vaccine. *Geez. Everyone has something to say whether it's based in fact or not. Look at all the damned memes.*

She hid her smile when she looked up from her tablet and saw Emmy stroking Tolvex's tail. *She's gotten past her fears if she's willing to show her affection for him publicly. Hmm, I wonder if Karid would like his tail stroked.*

Everyone paused when Vared's voice sounded over the speakers.

"Attention all hands. We are currently en route to Talonka Six to answer a distress call. There has been a collapse in an arbixium mine and 281 miners are trapped. It is unclear at this time whether all trapped beings are Ermipas. Prepare for search and rescue and massive casualties.

"We should arrive in approximately eleven hours. Medical personnel, gather your supplies and coordinate the loading. Section Leaders, prepare your shuttles. Adjust rest periods as needed to be prepared. When we have more information on what may need to be synthesized and loaded, I will send it to you. Commander Durek out."

Rachel looked at Tolvex who tapped at his tablet. "How can we help?"

"Lady Natasha, you will obviously be needed in the med bay. Medical personnel will be in charge of triage and treatment procedures on the planet. Perhaps Lady Lin could assist in gathering supplies."

"Of course. I'll have to ask the healers for information on Ermipa physiology, but I'm sure that won't be a problem," Natasha said. "Come on, Lin. Let's see if there are any natural remedies for Ermipas that you might be able to prepare in advance as well." She and Lin left the room.

Ava said, "I'll check with Talen and see if there are any special dietary requirements for Ermipas. I'll start making food for them, as well as for the warriors. I'll probably have to prepare some liquid and bland nutrition for some of the injured. I'll make sure the food for the Svesti is easily portable."

Tolvex smiled and nodded. "That would be helpful."

Ava hurried out of the room to the kitchen. She entered to find Talen directing his kitchen staff, having some continue making midday meal and others cooking large cuts of meat for sandwiches.

"Ava, good, you're here. Could you begin making bread? I think the warriors would appreciate sandwiches rather than ration bars while they're on the surface." Talen wiped his hands on his apron.

"Of course. I have a bunch of dough frozen already. Are there any ingredients I shouldn't use for Ermipas? I was thinking soup would be good for those who may need a liquid diet and it would go well with sandwiches." Ava set some ovens to preheat and grabbed her bread pans from a shelf. "I could make half with additional ingredients for anyone who isn't restricted."

Talen said, "No, there shouldn't be any problem with any of our food. Ermipas are hardy beings with strong stomachs."

Flashing him a quick grin, she lined up her pans and began coating them with a light butter-like substance. "Are you saying my food sits like lead?"

He barked out a laugh. "Hardly. I think we should save your frozen cookies for the surface. The warriors can live without them for today."

"You're the boss." She flipped him a quick salute as she activated a smaller maglev and headed to the secondary freezer.

They worked hard for the next eight hours. While the bread baked, Ava started making stock for her soup using whole *plostivs*, birds similar but larger than chickens, letting the meat fall off the bones. She chopped *sedapi*, a vegetable that tasted like celery but was white in color, and *horicar* which had a texture like carrots but looked like blue potatoes. Along with some herbs, she added chopped *sibella*, which tasted like onions but was tubular in shape. *I wish I had time to make noodles, but without a pasta making machine, it's just too much work. Oh, maybe some dumpling-like dough might work instead.*

"Talen, if we bake some *plostiv*, I can make something like Earth's chicken salad and have it ready to spread on bread for a second day of sandwiches."

He agreed and sent a warrior to get more *plostiv* from storage while she mixed the Svesti equivalent of mayonnaise and mustard together and chopped more *sedapi, sibella,* and herbs. *I think there are some nuts that will go well in it. I'll have to remember to add them in afterwards.*

While the soup simmered, Talen had a warrior synthesize hundreds of single-size bowls with lids that had a thermal quality.

Then he instructed the staff to slice and cut the cheese and vegetables for the sandwiches. Ava suggested they set up an assembly line of all the ingredients. One warrior cut the bread, another spread condiments on the slices, others added meat, cheeses, sliced *shurlix,* and more until each thick sandwich ended up wrapped in plasfilm and stored in cooling units to go to the surface.

Ava had warriors shred the cooled *plostiv* and mix it in with everything else including the nuts for the chicken salad. She instructed several warriors to slice more bread and add the Svesti version of lettuce before spreading the mixture to make the sandwiches after the chicken salad chilled overnight.

Talen sent all but a handful of staff to get some rest, leaving the others in charge of serving the warriors evening meal and prepping for morning meal. He limped toward the huge pots of soup.

"I'll get those," Ava said. "Rest that leg."

"No. I'm taller than you. I'll fill the bowls. You can seal them and put them in the larger heated containers."

"At least use a stool, Talen. You've done a lot of standing today and the next few days will be busy, too." Ava frowned.

He sighed and moved a stool to the stovetop.

"Better?"

"Yes. Thank you for humoring me." Ava put a tray of bowls next to the pot. "I know that injury doesn't bother you all the time, but when it does, you need to take it easy." She pulled two spoons out of a drawer.

He tugged the end of her ponytail. "As you wish, *picana.*"

She playfully slapped his arm. "Did you just call me little one?"

His fangs flashed white when he grinned. "Yes, you are a little female."

She mock growled at him. "You're lucky I like you. I'm very proficient with kitchen knives." Scooping up a spoonful of the soup, she held it out to him. "Taste."

"Needs salt."

She used the other spoon for herself. "It does not." She rested her hands on her hips and narrowed her eyes. "You'd better be teasing me."

Smiling, he said, "Of course I am. Everything you make tastes good."

He ladled the soup into bowls, and Ava covered and stored them.

"I have to admit, chicken soup looks so strange with Svesti ingredients, but it tastes close to Earth's version."

"I'm glad you were one of the first females to join us from Earth, Ava. I've learned a lot from you. It will make it easier to provide familiar food to future females."

"Well, I'm happy you love to cook as much as I do and have been so willing to let me play in your kitchen." She flashed him a smile. "I know there are many chefs who aren't willing to share kitchen space."

He leaned down and bumped shoulders with her. "You've been spending many late nights in here recently."

"I've been restless and cooking soothes me." She didn't look up.

"Missing a certain Lieutenant?"

Her shoulders tightened. "What do you mean?"

"I haven't seen Wurvez around lately. That's unusual if he's onboard. I know you've been spending time with him."

"I don't know what you're implying, Talen."

"Svesti have a highly developed sense of smell. I've noticed his scent lingering on you, but not lately."

She sighed and looked up at his concerned face. "He's not onboard, and I miss him."

"Has he treated you well?" His tail swayed.

"Yes. We're good friends and he makes me laugh." Staring at her hands, she added quietly, "I feel safe with him." She paused. "I feel safe with you, too, but you're like family safe—big brother safe."

"You haven't always felt safe, have you?"

She remained silent.

Blowing out a breath, he said, "Wurvez is a good male, but I think his humor hides a deep hurt."

"What do you mean?"

"I think he feels things more deeply than he shows the rest of us, *picana*. That's not a bad thing, but maybe he needs to feel safe, too. Perhaps differently than you do but no less important."

She mentally chewed on his words, her hands automatically working.

"You know, you're pretty smart for a big lug."

He grunted. "One last thing, Ava."

"Yes?"

"If anyone makes you feel unsafe, please tell me."

She tilted her head and looked into green eyes a few shades darker than her own. "I will. Thank you."

He tapped her nose with a finger. "Now let's finish up so we can get some rest. Talonka Six awaits."

"Uncle, we are responding to a distress call. Our arrival on Costonia will be delayed."

"That works out well. I have a meeting with our co-conspirators in two days. The delay will give us time to put everything in place." His uncle's voice sounded eager.

"What are your orders?" Muscles tense, the male held his breath. *I didn't like using Nerid. While he is weak, the male did not deserve to have his brain muddled. I feel as if I'm too exposed.*

"Take no action but keep alert for information that may prove useful. You must avoid suspicion. Do not contact me again until you reach the home world. Always Svesti."

The younger male released his breath slowly, and his shoulders relaxed.

"As you command. Always Svesti." Relief filled him as he disconnected the comm.

Chapter 5

"THE FOURTH STRIPPED world in three days. Why wouldn't the Zuvgran have their labs on the worlds where they live? Wouldn't it be easier to keep them safe and supplied?" Karid grumbled as he and Jevax watched the Frezzian freighter skim low over the planet's surface and drop crates.

Jevax made notations in their computer for the coordinates and everything they observed. "I don't know. It doesn't make sense."

Karid sat back, and his tail swayed slowly. He extended his claws and lightly tapped the console. "Secret labs. Stripped worlds. No outside contact." His eyes widened. "I think it's because they're working with biologics. If the scientists make an error and a virus gets loose, an unoccupied planet is easier to contain or destroy. Zuvgran deaths would be limited to those already on the surface."

Nodding, Jevax said, "Now that makes sense to me."

"Looks like they're changing direction. I wish I could get into their database."

Jevax tapped the console and entered a heading to follow the freighter. Frowning, he looked at the projected course. "They appear to be flying toward the asteroid field near Millus."

An angry rumble emanated from Karid's chest. "That's much too close to Costonia." The tails of both males flicked in hard movements. His jaw hardened. "Send an encrypted message to the *Invictus* with everything we've discovered so far and our heading. We'll wait until we know exactly where the next lab is before we check in."

Jevax grunted. "There are solar flares in the Lestanus system. The message may not make it through intact or at all."

"*Crek.* We'll have to try again later. Increase speed to get closer to the freighter. I don't want to lose them in the asteroid field. We need to know if there's a lab close to the home world."

"As you command."

After maneuvering through the asteroid field the next day, Karid and Jevax watched as the *Sept Reserve* conducted their low altitude run and dropped crates in the ruins of an ancient gladiator pit on Millus. Karid's eyes narrowed as numerous Zuvgran appeared as soon as the freighter left the atmosphere.

"Scans show a Svesti speedster approaching the planet."

"How far out is it?" Karid asked.

"A little over two hours at their present speed."

Karid's fingers drummed on the armrest. He turned to Jevax.

"Feel like hunting?"

"What are you thinking?"

"We know a Svesti noble has been working with the Zuvgran. This might be our chance to discover who he is."

"I like the idea of identifying a traitor." Jevax's eyes lit up. "What is your plan?"

"Land on the leeward side of the pit. Less chance blowing sand will reveal the ship and it's in the shadows of the walls. We'll leave the ship cloaked and get to high ground with our surveillance equipment so we can watch and if we're lucky, we'll be able to hear. We should still be able to track the freighter when we're done here."

Jevax tapped the console. "I'm not seeing any planetary defenses or active scans. There is a chance of passive scanning potentially revealing our presence."

"I believe it's worth the risk. Take us down. I'm going to gear up and gather the equipment. When I return, you can get ready."

"I'll try to send another encrypted comm to the *Invictus* with the latest update. Hopefully, it will get through."

"Good thinking." After he stood, Karid slapped Jevax's shoulder. "I'm looking forward to this."

"Sir, we will arrive at Millus in two hours," the Svesti warrior said.

The nobleman looked up from his tablet. "Thank you for the update." The warrior remained silent. "Was there something else?"

"May I speak frankly, sir?"

The noble waved his hand. "Yes, go ahead."

"Are you certain this is the best course of action? Meeting with the Zuvgran, especially so close to Costonia?"

"Do you doubt me?"

"No, sir. However, I do not trust the Zuvgran. I wonder if the risk is too great. Without you, the cause would falter."

The noble smiled, his fangs gleaming against his caramel bronze skin. "The Zuvgran emperor wishes the Sovex rule to end, just as much as we do. Our interests are aligned for now." With false modesty, he continued, "The cause would continue without me, because Svesti purity is paramount."

The male bowed his head. "I would feel more comfortable with additional warriors guarding you."

"I will be fine. Have faith in the Goddess, as I do. She will protect us as we are following her will."

"As you command, sir."

"I thank you for your concern and honesty. You will be rewarded when our objectives are met."

"The cause is just which is its own reward, sir."

"That is why you are one of my trusted guards—your commitment to our race." The noble paused. "Was there anything else?"

"No, sir. I will notify you when we begin our descent."

The noble dipped his chin imperiously. "Always Svesti."

"Always Svesti." The warrior returned to the cockpit of the luxury speedster.

Naroon. So easily led. How dare he doubt my decisions. The noble clenched his fist under his plush robe. *I will be king. Then I will defeat the Zuvgran and take their empire.*

The yellow moon provided minimal light as Karid and Jevax swiftly and silently made their way to the top of the seating surrounding the pit. Layers of brown dust stirred briefly as they lay prone and set up their surveillance equipment. Centuries ago, the Zuvgran invaded Millus, but the Svesti joined the fight and pushed them out of the solar system. However, they couldn't save Millus itself—it was now another lifeless world.

They watched as the speedster landed in the center of the pit. Three Svesti disembarked. One stepped forward to meet the Zuvgran waiting. Karid chest rumbled with a silent growl when he recognized the Svesti noble. He handed the magnifier equipment to Jevax. When he looked, Jevax's tail flicked hard once before stilling.

The long-range microphone did not catch everything discussed in the pit, but Karid heard enough to confirm that the noble informed the Zuvgran of the human females being on Theron the intent to infect them with the virus. Another Zuvgran approached the males and he heard, "We are not alone. Did you send others?" *Crek.*

"You recognized the noble?" Karid whispered. He quickly gathered the equipment and handed the packed bag to Jevax.

"Yes." Jevax's response was barely audible.

"Go back to the ship and depart. Hide in the asteroid field if you need to. Relay everything to Commander Durek or King Sovex—no one else."

"What are you going to do?"

"Be a distraction long enough for you to escape. This information must make it to the king."

Jevax shook his head. "Come with me."

"No." Karid's voice was firm. "The odds are better if we split up. Once you know they receive the intel, you can request additional warriors to return for me."

"I do not like this plan."

"Go now. There's little time. That's an order." Karid made his way in the opposite direction of the cloaked *Tenacity*. He glanced back to ensure Jevax followed instructions. *Good, he's no longer in sight.*

Hearing footsteps, he flattened himself against a pillar and pulled out two of his favorite knives. Sniffing, he attempted to determine how many Zuvgran approached. *Five? Six?*

He waited until the last passed him before attacking from behind. Stabbing two Zuvgran in their brain stems brought them down quickly. The other warriors turned at the sound. He dropped his head and rammed a third in the abdomen pushing him into the others. Two more fell, while one stayed on his feet. Using his extended claws, he sliced the throat of the one he originally tackled and stood quickly.

Karid launched himself at the one who still stood upright but dropped when a blaster stunned him. *That crekkin' hurt.*

"Bind his hands," the one with the blaster said to the others struggling to rise.

With his body unresponsive until the blaster's effects wore off, Karid had no choice to be compliant when they pulled his arms roughly behind him.

"Bring him." The Zuvgran hooked their hands through his elbows and dragged him. Fortunately, they took a ramp rather than stairs. *Maybe my knees won't suffer as badly.*

Karid felt tingles throughout his body as his nerves began awakening. He finally got his legs to walk shakily under his own power and began struggling. They reached the center of the pit and the Zuvgran forced him to his knees.

The Zuvgran leader said to the noble, "Is he one of yours?"

"No. He's loyal to Sovex."

"You *crekkin'* traitor. The king will have you executed," Karid said angrily.

"Who else is with you?" demanded the Zuvgran.

"No one."

"Where is your ship?"

"Hidden."

The Zuvgran nodded and one of the others punched Wurvez in the jaw. Blood droplets arched before falling into the dust.

"Try again. How did you know we would be here?"

"I didn't." Karid received a kick to the stomach. He bent over as far as he could and coughed.

"Keep him," said the noble. "Question him as you like. All I ask is you inform me of what you discover and he never returns to Costonia."

"You don't want him?" The Zuvgran sounded surprised.

"Consider him a gift from me to you. The virus?"

"I do not have it."

The noble growled. "Get it to me and I'll ensure it's done."

The Zuvgran studied the noble, then nodded. "I will pass along your request to the Emperor."

"It's not a request. It's the completion of our original agreement."

Karid growled low. "I will see you dead, traitor."

The noble crouched in front of Karid and drew an extended claw along his jawline leaving a trail of blood in its wake. Karid clenched his teeth against the pain.

"It is good that you are already kneeling in front of the future king. Too bad you won't live long enough to do it again."

Karid bared his fangs and spit on the noble. "You will never be king."

The noble backhanded him. "Watch how you speak to me." He stood and faced the Zuvgran. "We're done. Contact me when you are ready to uphold your end."

The Zuvgran dipped his chin, then ordered his warriors to take Karid who struggled more. Karid felt a flashing pain to the back of his skull and his vision went black.

When the Svesti noble rejoined his waiting warriors, the one who had questioned him earlier spoke.

"We are not taking the Svesti, sir?"

"No. It is not the Goddess' will."

"I know you're not a warrior—" The noble grabbed his throat, his claws pricking the male's neck.

"What was that?"

"Currently." The male choked out the word. His breathing calmed when the noble released him. "I only meant that those of us who remain in the warrior ranks have difficulty seeing a Svesti at a Zuvgran's non-existent mercy, regardless of our beliefs."

"It is not easy for me either. I do not wish any of us to have Svesti blood on our hands if there is a way to avoid it. We are brethren. However, we cannot have our brother impeding our plans. The best option is to leave him to the Zuvgran."

The warrior lowered his eyes. "As you command, sir."

"Exactly."

How did Wurvez know I was on Millus? And why is he alone?

When they entered the speedster, the noble ordered, "Scan for nearby Svesti ships. If you find any, contact the Zuvgran and relay its position."

How much does Sovex know?

Less than fifteen minutes later, the Svesti warrior approached the noble.

"Sir, we think there may be a cloaked vessel within the asteroid field. There was a shift of the rocks in one section that did not appear to be normal drift."

"Did you notify the Zuvgran?"

"Yes, sir. They've deployed some fighters."

"Good. Let them take care of it." The Svesti noble tapped his tablet and a holographic image of the asteroids appeared. He watched as the fighters peppered the suspected area with their weapons.

Moments later, an orange flash of light exploded debris scattered within the field. The warrior said, "Scans indicate a ship was destroyed. Survivors unlikely."

The noble smiled. "Take us back to Costonia." *No witnesses left. Perfect.*

"As you command."

Chapter 6

WHILE MOST OF the women took an earlier shuttle to the surface, Ava chose to be on one of the last ones to help Talen. On Talonka Six, she watched with awe as the Svesti warriors erected tents and transferred supplies. *Wow. They have a great system.*

Talen said, "Come. Let's finish setting up the dining tent so we're ready when everyone else is."

Lin met them at the tent. "What can I do to help?"

Ava glanced at her. "Where's everyone else?"

"Rachel and Emmy are setting up an information station for families and Natasha is helping set up the medical tents. Talia stayed on the *Invictus.*"

As soon as they entered the tent, Talen barked out orders to the warriors on how to arrange the tables, chairs, and counters.

"Ladies, when the counters are set up, if you could arrange the cooling and heating units so we can stock the dining line as we need to without having to go far for supplies, I would appreciate it."

"Okay."

Ava and Lin set up a beverage station in a corner, then decided what order items should be available for the warriors to serve themselves. They stacked the units behind the counter against the tent wall leaving several of each under the counter for easy access to put out.

"What do you want me to do with the maglev?" asked Lin.

"Tuck it back here. We can use it to take meals to the medical tents," Ava said.

"Good idea." Lin stretched her petite frame. "Has anyone told you the latest?"

Ava's forehead wrinkled. "About what?"

Lin beamed. "Some of us are fated mates."

"Fated mates? Who?"

"Me and Ash'n." Lin pulled down her collar and revealed her gold clan marking. "Talia and the commander and Emmy and Tolvex."

Ava peered at Lin's exposed skin. "That just appeared on your body?"

Lin's face turned pink, and she bobbed her head. "Yes, after we true mated."

"What does it mean?"

"According to Ash'n, fated mates are like soulmates. The Svesti believe fated mates are the two beings in the universe who are meant to be together and the Goddess leads them to each other. They haven't had fated mate bonds in over a hundred years."

"Wow. That's seriously cool and a bit scary. How do you feel about it?"

"Extremely lucky. I love Ash'n and this feels like added proof I made the right decision."

Ava hugged her friend. "I'm happy for you. You deserve a good man." She arched an eyebrow. "So how come this is the first I've heard about you two together? You've been keeping secrets."

Lin bit her lip. "You're not mad, are you? Initially, I felt so wrapped up in him, I wanted to savor it. Then Durek was attacked. It felt wrong to talk about my happiness when the focus needed to be on him."

"I'm just teasing you." Ava lowered her voice. "So Svesti are sexually compatible with humans?"

Lin's eyes became dreamy. "Most definitely."

Ava laughed. "That's good to know."

Several hours passed with little activity in the dining tent. Then groups of dusty warriors straggled in. Along with Talen, the women passed out food and beverages, and Talen asked Lin if she would load up the maglev and make rounds through the medical tents.

"The healers and medics probably need water by now," he said.

"Okay. I can do that."

Ava helped Lin place a few of the units on the maglev. Another group of warriors came in as Lin left. The warriors said they were taking shifts helping dig out a tunnel to a large group of survivors.

The sky turned dark before the Svesti reached the Ermipas and began transporting them to the medical tents. The dining tent became increasingly busy before it quieted again.

Talen said, "Ladies, go get some sleep. We'll be working hard again come sunrise. Tolvex wants the females are to sleep on one of the shuttles to ensure your safety and comfort."

"Are you going to rest, too?" Ava noted the exhaustion on his face.

"Yes, I'll grab some sleep in the warriors' tent."

"Okay. Which shuttle?"

"I'll escort you."

They walked to the improvised shuttle parking area. Ava watched with concern as Talen limped slightly but refrained from saying anything.

At the appropriate ship, the two warriors on guard duty smiled.

"Pick any quarters you like. You two are the first here."

"Thank you."

Ava turned to Talen before she followed Lin up the ramp. "We'll see you in a few hours."

"I do not expect you before sunrise and if either of you need longer to rest, please do so. I can always pull a warrior or two from another duty to help me."

"That won't be necessary, Talen. We're here to help."

"Stubborn female." He gave her a tired smile.

"Stubborn male," she retorted.

At the top of the ramp, Ava saw her overnight bag sitting with others. Picking it up, she took the first available room, undressed, and threw her clothes in the refresher. Too exhausted for a shower, she put on a T-shirt and flopped onto the bed. As she drifted off to sleep, she thought of Karid. *I miss you, you big naroon.*

Ava took a quick shower, dressed, and synthesized breakfast for herself as soon as she woke up. *Shit. Did we forget to pre-make breakfast for everyone?*

She hurried back to the dining tent and saw warriors carrying in more cooling and heating units and removing the empty ones from the prior day. Talen directed males to unload the new units. She saw fruits, *brellia*—a pastry filled with meat, and *pertiza*—a sweet yogurt being set out on the counters.

"Looks like someone remembered morning meal," Ava said as she helped arrange the fruits.

Talen grinned. "I've been doing this for some time. I had the warriors left on the *Invictus* send half of the normal morning food down here. Today's sandwiches should be here in a few hours."

"See? That's why you're the boss."

He mock growled at her. "Disrespectful female."

"That's me." Ava opened another container. Seeing it full of water pouches, she moved it to the beverage station and left it there so it would stay cold.

"We'll be busier today, *picana*. I hope you have comfortable shoes on."

"Have we heard how many miners are still trapped?"

"I think more than half have been rescued."

"That's good."

The rest of the day passed quickly. Ava barely had time to go to the bathroom when she needed it. If she wasn't putting out more food, serving the warriors, or loading the maglev for Lin, she cleaned tables and counters.

She sighed when evening meal supplies showed up. Huge sealed pots of *maxiem* stew and bread arrived. Talen lifted a pot onto the counter.

"Don't even think of lifting one of these," he said.

"Did you want me to serve?"

Shaking his head, he said, "They can serve themselves. Could you find the bowls?"

"Found them. I'll put them out with the utensils and keep it all stocked." She narrowed her eyes. "Did they send down any of the thermal ones so we can keep the stew warm for the patients and healers? We still have some of the chicken broth left from yesterday for the few patients on a liquid diet, so we're good there."

"I hope so."

Ava hummed when she found the heated bowls already filled and extra empty ones available if they needed them. *Good. Saves us time.*

By the time she made it back to the shuttle, she could hardly keep her eyes open. *At least tonight I should be able to get a full night's sleep.*

Plumping her pillow, she rested her head and thought about Karid. *Damn, I really miss him.* She sniffed. *What I wouldn't give for one of hugs right now.*

It wasn't until late the next day when Ava realized she hadn't seen Natasha since arriving on Talonka Six.

"Lin, has Natasha been sleeping in the medical tents? I just realized her overnight bag was still in the shuttle hall this morning. Wouldn't she have at least showered and changed clothes?"

Lin wrinkled her nose. "Now that you mention it, I haven't seen her since yesterday. I just figured I missed her moving from tent to tent."

Ava comm'd Emmy and asked her if she had seen Natasha. After several moments, Emmy said, "I'm coming to you."

Emmy and Tolvex entered the dining tent and questioned Ava and Lin. Tolvex tapped on his tablet and growled low.

"I can't find her tracker."

"Shit. Let me see when we last had it," said Emmy as she bent her head to work on her own tablet.

Tolvex comm'd Ash'n. "When was the last time you saw Lady Natasha?"

"Last night about sunset. I told her to take as much time as she needed to rest. She looked exhausted."

Emmy said with a frown, "Her tracker stopped transmitting near the rear of one of the medical tents last night."

"What does that mean?" asked Lin.

"Nothing good," said Tolvex. "I need to investigate."

"Would it be faster to send out a comm to everyone on the surface asking if anyone saw her near or after sunset last night?" Emmy's foot tapped.

"Excellent idea, *milara*." Tolvex looked at the women. "For now, none of you may leave a tent without a warrior escort. Until we know find Lady Natasha and know what happened, we need to take additional precautions with your safety."

Ava saw her concern reflected on Lin's face as they both nodded. *Shit. Where the hell is Natasha?*

Despite their protests, when it became evident that no one had seen Natasha for a full day, Durek ordered all the human women back to the *Invictus*. Sitting next to Lin in the shuttle, Ava looked across at Emmy and Rachel.

"How could Natasha just disappear like that?"

Emmy explained, "If someone removed her tracker and destroyed it or she's in a vessel with a dampening field, we wouldn't get any hits on it."

Rachel's blue eyes hardened. "That's what happened with Talia when she was kidnapped. The Durelians had a dampening field on their ship."

"So Natasha might not even be on Talonka Six anymore?" Lin bit her lip.

"It's a possibility."

"Devik says he's found no evidence that her tracker was removed or destroyed near her last known location," Emmy's knee bounced.

"Do you think it's the traitor?" Lin asked quietly.

Rachel sighed heavily. "My gut says no, but we have no evidence one way or another."

"I hope she's okay wherever she is." Ava chewed on her lip.

"Natasha's smart. She'll do her best to stay safe," Emmy said. "I'm sure we'll find her soon."

"At least we know the Svesti will do everything they can," Rachel added.

"Well, I know what I'll be doing when we get back to the ship. Stress baking. At least there are plenty of people to eat whatever I make."

The other women reluctantly laughed. Ava saw the concern on each woman's face. *We're all freaked out that Natasha disappeared without a trace. Why does this shit keep happening to us?*

Chapter 7

PAIN IN HIS head, shoulders, ribs, and hip penetrated the blackness of Karid's mind. Slowly opening his eyes partway, he refrained from groaning until he could remember what happened and who might be present. Sitting against a wall with one leg at an awkward angle accounted for the hip pain. Arms raised and spread above his head made his shoulders ache. Then he recalled being captured by the Zuvgran. *Crek. That's the headache and bruised ribs. My knees are crekkin' killing me from being dragged.*

Cautiously he looked around the white room through heavy-lidded eyes. A toilet and sink sat in the corner to his right while he faced a single bed opposite him. *I'm in some sort of cell. I really hate being a prisoner.*

Straightening his leg to let his hip rest and sensation return to his calf and foot, he maneuvered into a more comfortable position. He tilted his head back and saw his wrists bound in manacles attached by chains to the wall. *Not sure how they expect me to use the sanitary facility or bed from here.*

He clicked his teeth in the appropriate pattern and waited for cold to fill his mouth to let him know he activated his tracker.

Feeling nothing, he tried again. A low growl left his lips. *Crek. And I can't attempt it again with my claw since I can't move my crekkin' arms. Hopefully, Jevax contacted Vared already and they know I'm somewhere on Millus.*

When Karid tightened his jaw in frustration, soreness spread across his face reminding him of the noble digging his claw into his flesh. *He better hope the king gets to him before I do. I'll rip that traitor's crekkin' heart out.*

Karid listened but heard no one nearby. He perused his cell noting a single camera above the door. Eyes roving the room again, he looked for items he could use as weapons once he got his arms free. *Not a whole lot here, but I can make it work if I need to.*

Wincing, he rolled his head and stretched what muscles he could. Bringing his knees up to his chest, he pressed his back against the wall and stood. He sighed as the ache on his shoulders abated. Clicking his teeth again, he performed some leisurely squats taking care not to go too low and create pressure on his shoulders. Twisting his torso while doing leg lifts, he kept his body busy without straining himself. He stopped when he heard boots approaching.

Three Zuvgran entered the room—the leader from the surface and two others with stun rods. Karid snorted. *Guess it's time to get this party started.*

The leader narrowed his eyes. "What is your name?"

Karid stared back at him. "What's yours?"

The leader nodded at the warriors. One punched Karid in the face. The second used his rod to stun him. Karid's knees buckled and his hands gripped the chains above his manacles. *Crekkin' stun rods.*

When he was able, Karid straightened and grinned. "Is that the best you've got?"

"Why are you here?"

"I heard there might be a gladiator fight. I always wanted to see one."

Karid tightened his abdomen for the punch to his gut and air left his lungs when a fist hit his kidney.

"How many Svesti are here?"

"Zuvgran working with Svesti. How long has that been going on?" Karid received another fist to his stomach.

"How many were on the ship we destroyed in the asteroid field?"

Karid remained silent except for the occasional grunts and groans as they continued to ask questions and beat him. *Goddess, please let him be lying about Jevax.*

At some point, he went to the happy place in his mind. The other times he had been captured, he imagined patiently working on an intricate sculpture to distract him from the pain. This time, Ava's face filled his vision—her pale skin, full eyelashes over green eyes with hints of blue and gold, pert nose and rosy cheeks dusted with brown dots she called freckles, soft full pink lips, and rounded chin. Glorious red curls he loved to run his fingers through covered her small sensitive ears which she sometimes adorned with dangling gems that tinkled when she moved or laughed.

He came back to the present when both warriors stunned him simultaneously and his knees buckled. Breathing heavily, he hung from the manacles.

"Release him."

"Sir?"

The leader glared at the questioning warrior. "Do you want to clean up his piss and shit? That's what you'll be doing if he can't reach the sanitary facility."

The warrior unfastened the manacles and pressed a button that pulled the chains into the wall.

The leader turned back to Karid. "We'll continue this later."

Karid muttered, "Fun times. I look forward to it."

A foot struck his stomach. "I will break you, Svesti."

Karid raised his head and glared. "I doubt that, Zuvgran."

Laughing, the leader said, "You are correct. It will be fun times." He jerked his head at the other warriors and they left Karid bruised and bleeding on the floor.

It was some time before Karid mustered the energy to roll over and rise onto his hands and knees. Truthfully, his body hurt, but he played up his injuries for the camera. He staggered to his feet and relieved himself in the toilet before turning the water on in the sink. He bent to splash water on his face. Watching the bloody water swirl down the drain, he clicked his teeth again. When nothing happened, he extended a claw and tapped his tracker hard in the activating pattern. Cold filled his mouth for a few seconds which helped soothe the sensitive skin under his tongue where his claw bruised it. *It should stay cold longer. It would be my luck to have a defective unit.*

He took off his shirt and rinsed it in the sink. Checking his torso, he noted the bruises forming, but surprisingly no open wounds. Pressing his wet shirt to his stomach, the chill helped dissipate some of the heat.

Gingerly, he made his way to the bed and reclined. Taking measured breaths, he shifted to find the most comfortable position. He had no doubt his body would be taking more damage before he escaped or was rescued. *Might as well rest up.*

Karid closed his eyes as he thought of Ava. His lips turned up at the memories of her slapping his hand and teasing him when he attempted to steal cookies. Not long after the human females boarded the *Invictus,* she drew his interest. As the son of a merchant, he knew the females were meant for the nobility, but her scent intrigued him and her humor complimented his. Friends at first, he kept finding reasons to spend more time with her until they were together most evenings.

When she introduced him to Earth music and some dance steps one night, he loved the pink flush and slight sheen of perspiration on her face. Some of her curls laid damp on her forehead as she tried to catch her breath. He picked her up and pulled her to his chest to swing her around, her laughter ringing in his ears. When they stopped spinning, he stared into her happy green eyes and let her slide slowly down his body. Unable to resist, he bent his head and gave her a light kiss. Drawing back, he searched her eyes for her reaction. She tightened her small fingers on his biceps and pulled him back down to her.

Their second kiss ignited his blood. His hands on her luscious ass lifted her up. Carrying her to the couch, he sat with her atop his legs. His tail rested on her back and with his hands free, he cupped her face tenderly. Their tongues explored each other's mouths, gently at the beginning, then growing more insistent. She pulled back with a gasp.

"What are we doing, Karid?" She squeezed his shoulders.

He arched a brow. "Kissing. Many species consider it a sign of affection and use lips, tongue, or teeth."

Ava's blunt fingernails dug into his flesh. "Very funny, smartass."

"You think my ass is intelligent?" Grinning, he tilted his head.

"It means you think you're being amusing when you're not." She leaned back against his tail. "Seriously, Karid, answer my question."

All traces of humor left his face. He tugged on a curl.

"We are doing no more than you are comfortable with, *raralumia*. That I promise you." He dropped his forehead to hers. "You are a wonderful female, Ava, in so many ways. I find you very sexy and would enjoy pleasuring you in any way you like."

Green eyes widened and she bit her lower lip. Her breasts rubbed up against his chest when she inhaled deeply. His cock jerked.

"I'm not ready for more than a make-out session."

"Make-out session?" His forehead wrinkled in confusion.

"Just kissing, Karid."

"Then we will do nothing more." His fingers traced the lines of her cheek. "I'm honored and will treasure any affection you bestow upon me, *raralumia*."

She blew out a breath. "Very pretty words." Her hair brushed against his fingers as she squirmed. "What does *raralumia* mean?"

"My words are true. *Raralumia* means rare light." He gave her a hopeful look. "May I kiss you again?"

Laughing, she leaned forward and lightly pressed her full lips to his. "Clothes stay on."

"As you command."

He memorized Ava's moans and whimpers as he kissed not only her lips, but her face, ears, and neck. The warmth of her curves against him aroused and excited him. *Goddess, her swollen lips, flushed skin, and passion-glazed eyes are my favorite sight.*

Laying in his cell, Karid recalled how much he enjoyed their first make-out session. He fell asleep to dreams of Ava.

Chapter 8

IN THE KITCHEN the next morning, Ava answered her comm to see Talia's happy face.

"Natasha just contacted us and said she's helping with what she thinks is a measles variant outbreak with some group of kids."

"How the hell did she find herself there? Are we going to get her?"

Talia frowned. "She refused to tell us where she is. Rivezt thinks she's helping Zuvgran hybrids based on the information she asked him to test."

"Wow. Did she look okay? When is she coming back?"

"She seemed fine. I don't know how long she's going to be wherever she is, but Vared made her promise to check in twice a day." Talia raised an eyebrow. "He's really not happy she won't divulge her location."

"I bet. But I'm relieved she's alright."

"Let me contact everyone else and let them know." Talia shook her head. "One of these days I'm going to have to learn how to initiate a group comm."

"Ask Emmy. I'm sure she knows how to do it."

Ava smiled as she finished mixing the meat and spices for the morning meal's *brellia. How did measles make it way out here? And how did Natasha find out about it?*

The following day, Talia comm'd all the women to meet in the War Room. Ava's eyes widened when Talia told them mare about Natasha.

"Here's what I know. There are twenty-three Zuvgran hybrid younglings between the ages of four and sixteen as well as a Zuvgran warrior being held captive by other Zuvgran on Straxis. Natasha and a Svesti-Zuvgran hybrid named Ronan d'Olorg are meeting five Svesti warriors there to rescue them. We expect the Zuvgran who cares for the kids to be injured." Talia's eyes dimmed. "There is a high probability a young teenage girl is being sexually assaulted by their captors as we speak."

"Fuck. How long until they can rescue the kids?" Rachel bit out.

"Natasha and Ronan will be there in three hours. The Svesti will wait for them."

"Why not go in right away?" Emmy asked.

"Ronan said he has a plan to minimize the chance of additional injuries to the younglings, but he needs to be there to coordinate."

"Those poor kids." Lin's eyes watered and she shuddered. "That poor girl."

"I take it these aren't the children Natasha was treating," Rachel said.

Talia shook her head. "No. Vared told me if it would take Natasha that long to get to Straxis, she was most likely still on Talonka Six."

"Ash'n said he's almost finished developing a vaccine for the measles variant," Lin said as she wiped tears from her eyes.

"Will they bring the children here? If so, we should plan for what they'll need."

"Right now, I think they expect to take the younglings to Talonka Six. However, if some have critical injuries, I believe they will need our med bay," Talia said. "I'd like us to prepare for both scenarios. Those kids will have nothing at all for clothing or possessions."

"I'll take notes," said Emmy. "Let's brainstorm."

For the next half hour, the women discussed what they thought would work best for lodging, clothing, and food. Everyone volunteered to start doing what they could now and what responsibilities each would take on if the younglings came to the *Invictus*.

"I think we covered everything we can for now," said Talia. "I'm going to see if I can convince Vared to move our ship closer to Straxis, just in case. I know the mining collapse survivors have all been found. I just don't know if the Svesti can leave yet."

Before Ava left to talk to Talen about the food, she looked around the War Room. *What a great bunch of caring women. Every world needs more like them.*

Hours later, Talia informed the women the *Invictus* was picking up the rescued children with at least one medical emergency. She told them the younglings would receive medical checkups before heading to the dining area.

"Talen, it looks like we will be having guests," Ava said as she walked into the kitchen.

"Wonderful. The rescue mission was a success, then."

"Sounds like it. Although, I believe there were some injuries. The younglings will be here after the healers check them over."

Talen cocked his head. "I estimate it will take them about an hour or so. We should reserve some tables for them so they can remain together. After we spoke earlier, I asked Healer Rivezt what species to expect. Unless someone has an individual allergy, there aren't any dietary restrictions. All our food should be safe for the younglings."

Ava smiled. "That's good news."

When the younglings entered the dining area later, Talen smiled. "They appear healthy and nourished. Someone has been taking good care of them."

Ava said in a low voice, "Do you think any of the warriors will be mean to them because they're half Zuvgran?"

A growl emanated from Talen's chest. "If any mistreat them, you tell me. I'll take care of it. Younglings are a gift from the Goddess."

Ava patted his arm. "Relax, big guy." She gestured for the younglings to come closer.

"Hi, everyone. My name is Ava and this is Talen. Have a seat and we'll bring out some food for you. We heard you had a busy day."

Quietly, the younglings took seats. Their eyes grew wide when Talen and Ava returned with a maglev laden with food and drinks. Ava handed out plates and utensils while Talen began serving. Huge smiles broke out on the children's faces as they ate the tasty fare. As they relaxed, chatter broke out and young voices expressed their appreciation. Ava beamed in satisfaction.

"Lady Ava?" Hozan Crulex spoke quietly.

"Yes?"

He held something out to her. "I had this game in my quarters. I thought the younglings might enjoy it."

"What a wonderful idea." Instead of taking it, she pulled his arm and led him to the younglings.

"Everyone, this is Lieutenant Hozan Crulex, a science officer on our ship. He's brought a game he thinks you might like. Lieutenant, why don't you sit and explain the game to them?"

Crulex appeared uncertain. "I do not wish to frighten them."

A young blue Mostiffian-Zuvgran male with three oval eyes and four arms looked up at Crulex.

"I'm Yostal. I'm four and I like science and games. You can sit by me."

"That is very kind of you, Yostal. I am most pleased to meet you."

Ava turned away to hide her teary eyes. *Cookies. I'll go get them while I compose myself.*

When she returned, more Svesti sat with the younglings having brought games and toys. She made note of what games they played and comm'd Talia to see if she could synthesize more for the children's quarters. *I wish Karid were here. He'd love playing with the kids.*

Later, Ava smiled when Tolvex arrived with a Svesti-Zuvgran male. *He looks like a gray Svesti with horns.*

"You must be Ronan. I'm Ava." She gestured at the scene. "As you can see, the children are fine. Talen and I fed them." She waggled her brows at Tolvex. "And they love cookies."

Tolvex chuckled. "Everyone loves your cookies, Lady Ava."

"Anyway, while they ate, warriors returned with games and toys from their quarters and stayed to help occupy the kids." Ava's turned serious. "One told me it had been so long since having younglings around, he'd forgotten how joyful they are."

Tolvex tilted his head. "It's true. While we visit other planets, our missions rarely include interacting with younglings. And the last Svesti youngling just turned thirty solars."

"Talia and the other women came by, met them, and took measurements, so I imagine there will be clothing for the kids soon," Ava said.

Ronan said, "Thank you for welcoming them so generously."

After Ronan greeted each of the younglings, Ava helped him and the warriors take them to their quarters. She left them with Talia and the other women and went to check on the injured girl in the med bay.

"Where's Natasha?" Ava asked Rivezt.

"She's back there with the young female, Teeka, who was assaulted by the Zuvgran back there." Ash'n pointed to a closed off area.

"I'm going to check to see if the girl wants food."

"You may need to wait, Lady Ava. They hurt her badly." His tail flicked in short snaps.

"I understand. I won't stay long."

"Knock, knock," Ava said quietly as she entered.

"We're busy here, Ava." Natasha said softly while she gently cleaned Teeka's arm.

"I'm just determining which species we need to feed and making sure no one has allergies or anything like that," Ava said cheerfully in Galactic Standard as she stepped closer to the med bed. "Hi, there. I'm Ava. What's your name?"

Ava recognized the vacant stare in the teenager's eyes. Her heart squeezed in her chest. Taking a deep breath, she slowly approached the med bed.

"Oh, honey, I hope the assholes who did this to you got what they deserved. You're safe with us and Natasha's the best." Ava grabbed another cloth and started to wash one of Teeka's arms gently. With no expectation of a response, she kept up a soothing monologue commenting positively on Teeka's six toes, lavender skin, and white hair. She interspersed it with chatter about the other women and some of the people onboard. *No pressure. Just letting you know I'm here for you when you're ready.*

"Oh, when Natasha says you can leave the med bay, you can come by my quarters and soak in my bathtub. It's so big, I bet you could swim in it." Ava winked. "I have, but don't tell anyone."

Teeka snorted. *That's a good sign. She's paying attention.*

Natasha said, "Teeka, Ava is a great chef and she makes cookies that are so good, you'll want to keep them all to yourself."

"What's a cookie?" Teeka asked so softly it was hard to hear her.

"Just about the best snack you ever tasted. There are so many different kinds, you're bound to find some that you really like. I'll bring you several types and you can tell me what appeals to you. Are there any particular flavors that are your favorites?" Ava answered her with no visible emotional response to Teeka speaking.

Natasha glanced up with a grin. "That's one of the reasons we keep Ava around. Her cooking—especially her treats."

Ava stuck her tongue out at Natasha and tossed her cloth down. "Well, I need to get back to the kitchen before the other younglings riot and take down Talen." She looked at Teeka. "Talen Previv is the head cook on our ship and a great guy."

Natasha spoke to Ava. "I think Teeka can have soft foods—nothing larger than bite-sized—and slushy, cold drinks for now." She checked her tablet. "I don't see anything listed here as harmful foods for Praxites or Zuvgran, so no other restrictions."

"Got it. Fruit smoothies and gentle on the jaw." Ava gave Natasha a mock salute. "I'll be back with it." She turned to Teeka. "It was nice to meet you. I hope you feel better soon."

When Ava entered the corridor, she leaned against a wall and wrapped her arms around her abdomen. Seeing Teeka brought back some of her own worst memories. She closed her eyes and took deep breaths. Once she felt centered again, she squared her shoulders and went to get the girl something to eat and drink. *You can do this, Ava. Just be there for Teeka if she needs it.*

Later that evening, Natasha comm'd Ava asking if Teeka could stay with her. Ava happily agreed.

When her door chimed, Ava greeted Teeka with a wide grin.

"Come on in, girl, and let's get comfortable." Ava gave Ronan and Natasha an understanding look. "I've got her from here. If she needs either one of you, I'll comm." She turned around to follow Teeka, then said, "Oh, I left a meal for you both in your quarters, Natasha."

"Thanks, Ava. I think you're just what she needs right now."

When the door closed, Ava gestured to the couches. "Sit anywhere you like and I'll get us some snacks." Teeka sat gingerly and wrapped her arms around her waist.

Ava grabbed some fruit smoothies and cookies and placed them on the table before taking a seat across from the girl. "I know Natasha said soft foods, so I made some cookies that aren't crispy for you to try if you want."

Teeka reached for a cookie and nibbled the edge. A small smile graced her face before she took a larger bite. "Thank you," she said quietly.

Taking a cookie for herself, Ava said, "There are clothes in the bedroom for you. You can sleep in there alone tonight, or I can join you. I can rest in a chair or next to you on the bed. Or I can sleep out here on a couch. Whatever makes you the most comfortable."

Teeka's eyes filled. "You are all so nice."

Ava slowly put her hand out to pat Teeka's giving her time to draw away if she needed to. "Teeka, you need to know you did not deserve what happened. It may take awhile, but there will come a time when it won't feel as overwhelming as it does now."

Teeka squeezed her fingers tightly. "Truly?"

"Truly." Ava smiled gently. "If you want to talk, I'll listen. But if you don't, that's okay, too."

"I'm not sure I want to tell the story again tonight," Teeka whispered.

"Okay. Did you want to get changed into something more comfortable? We can watch an Earth movie or play a game until you're tired."

"Earth movie?"

Ava grinned. "It's like theater, but with video. We can watch a comedy, a love story, or an action-adventure. I think you'll enjoy it."

"Okay. Maybe something funny?"

"With real people or carton animals?"

"You pick."

The next day at lunch, Ava plopped down on the chair next to Natasha with a *leringa* pie.

"Here. Have a piece before everyone figures out there's pie." Ava cut a slice and placed it on Natasha's empty plate.

"Mmm. Thanks. I've missed your cooking," said Natasha between bites. "Synthesizer food all the time gets old, especially since they don't have any of your recipes."

"What had everyone looking so serious after the meeting this morning? You all looked shell shocked," Talia asked, concern in her voice.

"Some personal stuff for Ronan and Largon. I'm not sure how much I'm allowed to share. It was very emotional for both of them and for the rest of us," Natasha said with a frown.

Ava wagged her eyebrows. "So? You and Ronan? Are the rumors I'm hearing true?"

"What rumors?"

"That he is bunking in your quarters, not Largon's," said Emmy.

"Yeah, that part is true."

"Well, spill it. We want to hear all about your romance," said Talia.

"I also want to hear about the rescue of the little ones," Rachel said.

Ava listened intently as Natasha told them about the rescue, how a Zuvgran choked her, and she ended up killing him. *I'm glad she wasn't hurt.*

Rachel expressed her concern about Natasha's mental state and let her know to come talk to her if she needed it. Ava looked around at everyone. *It's good to all be together again.*

Ava laughed at Emmy's antics and felt bad about Natasha's embarrassment when Emmy started talking about Svesti versus Zuvgran cocks and their differences. There was a tense moment when she thought Emmy and Natasha might argue, but the women worked it out quickly. Ava's ears perked up when she heard Emmy say the Svesti had nodes, then she missed most of the following conversation as she got lost in her thoughts. *Hmm, I never felt nodes on Karid, but we haven't gotten naked below the waist yet either. I like feeling his hardness against me, knowing it's me that excites him, not just any body.* She squirmed in her seat. *Damn, Karid, you need to return soon.*

Ava thought it was strange to see blue, brown, and lavender skin among the mostly gray tones of the Zuvgran hybrids. Extra eyes, arms, fingers, toes, and various tail sizes and lengths became commonplace in her mind after she saw the Pellotian-Zuvgran hybrids Ronan and Natasha brought back from Talonka Six. *Wings. They have wings. How cool is that?*

They housed the additional seven younglings in the quarters already assigned to the first group, while Talos, the green Pellotian who had been caring for them roomed with Largon.

"I thought you told me that Zuvgran hybrids of all species were gray," Ava said.

"Most are. However, the Romittel, Mostiffian, and Praxite races can go either way," Natasha said. "How was Teeka last night?"

"Mostly quiet. She had a nightmare and I talked with her afterwards and held her. It seemed to help."

Natasha's brown eyes met hers. "Thank you for helping her. You were able to bring her out of her near catatonic state. She's already in a better place mentally because of you."

Ava glanced away. "I have some experience dealing with trauma. I'm glad I can make a difference for her."

"Do you want to talk about it?"

"Not really, but thanks."

"I'm here if you decide differently," Natasha said quietly.

Ava gave her a sad smile. "I know and that means a lot to me."

From his position on the other side of the aquiponics area, the Svesti male watched the hybrids shrieking with laughter and running around in no discernable pattern. Human females and Svesti males encouraged them, even Merix Hunnek, the old male who took care of aquiponics.

This is what our future looks like. Svesti hybrids every-where. Instead of all sharing the same gray skin, like the Zuvgran hybrids, Svesti hybrids will be smaller and weaker—probably in a myriad of skin colors like humans. Who knows if they'll have the natural defenses of the Svesti? Some of them might not have claws or fangs or, Goddess forbid, tails. They'll be strange and freakish—like the humans.

The Svesti-Zuvgran hybrid and his Zuvgran friend joined the happy crowd. The male snorted in disgust. *And now we're working with Zuvgran?* He ignored a persistent inner voice that reminded him his uncle had allied with the Zuvgran to obtain the virus that killed human fertility.

He internally noted who interacted with the humans and hybrids so he could relay the information to his uncle when the *Invictus* returned to Costonia. Even though he now had something to report, his orders were to remain silent until they reached the home world. Despite his best efforts, he failed to frighten the human females with his attacks. Although he switched out an upload, poisoned two females, subjected another to a broken ladder and dangerous gas, exploded an oven door, and even installed a tripwire that shot needles, the females seemed happy and whole. *I would believe they are protected by the Goddess, but I know that cannot be. The Goddess wishes us to remain pure.*

Leaving the area, he muttered under his breath, "Always Svesti. You'll see."

Days flew by and Ava kept busy with cooking and the children. The *Invictus* warriors and the human women began converting

Hangar Bay Alpha to house six hundred hybrids from different refuges. King Sovex offered to keep the younglings safely together while he and Largon d'Ayen, the rescued Zuvgran, determined a permanent location for them.

Natasha and Ronan left in his transport to deliver vaccines to hidden Zuvgran colonies that disagreed with the Emperor's expansionist policies and abusive tactics. Largon led the *Invictus* to the various refuges where he and Ronan had Zuvgran hybrid younglings hidden. The space cruiser began to feel crowded, but lively, with additional younglings.

Eleven days later when they planned to rendezvous with the traveling pair, Ava heard Zuvgran attacked them and they crash landed on Millus. Talia told her Durek, Tolvex, and Rivezt were going to the surface for the rescue mission.

"Why are all of them going?" Ava asked.

Talia looked around to ensure no one else could hear then leaned closer. "Before they went down, they reported intermittently receiving a weak signal from Wurvez' tracker. He's been on a mission and hasn't contacted the *Invictus* in weeks. There's no way any of them will stay behind if there's a chance of rescuing one of their best friends."

Ava's face froze and shivers ran down her spine. *Please let him be okay.*

"What about Jevax? Is he there, too?" Ava was pleased her voice didn't express the panic she felt.

Talia drew back and narrowed her eyes. "You knew about the mission?"

"Only that the two of them went on one and it was a secret. I have no idea what their orders were." Ava shrugged. "Besides the fact I definitely missed the two males who bothered me the most in the kitchen for snacks."

"They haven't received anything from Jevax's tracker."

"I hope they're both okay."

"Me, too."

Chapter 9

KARID LOST TRACK of how many times the Zuvgran came in to question and beat him. At one point or another, fists, stun rods, knives, and boots made contact with his body. He'd given up trying to determine a pattern as to when and how they would abuse him. Assuming he received one terrible meal a day during his captivity, two weeks had passed, but at least he could drink a steady supply of water from the sink.

Swollen face, cracked ribs, multiple bruises and cuts, as well as pissing blood were about all he had to show for his captivity. He tried to escape twice, but failed and endured longer beatings. However, he remained mentally strong and determined. No matter what, he would not divulge any information. He would die first.

Every time he went to his happy place to mentally avoid the pain, he thought of Ava. His memories of her, an imagined future with her as his true mate, having a family, and growing old together. Even now, laying on the bunk attempting to conserve his energy and heal, he drifted back.

He and Ava relaxed on her couch. When she complained about the small screen on her laptop, he comm'd Gat'n Wrox, the ship's head engineer, to ask if there was a way to transfer a video to a larger area from the device. Wrox talked him through the process and now they watched an Earth movie on the large wall in front of them.

Earlier, they gorged themselves on chips and cookies. Ava dimmed the lights for a better viewing experience. Her head rested on his thigh and his claws repeatedly combed through her curls.

"That feels so good. It's soothing."

"I enjoy it as well, *raralumia*."

Her fingers stroked his leg in random patterns as the movie about an Irishman and his father finished.

"Did you like it?"

"It reminded me of my own conflicts with my father," Karid admitted quietly.

She sat up and curled under his arm. One hand rested over his heart, the other on his thigh, her legs tucked sideways. *She fits perfectly against me.*

"He is a merchant and determined I should follow in his footsteps. When I decided to become a warrior, we argued as viciously as those characters in the movie. He threatened to disown me."

"Oh, you must've been upset." She looked up at him with concerned eyes.

"Yes. Even now, I have minimal contact with the male. If he can't accept me for who I am, then I see no reason to subject myself to his continued machinations and ire."

Her eyes dropped and she picked at nonexistent lint on his shirt. "I understand toxic parental relationships. I can't blame you."

"What about your family? We've never discussed them." Her shoulders tensed at his words and silence reigned for long moments. He retracted his claws and ran his fingers through her hair. His nose wrinkled when her *wimma* and sugar scent indicated anger, fear, and anxiety.

"My biological father was a nightmare that I'm not ready to talk to you about. My mother died when I was very young. My adoptive dad is wonderful and his mother is the one who taught me to cook."

"Please look at me, Ava." He waited until her eyes rose to meet his. "You do not have to share anything with me unless you want to. I admit I selfishly want to know everything about you, but not if you aren't ready. Just understand that I am here."

Her expression softened. "Thank you, Karid. Your patience means a lot to me." Her scent lightened again.

He stroked her cheek with a tender finger. "May I ask a question? You do not have to answer."

"Sure."

"Is whatever you're not ready to share the reason you hold back part of yourself when we kiss?"

"Do I?" Her brows came together. "Is that what it feels like to you? I don't mean to."

"It's not a criticism, *raralumia*, just an observation. At times, it seems you mentally go somewhere else in your head." He exaggerated a pout. "In the beginning I thought it was me, but then I realized I'm too wonderful."

She choked back laughter. "You are so modest as well." She paused and chewed on her lower lip. His thumb replaced her teeth and he softly rubbed the abused flesh. "You might be correct, though. I'm sorry."

His ponytail swung as he shook his head. "You do not need to apologize." He grinned. "It's probably for the best right now. If you completely engaged, you would melt me with your heat and I might not be able to resist taking our relationship further than you want."

"You are such a charmer." She playfully bit his thumb.

"May I kiss you now?" Her arousal scent filled his nostrils. *Crek. I love that smell.*

"Yes."

Their mouths met and they exchanged long, slow kisses. He worshipped her mouth, face, and neck with his lips and tongue. She tugged at his shirt to touch his skin. Her warm hands caressed him and his cock hardened.

One of his hands tunneled under her top to stroke her flesh. She wriggled when his hand traced a path to the underside of her breast. He gently circled her mound before cupping it. His thumb repeatedly passed over her engorged nipple. Kneading her breast, he pinched the bud lightly. He inhaled her gasp and deepened his kiss.

Her hands unbound his hair and she ran her fingers through its length before clenching it as her body pressed closer to his. *She's not holding back now and it's magnificent.*

Disconnecting their mouths, he raggedly whispered in her ear, "May I see you? Taste you?"

"Yes." She drew back and pulled off her T-shirt. "Now you."

Happy to comply, he reached to his back to draw his shirt over his head and tossed it aside. He gathered her close and groaned when her bare nipples brushed against his chest.

"You feel amazing." His lips trailed a leisurely path to her breasts while his tail stroked her back.

"Oh god, your skin feels like the softest suede. I want to rub myself all over you."

"Don't let me stop you." His mouth closed over a nipple and he tongued it before sucking it languidly. Her moans played like music in his ears. Restlessly, her hands stroked his chest before her fingers tightened on his own nipples and squeezed. A deep groan escaped him.

They explored each other's torsos with hands, lips, and tongues. Karid's cock felt trapped in his pants, hard and uncomfortable, but he wouldn't change this experience for anything. He kissed the scars he found on her stomach with gentle lips and her breath hitched. Freckles dotted the tops of her breasts and he licked them with the tip of his tongue.

His hand drifted to her waistband. Her fingers trapped his.

"I'm not ready for that." Not meeting his eyes, she chewed on her swollen lower lip. Her scent tinged with embarrassment.

His fingers moved upward. He kissed her earlobe before he spoke.

"As you wish, *raralumia.*" His hands cupped and kneaded her breasts while his mouth and tongue concentrated on her neck and face. When she relaxed, he smiled to himself as her scent grew heavy with arousal.

Eventually, Karid drew back and looked at her hooded eyes, flushed skin, and tousled hair. His long hair brushed over her breasts, and she shivered. His hands and tail caressed her back in long, slow strokes. He grabbed her T-shirt and drew it over her head to cover her beautiful body.

Cupping her face, he reverently kissed her. "Thank you, *raralumia*. You are even more glorious than I imagined."

The sounds of approaching warriors interrupted his recollections. *Crek. I need to think of something else quickly to soften my cock. I don't need the Zuvgran noticing.* Thoughts of arguing with his father did the trick. He sat up gingerly to await his next beating.

Four Zuvgran entered, three with blasters. The leader jerked his chin toward the manacles.

"You know the routine. Move."

Karid took his time rising and limping to the opposite wall. He held his arms up. One Zuvgran handed his blaster to another and stepped forward to secure him. Karid momentarily debated giving the male a head butt but refrained.

"Will you answer my questions today?"

Karid stared at the leader.

"I thought not. That's why we're doing something different." He nodded at the warrior closest to Karid. "Inject him."

"What dosage?"

"The Svesti is a large one. Give him double a female's dose."

Karid tried to evade the male but the chains securing him to the wall limited his range of motion.

"What did you give me?"

The leader ignored Karid's question. "Cut his pants off."

"What is going on?" Karid kicked at the male, but another joined the first to hold him.

"Be still or I'll have you stunned."

When Karid was naked, the Zuvgran backed away and left the cell. After some time, Karid's body became hot and his cock hardened. His brain felt fuzzy and he squirmed as he became sexually aroused. He tried thinking of arguing with his father, listing famous artists in alphabetical order, and even recalling the mission where Vared ended up trapped in rubble after an explosion, but nothing worked. His cock wanted friction.

The lead Zuvgran returned and smirked when he saw Karid's cock. "I see the sexual stimulant worked. Good." He glanced at the door to the cell. "Bring her in."

Two males roughly tugged a terrified young Jalaxian female into Karid's cell. The sheer white gown she wore contrasted with her blue skin and dark hair. *She looks like she's only fifteen or sixteen solars. Crekkin' Zuvgran.*

"A fine warrior such as yourself deserves some female companionship to pass the time. My gift to you."

The Zuvgran pushed the female at Karid. Her flesh made his body burn worse. His hips bucked once before he regained control.

"No! I won't touch her." Karid looked down at the youngling and whispered. "Go. Stay as far away from me as you can. They injected me with a sexual stimulant. I don't want to hurt you."

Her dark eyes flitted around the cell. Then she darted past the Zuvgran toward the corner furthest from Karid. She sat and curled herself tightly into a protective ball.

"Get back here, female," one warrior ordered.

"Leave her alone for now. He can see and smell her and it will only increase the effects of the drug since he can't reach her." The leader narrowed his eyes at Karid. "You'll have plenty of opportunities to act on all those lascivious thoughts in your head, Svesti. In the meantime, we'll let you simmer so the show is even better. Enough of this drug and you'd *grak* a *naroon* if we brought one in."

"If it gets that bad, maybe I'll *crek* you, Zuvgran."

The Zuvgran leaned toward him. "No, but you'd let me *grak* you."

Karid bared his fangs and growled. The Zuvgran laughed and left the cell.

Over the next few days, the Zuvgran continued to inject Karid while leaving him chained to the wall. At some point, they extended his chains so he could reach the sanitary facility. His cock remained stiff and painful, even as he tried to masturbate with his back to the female. He apologized to her over and over and instructed her to move slowly in the cell so she wouldn't trigger his prey instincts.

Karid fought to retain some semblance of control over his mind and body. The drug fogged his brain to the degree that he felt himself reverting to a primal, instinctual state.

One day the Zuvgran came in, stunned him, then removed the manacles before exiting the cell. Karid moaned in despair. He punched the walls until his hands were bloody, broke apart the bunk in a frenzy, and used one of the supports to stab himself in the leg. Pain helped him keep away from the female who remained huddled in the corner except when she used the sanitary facility. When the pain and frustration became too much, he laid down in a corner away from her and cried.

Karid had no idea how long it was before the Zuvgran returned. He fought them with all he had until they stunned him unconscious. When he awoke, he hung from the manacles with another set around his ankles.

"Since you're not male enough to *grak* a female, your body should reflect it," the Zuvgran leader said holding a large knife. "I'm going to enjoy this, Svesti."

When the Zuvgran used the sharp weapon, Karid howled in anguish, then released a series of long, agonized screams before passing out.

Karid awoke in excruciating pain. The female knelt by his head and held her cupped hands near his mouth.

"Good. You're awake. Drink." Water dripped down from her hands. Karid tried to move his head to catch it. "No, stay still and let me adjust for you."

After he drank what he could, he asked, "How long was I unconscious?"

"A full day, I think. They haven't come back. Is the drug out of your system?"

Karid nodded tiredly. "I think so. I apologize, female."

"You have done nothing wrong. I wish I knew what I could do to help."

"I appreciate your kindness, but I think it's best if you return to your corner. I'm not fit company, and I am still exhausted."

She whispered as she stood, "You are an honorable male. You did not deserve this."

"Neither did you." Defeated, Karid found himself in a fetal position before his vision turned black again.

In a pain-induced haze, Karid heard blaster fire, then Vared's voice yelling, "Lady Natasha, come help the female. Someone find a stretcher." *I must be dreaming. Vared would never bring a human female on a rescue mission.*

"They won't hurt him, will they? He is an honorable male," the Jalaxian asked.

"They're his brothers. They're here to rescue him," Lady Natasha said.

"Karid, can you hear me? It's Ash'n." Gentle hands turned him over. *Goddess, are they really here?*

Karid groaned and tried to open his eyes.

"Sweet Goddess, what the *crek* did they do to him?" *Devik is here, too? Now all my friends know my shame.*

Karid's best friends gently lifted him onto a stretcher and placed a blanket over him. Then he heard Vared again.

"Move everyone out. Make sure there are no others to be rescued, then destroy this place once we have the data."

Multiple boots sounded loud in Karid's ears and his stomach roiled as the stretcher moved.

An unfamiliar voice said, "He's not going to hurt you, young female. He's with us. No one will hurt you with us."

Devik sounded distressed. "Rivezt will care for him, Lady Natasha. No one else." *I don't even want Ash'n to see me.*

Karid lost consciousness again.

"You will let me see him right now."

Ava's angry words roused Karid. Opening his eyes, he squinted at the brightness of the room. Memories of his ordeal assaulted him, and he blinked back tears.

"I'm sorry Lady Ava, but he remains unconscious. No visitors while he heals."

"I just want to sit with him." *Oh, raralumia, it's better this way. I cannot bear for you to witness my shame.*

Compassion laced the healer's voice. "I cannot let you in."

Karid strained to hear when Ava said quietly, "Can you tell me what they did to him?"

"The Zuvgran inflicted multiple injuries, some worse than others. There is scarring the med bed is unable to correct. I cannot be more specific." Ash'n paused. "Thank the Goddess he still lives. However, recovery from his ordeal will take time."

After Ava left, Ash'n entered the room.

"Good. You're awake. How do you feel?" Compassion laced his friend's voice.

"How long?" Karid croaked.

Ash'n raised Karid's head, then handed him a water pouch. With a shaky hand, Karid sipped the cool liquid.

"We rescued you six days ago. We should reach Costonia in four days."

"No. How long was I there?" Karid stared at the pouch.

"We believe three weeks. We've been very worried about you."

Karid quickly withdrew his hand when Ash'n squeezed it.

"Who knows?" Karid's shoulders tensed.

Wrinkles appeared on the healer's forehead. "About what?"

Karid gestured toward his body and kept his voice low. "What was done to me."

Understanding showed on his friend's face. "Myself, Vared, Devik, and Traxen. I've allowed no one else to treat or visit you. I also sealed your medical file with a password."

Karid closed his eyes. "I'm tired."

"Lady Ava would like to see you. She's been very persistent."

"I wish to be left alone."

"We should discuss your treatment." Ash'n sounded concerned.

"No. I don't care what you did to heal me."

"I believe it would be helpful for you to speak with a mind healer when we reach the home world."

"Absolutely not." Karid's tail flicked and he growled as he glared at Ash'n. "I have no desire to talk with anyone. Not even you. Please leave."

"My friend, you've been through an ordeal."

Karid pointed at the door and yelled, "Go!"

His friend sadly shook his head. "I'll let you rest." The door closed quietly behind him.

Karid stared at the wall several hours later when Vared, Devik, and Ash'n came in with a tray of food.

"It's good to see you conscious," said Vared.

"Lady Ava sent cookies with your meal," Devik said with a small, sad smile.

"I'm not hungry." Karid refused to look at them. "I think my tracker was defective."

From the corner of his eye, he saw his friends exchange glances at his sudden subject change.

"How so?"

"It failed to activate multiple times when I clicked my teeth. When I used my claw, it turned cold only for a few seconds."

Devik tapped on his tablet. "I'll make a report."

Vared's scar whitened as his lips turned down. "Ash'n tells me you refuse to talk with a mind healer. Perhaps you should talk with us."

"No."

Silence filled the room. Vared's tail flicked and he crossed his arms.

"As is customary, you are on medical leave until you've healed."

Karid nodded curtly.

"I'm assuming you will not be residing with your father when we get to Costonia. Would you like to stay with one of us instead while you heal?" Ash'n asked.

"I wish to be alone. I will deal with this on my own."

"That's unwise, my friend," said Devik. "You should be with those who care about you."

"No."

"Why won't you look at us, Karid? We only wish to help," Ash'n said sadly. *Because I don't want to see your pity.*

Karid could only say, "I thank you for rescuing me and your concern. I need nothing else except to be alone. Please leave."

Vared's chest rumbled. "We'll go for now, but this discussion is not over."

Yes, it is.

Each day, his friends showed up at mealtimes, either singly or together. Karid steadfastly avoided any talk about his captivity, injuries, or anything at all. He barely ate. His room in the med bay felt like another cell.

Vared strode in and tossed a bag on a chair.

"Take a shower and get dressed. I will shuttle you to where you will be staying on the planet. King's orders."

Karid stared. "Where?"

Vared raised an eyebrow. "Does it matter?"

"Guess not if I can be alone." Karid stood and took the bag to the sanitary facility.

When Karid was ready, Vared led him through the darkened corridors to Shuttle Bay Bravo. Being late at night, they didn't encounter many warriors, and the few that they passed simply nodded respectfully. Karid's forehead wrinkled when he saw the bay stuffed with more spacecraft than usual.

Vared noticed his expression. "We moved the ships from Shuttle Bay Alpha to the other bays to make room for the younglings."

"I don't understand."

His friend gave him a disappointed look. "I don't think you're in the proper mindset for me to explain." He pointed to a small shuttle near the bay exit. "That one is ours."

Vared coordinated their departure with the bridge. He remained silent until they entered the atmosphere of Costonia.

"It's good to be home. I wish you looked happier about it."

Karid grunted and watched as the planet grew larger in the viewscreen.

"We'll be escorting the human females to the palace before daylight to keep them from being overwhelmed by the court leeches. Traxen wants to meet them before deciding whether Ladies Rachel and Ava should be participate in a Choosing," said Vared.

Karid's tail whipped and slapped the back of his seat.

Vared landed in the forest about twenty miles north of the palace. When the pair disembarked, a cabin stood not far from the ramp.

"Traxen had the locks are keyed to you, me, Devik, Ash'n, and him. Food will be delivered every few days. You can make any requests through the staff or comm one of us. There are no other cabins nearby."

"Thank you." *Finally, I can be alone.*

"One last thing." Vared clasped Karid's nape and touched foreheads. He held tight as Karid attempted to twist from his grasp. "I think you're making a mistake pushing away those who love you most. Ash'n talked me out of sparring with you to beat some *crekkin'* sense into your thick skull." He released Karid and his lips thinned. "This is not a permanent solution. I don't like it, but we will give you some space to work through your pain. You are a brother of our hearts. We are here for you, no matter what. You never have to be alone."

Karid couldn't speak and didn't know what he would say even if he could. He just clasped his friend's forearm and nodded solemnly. He turned and opened the door, never looking back as Vared left to return to the *Invictus*.

Chapter 10

AVA TOSSED THE bread dough on the counter harder than she normally would. Using her palms, she pushed the dough forward before grabbing the top and folding it toward her, then repeated her actions. The rhythmic motions calmed her as she worked through her anger and worry about Karid. Nine days ago the Svesti rescued him, but no one would let her in to see him. Lin told her that Ash'n said Karid remained insistent he wanted to be alone—even ignoring his best friends. *I'm not the only one concerned.*

Even though Ava spent part of her day with the young-lings, she couldn't escape her chaotic thoughts. Teeka moved back with her friends saying she needed some normalcy. *I should check on her before we go to the planet.*

"Ava, you should be resting. You've been here late every night for weeks," Talen said from behind her.

Keeping her gaze on the dough, she said, "I'm trying a new recipe. A different type of bread. And I like the quiet."

"The freezers are overflowing, *picana*. We are all worried about him." Talen reached out one his large hands to still hers. "Exhausting yourself will not help him."

She blinked rapidly as she attempted to keep her voice even. "It's the not knowing that's making me crazy. I don't know how to prepare myself to help. Even though he's on the ship, I still feel like he's gone."

He gently used his other hand and tail to turn her toward him and hugged her. "I know. But you're a strong female with a good heart. You can handle whatever comes. The other females and I will always be here for you."

She rested her head on his chest and finally let the tears come, dampening his shirt. He held her until her sniffles abated. Leaning back to look her in the eyes, he said, "Go. Rest. Tomorrow, I don't want to see you here. Use the time to pack. We should arrive at Costonia soon." He smirked. "You'll be able to fill the palace freezers instead."

Ava choked back an involuntary laugh. She patted his cheek. "Thank you for being such a good big brother and putting up with me."

"I am honored you think of me that way." Quickly giving her another hug, he said, "Now go."

Ava took Talen's advice and let fatigue finally overtake her. She didn't leave for the kitchen when she woke from a restless sleep. Not wanting company, she chose items from her cooling unit to eat rather than go to the dining area. *I should probably clean the perishables out today if we're going to the surface soon. No sense stinking up the place.*

Munching on some cheese, she padded barefoot to her bedroom. *Despite everything that's happened, somehow the Invictus feels like my home. I'm a little sad I have to leave soon.*

She pulled a suitcase from the hidden storage closet and placed it on the bed. Pressing the wall to open the drawers, she slowly began packing. She froze when she pulled out one of Karid's shirts before burying her face in it. Irritated it no longer had his scent on it, she brushed the silky blue material with her fingers and found herself smiling when she recalled why she had it.

It was from the night Karid sweetly said, "I have been researching on Earth's internet. Would you go on a date with me?"

She raised an eyebrow. "What do you think we've been doing? We're together almost every day."

Karid's forehead wrinkled. "Do you consider those dates?"

"If I kissed you, then I call it a date."

"So I do not need to do anything special to show my interest in you as a female?"

"Well, I didn't say that. A woman likes to be treated well."

"This is a little confusing." He tugged absently on his ponytail and crinkled his nose. "I thought I always treated you well." *How can a huge warrior be so adorable?*

She laughed. "You do. What were you thinking for this date?"

"I thought we could dress up, and I could surprise you."

"Yes, Karid, I would love to go on a date with you. When should I be ready?"

"This evening at our usual time?" His gray eyes lit up.

"I look forward to it."

Wearing a satiny green shirt Natasha made for her with material they purchased on Theron paired with a black skirt, she opened her door and admired Karid in a color other than his usual black. The blue silk lovingly outlined his wide shoulders, muscular arms, and trim torso. *Lucky shirt.*

He drew in a breath when he saw her. "You look beautiful, Ava."

"Thank you. You look very handsome." She caressed the shirt over his pec. "This color brings out the gray in your eyes."

He dipped his chin, and his fangs gleamed white against his reddish bronze skin. "I am glad you approve." He offered his arm. "Shall we?"

With a huge smile, she wrapped her arm around his. "Of course."

With his tail lightly touching her back, he led her to the aquiponics area and they sauntered along the pink gravel path. Exchanging humorous anecdotes, she told him of an incident at her first job in a restaurant.

"It was a busy Saturday night and we had a new busboy. We needed more supplies kept in the basement. Cooks were yelling out what they wanted the busboy to bring up to the kitchen. In the middle of the chaos, the head chef said he needed a bucket of steam and told the new guy they kept it next to where they stored the salad dressings. The poor kid came back all worried because he couldn't find the nonexistent bucket."

Karid chuckled. "How long before he realized he was being pranked?"

"About the time we couldn't hold in our laughter anymore."

After the aquiponics area, they strolled to Karid's quarters. She halted just inside the door. The low lights cast a romantic glow, and white linen decorated his dining table. A hurricane lamp centerpiece sat among strewn flower petals. On the counter, ornate silver cloches that looked remarkably like the ones on Earth covered their meals. Soft instrumental jazz emanated softly from somewhere. She turned her gaze to see his hopeful expression.

"Karid, this is amazing. It feels like a restaurant on Earth."

He beamed. "I hoped you would like it. I asked Talen to make some Earth specialties he learned from you."

Conversation never lacked as they ate the delicious meal. The entree was a beef bourguignon recipe made with *maxiem*. Ava hid her smile when he pulled out the cheesecake with *leringa* sauce. *I won't tell him I actually made that. Talen is a sneaky one.*

Afterwards, Karid asked her to dance. Snug in his arms, she closed her eyes and inhaled his scent—musk with cinnamon and pepper. His tail wrapped around her bare ankle and lightly caressed her, while his hands smoothed her shirt against her back. Their bodies swayed with their legs touching. Separated by their shirts, her nipples pebbled against his lower chest and heat built in her veins.

Breath hot in her ear he whispered "Are you enjoying our date?"

"Yes. It's wonderful." She tilted her head as he licked the shell of her ear and kissed her neck.

"You deserve it. I've never met a female as incredible as you, *raralumia*."

She mewled and shivered when his fangs nipped her pulse. Her fingers found the leather tie securing his ponytail and tugged. Unbound, his light brown hair created a curtain between them and the rest of the room when he kissed her lips. *I love his hair*.

Her hands slid under his shirt. Flattening her palms and spreading her fingers, she explored his back from his neck to his waist. Greedily, she said, "Take it off. "

He sucked on her lower lip before taking a step back, removing his shirt, and tossing it onto the couch. His hands reached for the buttons of her shirt.

"May I?"

She nodded and trailed her fingertips over his pecs. His mouth lingered over each new bit of her skin he exposed sending quivers down her spine. Pulling her shirt down her arms, he used it to drag her arms together behind her back. Her breasts heaved upward in her lacy bra and his eyes turned molten silver.

"So bountiful and so beautiful." He held her arms captive with one hand clutching her shirt. He raised his tail to tease her mounds. The light touch drove her insane with the need for more. With his other hand, he extended a claw and traced her curves before circling a nipple.

Leaning down, he sucked on an erect bud. She moaned and her head fell back as he licked and nipped her through the lace. Giving her other nipple similar attention, he groaned. Her panties dampened.

"Your scent makes me hungry for more."

Panting, her head fell forward. "I'm not ready."

"I just want to taste and pleasure you, *raralumia*." Wild silver eyes caught hers. His tail dropped to caress her inner thigh. "You can keep your skirt on and I will stop whenever you say." He licked his lips and stilled.

She rubbed her thighs together trying to ease her arousal. Gazing at him, she realized if he pushed the issue, she'd have sex with him. Her eyes dropped to his mouth. *He's asking, not taking.*

"Pleasure me, Karid," she breathed.

"Are you certain?"

"Yes."

"Thank the Goddess," he said as he released her arms and knelt at her feet. Keeping his eyes on her face, his hands caressed her ankles and burned a path of tingling heat as they rose higher. When he reached her panties, his fingers slid underneath and squeezed her ass before he tugged them down her legs.

Her hands gripped his shoulders as she stepped out of her underwear. He raised them to his face. His eyelids closed as he inhaled deeply. *Fuck. Why is that so hot?*

Growling, he reopened his eyes and his hands slid back under her skirt to cup her ass. She squealed as he lifted her off her feet and knee-walked a short distance. He gently lowered her to sit on the arm of the couch, his tail supporting her back.

Pushing her skirt to her waist, he pulled her legs over his shoulders. His gaze dropped to her pussy.

"Beautiful and so wet for me." His tongue swiped upwards and her hips jerked when his tongue met her clit. Smiling silver eyes looked up. "Delicious."

A long moan fell from her lips as his tongue licked and his mouth sucked. Quivers shook her when he growled lightly against her hidden flesh. His tongue pierced her pussy and her hips jerked when he found sensitive areas she didn't even know she had. Her fingernails bit into his scalp when he returned and explored her clit. Her legs wrapped around his head as he experimented with different motions and pressures. She wailed his name when a fang grazed her swollen clit.

Large, warm hands wrapped around her thighs to keep her spread for his ministrations and hold her in place. Tingling started at her toes and traveled throughout her body as it bucked hard against his mouth.

"More, Karid. More. That feels so good." Shuddering through the most intense orgasm of her life, she was unprepared for a second one on the heels of the first. She screamed his name as uncontrollable spasms shook her. Before the third climax she absently started pulling his hair. She released him and he growled a loud "No" against her. She burrowed her fingers in his tresses and he smiled against her pussy. After he made her come again, her limbs fell limp.

"Too sensitive," she mumbled.

He gave her pussy a last gentle lick and turned his wet face to nuzzle and nip her inner thigh. His hands pulled her skirt down. He stood and lifted her. Flopping to sit on the couch, he arranged her on his lap before pulling his shirt over her head to cover her. The silky material was cool on her heated flesh and the collar slipped down exposing her shoulder.

His cock pressed against her ass. She tasted herself on his lips and tongue as he kissed her.

"I knew you would be glorious in your passion. You are *crekkin'* exquisite."

Heat rose on her cheeks. "Thank you." She wriggled. "I didn't take care of you."

"Giving you pleasure gives me pleasure, Ava. Just let me hold you."

His tail wound around her ankle and the fingers of one of his hands combed through her curls. A purr emanated from his chest and her eyelids drooped. She fell asleep in his arms.

And when I woke, I was tucked into my own bed still wearing his shirt. Underneath all that muscle, he's exceptionally sweet.

Tears running down her face, Ava continued packing her belongings. Karid didn't want to see her and her heart hurt at the thought she might never get the chance to find out where their relationship could go. Anger at the Zuvgran for hurting him, at his friends for keeping her from him, and even at Karid himself for hiding himself away burned through her veins before waning, leaving her emotionally exhausted. *I have a right to be angry, but it serves no purpose and certainly doesn't make me feel better. I can't change it.*

Wiping her arm across her sniffling nose, she mourned the loss of his presence. She missed laughing and talking with him, smelling his unique scent and hearing his heartbeat when she rested her cheek on his chest, and how safe she felt to be herself with him. *He could've been the one I could truly trust with everything and now I'm in this painful limbo.*

The quiet click of the suitcase lock sounded loud in her silent quarters. *Somehow, I'll get through this.*

Ava was the last woman to reach Rachel's quarters where Talia asked them to meet after evening meal. She hopped up on a couch.

"Vared said he will be flying us to the surface at four in the morning—about eight hours from now."

Confused, the women glanced at each other.

"That seems like a strange time," said Emmy.

"He said Traxen wants us to be able to arrive and settle in without all the fanfare of the court."

Rachel shrugged her shoulders. "It's certainly easier that way."

"If it means we don't have to be on display and worry about embarrassing ourselves by not remembering protocol, I'm good with an early morning arrival," Lin agreed.

"I'm assuming Ronan and Largon will go with us," Natasha said.

Talia nodded. "As will Tolvex and Rivezt. Then I believe Largon will return to the *Invictus* with Tolvex to help relocate the children while Ronan coordinates from the planet."

"What about Karid?" Ava asked quietly.

"I don't know." Talia's lips thinned. "Vared won't tell me anything about his injuries or progress."

"Neither will Devik," Emmy said.

Lin added, "Ash'n is the same. I can tell he's worried, though." Talia and Emmy nodded.

Natasha stood and moved towards Ava. "Ash'n added a password to Wurvez' medical files. None of the other healers know what's going on."

"I can probably get into the files."

"No, Emmy," Ava said firmly. "As much as I want to know, we will not invade his privacy that way."

"You sure? I'll face Devik's wrath if you want me to hack his records."

"I'm positive. Promise me you won't. Not just for Karid's sake, but also yours. If Devik isn't confiding in you, then you can't betray his trust again."

Emmy huffed and crossed her arms. "I promise."

Talia's expression softened. "Is there something you haven't told us about you and Wurvez?"

Ava stiffened, then let out a slow breath. She looked at their concerned faces. *I guess it's time.*

"Karid and I were dating before he left on his mission. He said he wanted to have a serious discussion when he got back. Now he won't even see me, let alone talk to me."

"It seems pretty obvious that he's withdrawing from everyone. Something traumatic happened to him," said Natasha.

"I know," Ava said quietly. "I understand that. It hurts here," she spread a hand over her heart, "to know he's in pain. I want to be there for him."

Natasha shifted in her seat and fidgeted with the end of her braid. "I don't know if I should tell you this."

"What?"

"The night before we were rescued on Millus, Ronan and I heard someone howling in pain. We both believe it was Wurvez. And during the rescue, Ash'n, as well as his other friends, refused to let me assess Wurvez." Her brown eyes turned sad. "I'm certain all of that adds up to some type of severe injury."

Ava's heart stopped, then raced. She leaned over and squeezed Natasha's hand. "I came to that conclusion myself with the way the males have been acting but thank you for sharing what you know with me."

"So you and Wurvez, huh?"

"Emmy, not the time," said Rachel with an indulgent shake of her head. The other women agreed with forlorn faces.

"Oh, alright. I'll wait for a better time to be nosy." Emmy smiled at Ava. "At least you have good taste."

Ava snorted involuntarily and swiped her hands under her eyes. "Thanks." *If I weren't so worried about him, I'd let her be nosy now.*

Pale yellow light on the horizon pierced the darkness as the shuttle silently approached Costonia. Vared piloted the craft with Talia sitting next to him while everyone else sat in the back. Ash'n activated a viewscreen so the other women could watch their descent.

"I can't wait to see the flora growing in its natural habitat," said Lin excitedly.

"Where are we going?" asked Rachel.

"Trezoura, our capital city. You'll be guests at the palace," said Devik.

"Even us?" Emmy looked at her mate. "We're not going to your home?"

"We'll visit my brothers and father later, but for now, we have a room here." Devik smiled.

"Will our presence create problems for the king?" Largon asked with a frown.

"Possibly, but I doubt he'll care. Traxen does what he believes is right." Ash'n grinned.

"You call the king by his first name?" Ava's forehead wrinkled.

"Traxen is only a few years older than Vared and was still at the Warrior Academy when our group arrived. He spent time with his cousin, which meant he also befriended us. It continues to irk him when we use his title." Devik explained. "He is a good male. Much more even-keeled than Vared."

The women softly laughed—they all knew about the commander's temper.

"We're approaching the palace now."

"Oh," exclaimed Lin. "It doesn't even look like a building is there."

"Most of our structures integrate with nature," said Ash'n.

"That's wonderful." Lin bounced in her seat before leaning on Ash'n. Her hands wrapped around his elbow. "You'll have to show me everything." He kissed the top of her head.

Ava turned her attention back to the viewscreen and schooled her expression. She was happy for her friends with their fated mates but also feeling a little jealous. *Karid wanted to be here to show me his home. I know he's hurting, but he's hurting me now, too.*

The shuttle landed in a designated area on the roof of the palace. When they disembarked, King Sovex awaited them with two older males, one female Svesti, and two male guards. Several others discreetly entered the ship with a maglev. *Probably going to get our belongings.*

Ava smiled when she was supposed to, but her heart wasn't in it. Now that she felt comfortable with the Svesti, she normally would have been thrilled to meet the group and learn more about them. Instead, she listened apathetically as the King greeted them by name and made introductions. The commander's father, Canaan Durek, hugged Talia and his son, while the king's admin, Ril'n Xeliv smiled and nodded. Ash'n hugged and touched tail tips with the female, his grandmother, Narilla Rivezt. *What striking silver hair she has.* She appeared especially delighted to meet Lin.

She did take note that King Sovex and Canaan both greeted Ronan and Largon with respectful warrior clasps of the forearms. Canaan invited both to visit his estate after getting the younglings settled so he could learn more about them and tell them stories of his cousin, Ronan's deceased mother. She saw Natasha's eyes fill with tears at the kindness before she schooled her expression.

As the group escorted them to their rooms and made plans to meet later, one of the guards approached her.

"Lady Ava, I have heard so much about you from my brother, Talen."

Surprised, she really looked at him, then a heartfelt smile grew on her face—her first since landing on the planet. "You must be Madix. He speaks of you often."

"None of it is true, I'm sure. He likes to exaggerate my shortcomings. Not that I have any." His fangs flashed against his reddish bronze face. "I already spoke with the king and the head cook. You will have access to the palace kitchens to make your wonderful cookies. I can't wait to try some."

"Thank you, Madix. I appreciate your kindness."

He dipped his chin. "Talen instructed me to ensure you have what you need. I am honored to help." *What I need is Karid. I wish you could help with that.*

Chapter 11

MOONLIGHT STREAMING THROUGH the windows provided enough illumination for Karid to navigate the cabin. He dropped his bag in the first bedroom he found before heading to the living area. Searching a side cabinet, he came across a bottle of Estalan liquor nestled amongst a number of others. Pouring himself a large portion of the coveted amber liquid tinged with pink, he collapsed into an overstuffed chair—glass in one hand and bottle in the other.

He stared into his glass as if it held the secrets to the universe. Taking a large swig, he closed his eyes briefly and concentrated on the burn of the alcohol traveling down his throat. *Maybe this will keep the nightmares away.*

When he finished his drink, he began to pour another. He hesitated. Carefully placing the glass on the table near him, he tightened his grasp on the bottle's neck. *Crek it. I can just drink from the source.*

Although his eyes traversed the room, in his mind he only saw his cell. Swigging occasionally, he tried to forget his captivity. Time had no meaning for him until his body protested. Feeling nature's call, he stumbled his way to the sanitary facility gripping the bottle before putting it down on the counter. Glaring at the wall above the toilet with his jaw clenched, he took care of business. He washed his hands, then cradled the bottle to his chest as he made his way to the bedroom. Pushing aside his bag, he flopped onto the bed and fell asleep.

When the nightmare woke him, Karid's heart thundered in his chest. Sweat beaded on his body and blood pounded in his ears as his tail moved erratically. Grimacing in the growing morning light, he discovered the bottle of liquor still clutched in his fist. Raising it vertically, he finished the last of it before tossing the bottle aside barely hearing the soft clunk on the carpet. *That didn't work as well as I hoped. I didn't get drunk enough to silence the nightmares.*

Crek. I didn't even undress. He fumbled into a sitting position and took off his boots. His shirt ended up on the floor somewhere near the empty bottle. He left his pants on and rolled onto his side forcing himself to keep his eyes wide open. He feared falling asleep again. He tried distracting himself with thoughts of Ava, but the pain of giving her up warred with the memories of his trauma. *I had such hopes and plans for us and now they mean nothing. She deserves better than the weak male I've become.*

Grunting, he decided to rise and see what there was to eat. In the cooling unit, he found some *pertiza* and *brellia*. Take several bites from each, he frowned at the sour taste left in his mouth. The *brellia* thunked on the floor when his toss at the recycler missed. He stared at it for a long moment, then shrugged. Leaving it where it lay and the half-eaten *pertiza* on the counter, he stomped back to the living area. He grabbed another bottle and took a long swallow. Grimacing, he squinted at the label. *Durelian whiskey. Tastes like rulah dung soaked in grease.* Sighing heavily, he kept drinking until the room spun, the pain ceased, and he faded into blackness.

A crick in his neck and cramp in his shoulder eventually penetrated Karid's stupor. He rearranged his body in the overstuffed chair trying to find a new position. Extending his claws, he lazily scratched his stomach near the scars Ash'n hadn't been able to erase completely.

Waves of guilt rocked him as he thought of how he had treated his best friends and Ava. *I don't want their pity. I may not be a warrior any longer, but I have some pride.*

He ignored the small voice in his head that chastised him about his behavior. He couldn't muster the energy to argue with himself so he went with the loudest voices that sounded suspiciously like the Zuvgran leader and his father in stereo. *I'm no longer a real male. I'm worthless.*

Growling and tail whipping frantically, he abruptly stood and staggered for another bottle. Startled, he froze at his reflection in the mirror above the cabinet. Unable to meet his own eyes, he roared and punched a hole in the wall, bruising his knuckles. Wild-eyed, he searched the room for something, anything he could use. When he saw a lightweight afghan, he grabbed it and covered the mirror. *I need to cover all of them. I can't look at myself.*

Suddenly panicked, Karid lurched through the cabin, tossing any material he could find over every mirror. Hyperventilating, he found himself gripping the edges of the sink in the sanitary facility. His long hair hid the room around him as he stared at the drain and worked at slowing his breathing. *I feel so dirty.*

He released the fastening on his pants, kicked them off when they fell to the floor, and got into the shower. The hot water pelted him, and he scrubbed his arms and chest raw. He couldn't make himself wash lower. He couldn't look. He couldn't... The voices grew louder and he collapsed onto the floor of the shower, head down on his knees while his arms hugged his calves. Sobbing, he rocked long after the water turned frigid. *Make it stop. Dear Goddess, please make the voices stop. I just want to forget.*

Several days later, Karid answered the kitchen door chime. Two males stood there with a small maglev.

"Who are you?"

"We're from the palace. We were ordered to bring supplies."

"What supplies?"

"Food and whatever else you request."

"How often are the deliveries?"

"Every four days."

Karid stared at the males. "Do you know what liquor was originally stocked?"

"Yes, sir." The males bobbed their heads.

"Add double that to every delivery." Karid paused. "Except for the Durelian whiskey. Don't bother bringing that."

"Sir?"

"Is there something wrong with your hearing?"

The males looked at each other.

"No, sir," one said. "We'll add your request to your next delivery."

"That will be fine. I'll leave this door unlocked every fourth day and you can leave the delivery in the kitchen."

"As you wish, sir." The males hustled and carried in the food. They stocked the cooling unit and stacked thermal containers on the counter.

"Everything is marked for you, sir."

Karid dipped his chin. "Be off with you then."

The males hurried off with the maglev to the small flitter parked nearby and departed. Karid closed and locked the door. *I've been here four days already?*

He set a repeating reminder on his comm to unlock the door for the subsequent deliveries. Opening one thermal container, he took a few bites before tossing down his fork in disgust. *Nothing tastes right.*

Karid picked up a bottle and took a swig. *I'll eventually discover the right amount to stop the voices and the nightmares. I just need more to quiet my brain.*

"That was delicious." The Svesti noble wiped his mouth with a cloth napkin.

"Thank you. I'm glad you could make it to your nephew's welcome home celebration. I know how busy you are with all your Council duties."

"I try to make time for family. After everything our race has suffered, one should prioritize the important matters." *Goddess, will this meal ever be over? She's as dull-witted as ever. At least she cooks well.*

She smiled. "Father and Mother would be so proud of the male you've become."

He dipped his chin in acknowledgment. "Would you mind if I stole your son for a bit? He hasn't had a chance to ride in my new speedster. I think he'd enjoy it." *I need to speak with him alone.*

Tittering, she said, "Males and their technology. Go, have fun."

Her son rose from the table and bent to kiss her cheek. "Thank you, Mother. I promise to spend all day with you tomorrow."

"I will enjoy that. You can tell me your impressions of the human females and all your adventures on the *Invictus*. The changes are so exciting." She patted his hand, then looked to her brother. "Would you like some leftovers for your guards and pilot? There is plenty."

"That's kind of you, but they are fine." *Why would I take their attention from their primary duties and spoil them? Simple female.*

Uncle and nephew spoke of inconsequential topics as they walked to the ship with two guards trailing them. Once onboard, the older male instructed the warriors to give them privacy and told the pilot to fly over popular sites as if giving a tour.

Once they were alone and underway, he said, "Report."

His nephew detailed all his actions for the cause while on the *Invictus*. He spoke of the Zuvgran hybrids and the rumor about the king settling all of them on Costonia.

"Unacceptable," the older male said. "Sovex goes too far."

"Also, there was a rescue of a Svesti almost a month ago. The commander led the mission himself on Millus with a large contingent of warriors. I haven't been able to confirm it, but the rumblings are it was Lieutenant Wurvez."

The noble froze. "Are you sure?" *Crek. The Zuvgran were supposed to kill him. He's seen my face.*

Confused, his nephew said, "That there was a mission. yes. Who it was? No. Although, whoever they rescued spent the rest of the time in the med bay and refused all visitors. It's said he's badly injured and traumatized."

"Where is he now?" *If Wurvez had spoken of what he saw, Sovex would have already arrested me. I need to find him and end him myself before he can ruin my plans.*

"I do not know. When I manufactured a reason to visit the med bay before the shuttles began transporting us to the planet, the private room was open with no one there."

"Why did you not tell me this before?"

"You ordered me to not contact you until I was home. I had to remain on the *Invictus* to help with the inventory and resupply before coming to the surface."

"You did not think this was important?" The older male's tail whipped behind him.

"Important enough to report when I saw you, which I did. Uncle, I am uncertain what I did to upset you."

Relax, he doesn't know about Millus.

Consciously restraining his anger, his tail slowed and he said, "I apologize, Nephew. I have many moving pieces and you surprised me with this addition."

"I understand."

"Continue to see if you can determine who they rescued and his current location. I think it may be helpful to the cause."

"I'll try, but I am very low in the command structure and a lot of secrecy surrounds it all. I don't even know when they transported the human females to the planet and you know I've been on the *Invictus* for an additional two weeks since the ship arrived. I should've have heard something but no one knows how they got here."

The noble waved his hand. "That's not important. I'm sure Sovex arranged it so he was the first male they saw on the planet. His ego knows no boundaries."

After dropping his nephew back at his sister's home, the noble sat back in the plush seat as his pilot flew him back to his own estate. *How do I find out for certain if they rescued Wurvez and where he is?*

An idea finally came to him and he slowly smiled as he worked out the details on how best to manipulate the male to do the work for him. *Yes, he's perfect. I'll have him followed and then arrange to kidnap Wurvez again to find out what he's said before I kill him myself.*

In a much better mood, he called one of his guards and gave him instructions. He sipped some Estalan liquor and his tail slowly swayed. *No one will stop me from regaining my birthright.*

Chapter 12

THREE WEEKS AFTER arriving on Costonia, Ava walked the familiar path to the palace kitchens. The head cook, Reesa Naturu, was a pleasant older female who survived the Zuvgran virus and had been working at the palace for fifty solars. Fortunately, she welcomed Ava and gave her use of one of the kitchens to experiment. Reesa said she only needed it for large events. Like Talen, she eagerly absorbed the recipes Ava introduced to her. She especially liked the different types of bread and the ease of sandwiches for casual lunches.

Ava stayed busy making treats for the hybrids and those in the palace. The younglings stayed in temporary housing near the site of the new building. Largon and Ronan asked for input from all the human women, as well as the long-time carers of the children. Ava suggested a large dining area with some smaller tables around the edges for those who liked it quieter and kitchens with lots of storage.

Natasha advocated for a small onsite clinic, while Talia wanted classrooms and a large library. Given Emmy's history in foster homes, she said she wished the group homes had more bedrooms where only two to four people would share, rather than dormitory style bunks. Lin thought a garden area where they could grow their own herbs and vegetables would be helpful. Playgrounds for the youngest and training areas for the older younglings were high on Rachel's wishlist. Ava wanted smaller recreation rooms be spread throughout the building. Herrah, a Wrestikan-Zuvgran hybrid who had spent years in caverns on Talonka Six, insisted on lots of natural light. Ronan and Largon worried about security measures and having offices and storage areas for all the items the younglings might need.

When they discussed a name, both Ronan and Largon liked Phoenix House when Talia explained the mythical concept of an immortal bird that rises from the ashes of its previous incarnation in a burst of flame as a symbol of hope and renewal. The king supplied architects and engineers to design the structure and everyone applauded how fast plans got approved and building began.

Ava tried to get to Phoenix House every couple days to bring snacks and check on the children. Teeka met regularly with a Svesti mind healer and started to increase her comfort level around larger groups of people. Ava checked in with the youngling regularly and couldn't be more pleased with her progress.

Finally arriving in the kitchen, Ava pulled her hair up in a ponytail and donned an apron. Humming softly, she took out some ingredients to experiment with fish recipes. Fresh fish arrived regularly at the palace. Reesa patiently listed the various types of fish and which were fatty or lean, meaty or flaky, and mild or strong flavored. She also told Ava how each was normally cooked. Ava couldn't focus and quickly lost herself In her own thoughts until she slowly became aware of voices in the storage hall behind the kitchen.

"He looks awful."

"And the waste of food. It's disgusting how he's living."

"I can't believe how much alcohol he's consuming."

"Should we tell the king?"

"I don't think so. The king told us to give him whatever he wants."

"I can't imagine the king expected this rapid decline."

"It's sad. He was such a fine upstanding warrior. Now he's an embarrassment to our race."

"Don't let the king hear you say that. I don't know what happened to him, but the rumor is he was held captive by the Zuvgran. It's not like either of us would fare much better."

The voices faded as the males finished whatever they were doing and walked away. Ava's eyes filled with tears, and she impatiently wiped them on her arm. *I'm sure they were talking about Karid. He needs an intervention. What should I do?*

Despite Ava's protests that she wanted to eat in her room, the other women insisted she join them for evening meal with the king and some of the nobility. Natasha joined her in her room to get ready.

"I have to wear that?" Ava groaned.

"Yes. It's as close to black tie as they get on Costonia, so dressing up is mandatory."

"I don't want to."

"Stop whining. We've covered for you as much as we can because we know you're worried about Wurvez, but you have to make an appearance." Natasha gestured to the gown. "Come on. I made it for you."

Ava picked up the cream silk gown with brown lacy accents. "It's not my normal style."

"Of course it isn't, but jeans and T-shirts aren't going to work." Natasha lifted an eyebrow.

"Fine." Ava headed for the bathroom.

"Oh, I sewed in a built-in bra."

"Perfect," Ava muttered. Once she changed, Ava had to admit Natasha did a great job. *It's just it feels wrong to look this good and pretend to be happy without Karid escorting me.*

She walked barefoot into the bedroom and spun slowly for Natasha.

"Where they hell did you find the lacy stuff anyway?"

"You'd be surprised what you can find in palace storerooms," Natasha whispered. "It looks even better than I imagined. Let's do your hair and find you some shoes."

"Why are you doing this, Natasha?" Ava sat as her friend wielded a hairbrush and pointed.

"Because you've been hiding and we miss you." Natasha gently brushed Ava's curls and swept her hair into an updo securing it with some sparkly combs she'd brought with her.

"I don't feel like making small talk with a bunch of men sniffing at me, hoping for a fated mate bond."

"Poor Rachel has been dealing with it for weeks."

"Yeah, but Rachel can kick all their asses." Ava met Natasha's eyes in the mirror and they both laughed.

"I can't argue that." Natasha fluffed some of the curls and pulled a few out from the side to frame Ava's face. "Now some earrings."

"I'm choosing those." Ava rooted around in her jewelry bag and pulled out a pair of dangling miniature rolling pins. "Perfect."

"Are you serious? This gown deserves gemstones."

"The rolling pins match the brown on the dress and suit me."

"You know what? I'm not even going to argue with you. Now where are your shoes?"

Ava gestured to the closet. Natasha found a pair of brown sandals with delicate ankle straps.

"I guess these will have to do. I should have synthesized something for you."

"Thank goodness for small favors."

"Hey, at least I got the better end of the deal. Rachel is helping Emmy get ready." Natasha mock shuddered. "I'm sure they're arguing about Emmy wearing one of her politically incorrect T-shirts." She perused Ava's face. "Maybe a little bit of lip gloss."

"No, I do not want kissable lips."

"You're still waiting for Karid, aren't you? You know the chances are slim with him now, right? Maybe you're better off without him."

Ava's temper flared. "You know nothing about it. If I want to wait for him, that's my fucking choice."

Natasha crossed her arms. "Then stop moping and do something about it."

"What the hell can I do? He won't see me. He won't see anyone." Ava threw her hands up in the air. "Don't you think I've thought about it?"

Natasha's voice gentled. "Ava, I think you're the only one who *can* reach him. He's pushing away his best friends—males who have been by his side for decades. If he feels for you half of what you feel for him, then he needs you desperately right now. I know you have an instinctive knack for helping people with trauma. Just look at Teeka." She narrowed her eyes. "I believe you have much more experience with PTSD than you have shared with us. That's okay if you don't want to tell us. But if you want more with Karid, you're going to have to work for it. Sooner rather than later for his sake."

Ava's eyes watered. "Fuck, Natasha. Is this your version of tough love?"

Natasha hugged her tightly. "We just want you to be happy. It's killing all of us to see you so miserable. Just get through tonight and we'll help you come up with a plan tomorrow."

Sniffling, Ava said, "I'm not sure I deserve such good friends."

"Of course you do. Now move your ass. We're going to be late."

Chapter 13

ANGUISH. DESPAIR. SELF-LOATHING. Fear. Anger. Apathy.

Anguish at the loss of being a male and warrior. Despair at the loss of Ava and hope for the future. Self-loathing for being a weak male and amounting to nothing, just as his father predicted. Fear when he relived his ordeal. Anger at himself for not being stronger—then and now. Apathy at his spiraling descent.

The never-ending cycle of negativity consumed Karid's days and nights. He eschewed contact with the outside world as much as he could. Every four days, his comm would alert him of a delivery. After unlocking the kitchen door, he remained in his room with the last few bottles of alcohol until the new delivery arrived. He relocked the door afterwards so his friends couldn't enter without him hearing. Only once had he forgotten the day and saw the delivery males again.

Vared, Devik, and Ash'n comm'd him every day, but he refused to answer. Occasionally, Karid would tap out a message telling them he did not want company. He briefly considered asking about Jevax and the ramifications for the Svesti noble, but he couldn't manage a conversation with anyone. A mind healer comm'd every few days and he deleted the messages without listening to them. Ava comm'd after she settled into the palace, but he didn't respond. But in his weakest moments, he would replay it to see her face and hear her voice. Her longing when she told him she missed him and her concern when she expressed her worry pierced his heart. *I hate the sorrow in her beautiful green eyes. She deserves so much better than me.*

Food still tasted horrible, so he barely ate. He lost large periods of time. Once, he came to huddled in a corner, bottle clutched in his bloody hands. His stinging, red-rimmed eyes eventually noticed several new holes in the walls.

Another time he woke shivering—still wearing his pants—sitting in a cold bath with no memory of even stepping foot into the sanitary facility. He had to dunk himself in the water afterwards to get the vomit out of his hair.

If he didn't keep himself right on the edge of drunk and unconscious, the nightmares tortured him. He relived the worst moments of his captivity, then Ava would appear with pity in her eyes. "I'm sorry, Karid, but I want a real male—a warrior, not what you've become." Then she'd walk away from him resolutely, her plump ass swaying, and never look back. In his dreams, he dropped to his knees begging her to stay, but every time she faded into nothingness.

The first time he had that nightmare, he sat up straight in the bed, clutching his chest and gasping for air. Alone in the darkness, he watched the moonlight reflect off his favorite knife on the nightstand. He studied it for long moments before tentatively picking it up. Turning it from side to side, the metal gleamed—one edge jagged and the other sharp.

"Not a male." "You're worthless as a warrior." "I'm sorry, Karid." Echoes of the voices reverberated in his skull and grew louder as he saw distorted reflections of himself in the tempered valadium. *It would be so easy to end it. A fitting end for a weak male.*

He lifted the point to his neck and held it against his flesh. Harsh breaths ripped through his chest. *Just one decisive slash and it's over. No more pain.*

In his mind's eye, he saw his best friends shaking their heads, heartbreak in their eyes. Ava's agonized face filled his vision with moisture wetting her lashes. His hand wobbled. Silent tears ran down his face. He lowered the knife and bowed his head. *I'm too weak to even do this.*

Karid stared at the weapon on his lap. The irony of its position struck him and he snorted and wept simultaneously. When he regained control of himself, he carefully placed the knife in its sheath and stuck it under the mattress to keep it out of sight.

He stumbled to the living area and chose another bottle. *It'll kill me slower, but maybe that's what I deserve.*

The Svesti noble entered the store and refrained from showing his distaste at the mediocre quality of the displayed items. His guard's information had better be correct and his target here. It took him five days to track him down. He stepped closer, pretending to look at some figurines.

A salesman approached. "Councilman. How may I help you?"

At least he trains his staff to recognize their betters.

"I'm looking for a gift for my sister, but I haven't decided on what would please her best."

"What are her interests and hobbies? Or perhaps you believe she would prefer a decorative item such as a figurine or jewelry?"

"She enjoys cooking and gardening."

"If you like, I can show you to those sections. We also keep higher quality, unique items in a separate area for our discerning friends."

"That's the area I would like to see. My sister deserves the best."

"Of course."

The noble followed the salesman and noted an office door just beyond their destination. He told the salesman he would like to browse. He pretended to examine various items while watching for his target. Becoming frustrated, he chose a set of bowls hand carved from trulet wood.

As he waited for the salesman to wrap his purchase, he saw the male he wanted leaving the office. Acting surprised, he said, "Drikon Wurvez. I was not expecting to see you."

"Why not? This is one of my establishments." Then he said with pride, "But I have many all over the planet."

The noble lowered his voice. "I thought you would be caring for your son."

The reddish bronze male frowned and said aggressively, "Why are you talking about my son?" He shook his head and mumbled to himself, before lowering his voice. "My apologies. What did you mean?"

The noble pasted an embarrassed expression on his face. "Oh, perhaps I misheard."

"Councilman, please do me the courtesy of explaining." Wurvez crossed his arms.

"I heard your son was recently rescued from the Zuvgran and hidden away to recuperate. No one has seen or heard from him and I assumed you would be overseeing his care. But I must have misunderstood. As his father, you would be kept informed."

Wurvez grunted. "As far as I am aware, my son is fine." He mumbled to himself again. "He had better be fine. He is my heir." *There's something not right about this male.*

"So you've heard from him since the *Invictus* entered orbit. That's a relief. If I remember correctly, he's your only child. I've never been so happy to be misinformed before."

"No, I haven't spoken with him, but that's not unusual. We're both busy males."

The noble dipped his head. "Of course. I apologize for any worry I may have caused."

"No need to apologize. You were only expressing concern." Wurvez' face looked pinched. *Excellent. I've wound up the hothead. Now let's see how he spins.*

"I must be going, but I enjoyed my visit to your establishment. I'll be sure to recommend it to others."

Outside, the noble comm'd one of his men. "Do not lose him. I want to know everything he does and where he goes."

Chapter 14

RRANGING THE TABLETOP comm, Ava sat cross-legged on her bed and checked the time. She entered the information as instructed and waited impatiently.

"Hello."

"Dan? Turn on the video on your phone." Ava beamed when she saw her adoptive father's face appear. "Can you see me now?"

"Sunshine! Where are you?" He grinned happily. The familiar brown hair with flecks of silver at his temples and laugh lines that wrinkled the skin beside his warm brown eyes always made her think about how his looks foreshadowed his personality. Wisdom tempered with humor.

"I'm on Costonia. It's amazing here. The Svesti are building a communications array to allow for more frequent contact with Earth. It's not finished yet, but after the military, we human women have priority to use it. At least for now. I have to schedule the time in advance, though."

"I'm so glad to hear from you. So we can chat while you're away?" He frowned. "Gram will be sorry she missed you. She's out grocery shopping."

"Tell Gram I love her and the Svesti are enjoying all her cookie recipes."

"I saw the videos the American ambassador disseminated." He shook his head curtly. "I wasn't surprised at the governments' actions." Concern crossed his face. "But the aliens aren't making you mate or anything, right?"

"Honestly, Dan, they treat us better than most human men do." Ava's lips quivered.

"What's wrong, Ava?"

She drew in a shaky breath. "I need your advice."

"Tell me."

"I met a wonderful male. I know you'd like him. We became friendly and dated. He was sent on a mission and captured by the Zuvgran. The Svesti found and rescued him a month ago, but he refuses to have anything to do with his best friends or me."

"Sounds like he's suffering from PTSD." He looked confused. "I'm sure you already figured that out."

Ava nodded and tucked a curl behind her ear. "Of course. He's sequestered somewhere. No one will tell me what happened or where he is. I'm really worried. I don't know what to do."

"How do you feel about him? Deep down where it counts."

Ava bit her lower lip. "Before all this, he made me feel truly alive and willing to risk my heart. I think he's my person, Dan. The one I can trust with everything."

"Everything?"

"Yes."

"Then go to him. Help him. Trust your instincts." He tilted his head. "Just be sure to protect yourself. You don't know how PTSD may be affecting him."

"I can't see him hurting me physically, Dan. He's like you. He has a deeply ingrained need to protect and serve, especially females."

Firmly, he said, "Take precautions, Ava."

"I will. But how do I go to him when I don't know where he is?"

"Someone has to know. Who would that be?"

Ava thought for a bit. "Probably his friends, but they won't tell me. The king, maybe?"

"I would think the king could find out even if he didn't know. What's the point of being king otherwise?" His eyes lit with humor.

Ava smirked. "You've got a point. I knew you could help me."

"So this means you might be staying there?" Shadows clouded the warmth in his eyes.

"I honestly don't know what it means. A lot of it depends on Karid."

"So that's his name?"

"Yes. Lieutenant Karid Wurvez. Second in command of the space cruiser *Invictus*."

"Military, huh?"

"If he returns to his position, then I might be traveling with him back to Earth to pick up some diplomats."

"Well, if that happens, you'd better let me know so Gram and I can see you. I miss your hugs."

"Definitely."

"Now that the advice is out of the way, tell me about your person and what's been going on."

After Ava disconnected the comm an hour later, she felt freer and lighter. *Dan always knows how to help me. Damn, I'm lucky he's my dad.*

Smiling, she made arrangements with Xeliv to get on King Traxen's schedule.

"I have an appointment with the King," Ava said to the two warriors guarding the outer sanctum of the royal offices.

One spoke into his comm quietly, while the other smiled. "How are you today, Lady Ava?"

"Fine, Madix Previv. It's another beautiful day on Costonia."

"Would you have spent time in the palace kitchens recently? Perhaps making some of those Earth cookies?" Previv hinted.

She laughed. "You obviously take after your older brother. As wonderful a chef as Talen is, somehow he always requires me to make the cookies."

"I enjoy all the different kinds you prepare. I think it's one of Earth's finest accomplishments—the invention of the cookie."

"You warriors all think with your stomachs."

The other guard said, "You may enter, Lady Ava."

She nodded. "Thank you." As she walked between the two, she whispered, "There should be some cookies at midday meal.

They're called thumbprints, and I used a *tempika* berry filling." She grinned as their eyes widened. "Enjoy."

Xeliv, King Sovex's admin, welcomed her and announced her after they reached the king's office.

King Sovex stood and smiled as she entered. "Lady Ava, please come in and have a seat."

"Thank you for agreeing to see me, Your Majesty."

He sat again. "I'm curious why you requested a private audience."

Ava laced her fingers together in her lap. Drawing in a deep breath, she said, "What is the status of Lieutenant Wurvez? It's been over a month since his rescue, and there has been no word on how he's doing."

His face became unreadable. "He's recuperating from his ordeal."

She stared into his lavender eyes. "No, he's not."

"What makes you say that?"

"You are aware I spend a great deal of my time in the palace kitchens when I'm not at Phoenix House?"

"Yes. Many are enjoying your meals."

"I hear the whispers, Your Majesty. Karid is not eating; food is going bad. But he's going through alcohol at record levels. I've heard he's lost significant weight and looks sickly."

"The staff should not be gossiping," the king grumbled.

"That's like asking the sun not to shine." Ava grinned. "It's not going to happen."

"True. What is your interest in Lieutenant Wurvez, Lady Ava?"

"We were friendly on the *Invictus*. I believe I know some of what he is experiencing and I can help."

"I doubt you know what he's going through."

Ava's eyes narrowed. "Did Rivezt ever show you my medical records?"

"No. As far as I know, there was no reason to."

"May we comm him now? I think it's relevant to our conversation."

Tapping his tablet, he initiated the connection with Rivezt.

"King Sovex. What can I do for you?"

"Lady Ava asked that we speak. I'm not sure why."

Ava stood and moved behind the king. "Rivezt, when you treated me the first day we met, did you take scans of my body?"

Rivezt nodded. "Of course."

"Did you keep notes about your speculations on what you found?"

Cautiously, Rivezt said, "Yes. I healed what I could. I never discussed it with you since it had no bearing on any future treatment."

"I appreciate your past and continued discretion, Rivezt. However, I need you to share those scans and notes with King Sovex. I think he needs to see them to have a better understanding of why I believe I can help Lieutenant Wurvez."

Rivezt's blue eyes widened. "Oh." His face turned hopeful. "It hadn't occurred to me, but Karid may need to hear what you have to say." He tapped some buttons. "I just sent it to King Sovex."

"Thank you, Rivezt." Ava smiled sadly. "Obviously, this stays between us."

"Of course, Lady Ava. Anything you can do to help Karid would be welcome. He's one of my best friends." Rivezt dipped his chin.

King Sovex disconnected the comm and read the file while Ava returned to her chair. A muscle in his jaw flexed when he looked at Ava. "It says that these injuries would have taken place when you were a youngling."

Ava nodded, her own jaw hardening. "I don't wish to discuss the causes of the injuries, but if you consider where I am now versus where I was then, you should see that maybe I do have something to offer toward Karid's healing, Your Majesty."

"Call me Traxen."

"Then please call me Ava."

Traxen leaned forward. "Karid suffered greatly while in captivity, Ava. I can't reveal what he endured. I'm not even sure he's told us everything because he won't speak to anyone. But you are correct. He isn't getting better. He refuses to meet with a mind healer and chases away all that care for him. He probably won't talk to you, and he may get violent."

"I understand that, Traxen. But I'm not so easy to chase away." She straightened her shoulders. "I also don't believe Karid would ever knowingly harm me or any other female."

"What do you need from me?"

"Is there an extra bedroom where he's staying?"

"Yes, he's in one of the cabins in the King's Forest."

"Then I need your permission to stay with him. I'd like food deliveries per a list that I'll provide weekly and no more alcohol unless I order it. And no visitors without my approval."

Traxen inhaled deeply, his tail swaying. "Do you think you can bring him back?"

Ava shrugged. "I doubt I'll make him any worse than he is." Her face tightened. "You do realize he may never return to the way he was, right? He can't help but be different."

Traxen's eyes were sad. "Yes, I know." His face softened and his voice was quiet. "I don't care if he ever returns to his warrior status. I just want him to find enjoyment in living again. Right now, he's barely existing."

Ava reached out and squeezed his hand. "I don't know how long it will take or how much help I will be, but I have to try."

Traxen squeezed back. "When do you want to leave?"

"As soon as we can coordinate it. I have the first grocery list ready and two bags packed in my room."

"Then let's get an escort to take you." Traxen stood and offered his arm. "Please update me regularly and let me know if you need anything more."

Ava placed her hand on his forearm. "You've got a deal, Traxen."

After her escort left in his flitter, Ava stood in front of the cabin, and wiped her sweaty palms on her jeans. *Cabin, my ass. Geez, it's bigger than a normal house on Earth even if it looks like it*

grew from nature. Guess royalty doesn't rough it. Traxen told her male delivered the food and left her bags in one of the guest rooms. No one saw Karid while they were there.

Opening the door, she scrunched her face at the smell. The main living area was a mess. Empty liquor bottles, barely eaten food, and dirty clothes littered every surface. She slowly walked towards the kitchen, noting a couple of walls had fist-sized dents in them. The kitchen looked and smelled as bad as everything else.

She found five sanitary facilities. Most sat unused and needed nothing more than a spot cleaning. One was in better shape than the living area, but even there, empty bottles abounded. *Shit! He's even worse than I thought. He's covered all the mirrors.* She frowned. *Where to start?* She straightened her shoulders. *Bottles first.*

Picking up as many bottles as she could manage, Ava dumped any contents down the sink and tossed the empties in the recycler. She finished cleaning the bathroom and headed back to the kitchen. *I won't be able to cook without a clean kitchen.* She shuddered at the filth and started tossing things in the recycler. *I should've brought hazmat gloves.*

She didn't know how long she'd been working when she heard Karid growl, "What the hell are you doing here?"

She looked up from scrubbing the counter and tried to keep the shock from showing on her face. Karid had lost a lot of weight. He had deep set, almost purple bags under his eyes, and his pants hung loosely on bony hips. Partially healed scars riddled his torso, marring his reddish bronze skin. She slowly set down her sponge—giving her a second to close her eyes and pray she had it in her to help him before she turned to face him.

Leaning back on the counter, she shot him a carefully crafted grin. "Well, I must say, Karid, your decorating taste leaves much to be desired. Frat boy combined with toxic landfill just isn't going to cut it."

"Leave," he growled. "I don't want you here."

"Sorry. I'm staying. I just need to get the kitchen clean enough to make something for evening meal."

She kept her body relaxed as he stalked toward her. The scent of stale liquor and sweat emanated from him, masking his normally decadent odor. She wrinkled her nose. "You, my friend, need to take a long hot shower using lots of soap and shampoo. Get dressed in clean clothes and then tackle cleaning the living area. I refuse to dwell in a dumpster while I'm here." She lightly tapped his chest with a finger. "You stink, Karid. It offends me."

"Then leave, Ava." Fists clenched, he stood close to her, but didn't touch her.

You poor male. What did they do to you? And what are you doing to yourself? She tilted her head back to stare into his gray eyes, fuzzy with inebriation. "No."

One of his forearms brushed her breast when he crossed his arms. Her nipples pebbled. *Fuck. Even as shitty as he looks and smells, he still turns me on.*

"Why are you here?"

"Because you've been ignoring me. Besides, they ran out of room at the palace."

"I doubt that." He glowered at her. "Why won't you listen to me?"

She smiled. "I will when you have something worth hearing, Karid." She pushed lightly against his warm chest. "I mean it. Go shower."

His brows knit and he looked confused. Turning abruptly, he left the room. Ava let out her breath. She picked up the sponge to finish cleaning. *If there is a God or Goddess listening, please help me help him. I can't lose him now that I found him.*

Chapter 15

Clenching his fists, Karid stood in his sanitary facility. *Why is she here?* Surfaces gleamed in the sunlight streaming through the window. Sniffing, he noticed the scent of cleanser. Then he noted his own odor and wrinkled his nose. He undressed, tossed his clothes in the refresher, and stepped into the shower. *I'm cleaning myself because I want to, not because my filth offended Ava.*

The hot water pelted his abused body, easing some of his muscle aches. Soaping a cloth, he washed quickly, flinching as he brushed his hands across his genital area. The fogginess of his mind cleared a little as he shampooed his long hair. *I don't want anyone to see me this way, especially her. How do I get her to leave?*

Finishing up, he dried himself and realized he had nothing to wear. *Crek! I don't want her to see me naked. I couldn't bear the shame.* He wrapped a towel around his waist and hurried to his bedroom. After combing out the knots in his neglected long hair and pulling it into a ponytail, he dressed in a black T-shirt and pants.

He looked around the room. *Goddess, I really have been living in a cesspool.* He made quick work of throwing his dirty clothes and sheets in the refresher before making the bed with clean linen. Grabbing food remnants and empty bottles, he tossed those in the recycler and opened a window to let the fresh air in.

In the main living area, Karid's embarrassment rose. *Ava saw this. What must she of me? Whatever it is, she wouldn't be wrong.* He growled low and his tail flicked rapidly. With jerky movements, he opened the windows and cleaned up the mess. He programmed the cleaning bots to clean the floors throughout the cabin. Finished, he hesitated. *Do I go back into the kitchen? My room? Stay here?*

Grunting, he berated himself. *Look at you, you weak naroon, paralyzed with indecision. Go into the kitchen and convince her to leave.*

Squaring his shoulders, he strode into the now clean kitchen. He sucked in a quick breath at the sight of Ava's plump ass outlined by her jeans as she bent over to pull items from the cooling unit. He mentally shouted at his hardening cock. *She can never be yours. When she knows the truth, she'll want nothing to do with either of us.*

Karid sat at the table, both to hide his erection, and watch Ava wash some vegetables.

"I don't want you here," he said gruffly.

She glanced over at him. "I know. But I'm here and I'm not going anywhere anytime soon." She picked up a knife and began slicing and dicing *shurlix*.

"I'm not going to talk about my captivity with you."

"I don't recall asking you to," she said calmly, motions steady.

He crossed his arms and huffed. "You have no idea what I'm going through, Ava. And I don't want to share."

She stopped and stared at him, her green eyes serious. "You are correct. I don't know what happened. But I am familiar with what you're going through now."

Snorting, he said, "You couldn't know. Your life is perfect."

Sadly, she said, "Yes, I've had a perfect life. Let me tell you about some of it." She turned back and continued preparing the food.

"I told you my biological father was a living nightmare. He was also a very rich, powerful man who believed the rules of common decency did not apply to him. He used to beat my mother...and me. She tried to protect me as much as she could, but I couldn't escape his wrath totally. When I was five, she mysteriously died. I believe he killed her."

"Ava..."

She ignored him. chopping steadily. "When I was six, my father sexually molested me and continued to do so for years. When I was eight, he began sharing me with like-minded degenerates. Unbeknownst to any of us, he was also filming when they raped and hurt me. He allowed them to do almost anything they wanted, so long as they did not leave visible marks that clothing couldn't cover. He blackmailed them and used those videos to make more money or garner more power."

What? Karid's tail whipped behind him as his entire body tensed. His claws dug into his palms, causing them to bleed. *I'm going to go to Earth and kill all those the males.*

Tonelessly, she continued. "I tried to tell people, but some of those men he shared me with were police officers and judges. Like I said, my father was a powerful man. And anyone he couldn't blackmail, he paid off to look the other way. I was almost eleven years old when someone took me seriously."

She stopped chopping and turned her head. Dry, green eyes stared into his. "I'm twenty-five. I've spent over forty percent of my life being tortured and abused in some fashion, Karid. The vast majority of my childhood was a living hell. You are the first person I've told outside of the legal proceedings and therapists I've had. The most I ever told anyone else was that I was sexually molested as a child."

Karid felt hot tears running down his face. "I have no words, Ava. Your ordeal was worse than mine." He bowed his head. "I am obviously weak."

"Trauma isn't a competition, Karid. It just is. The only reason I told you is I want you to understand that I do have some knowledge of what you're dealing with now. It took me many years and the help of some very good, caring people to get where I am today."

"But you're over it now?" he asked quietly, eyes downcast.

She grabbed a med kit from a cabinet and moved to the table. "You don't get over it, Karid. You learn to deal with it, accept it, and make better memories that remind you life is worth living." Her red hair brushed her shoulder when she tilted her head. "It becomes smaller—less important if you will. Your trauma isn't who you are, although I know it feels that way at the moment."

Tenderly, she took one of his bleeding hands and wiped it with a sterilizing cloth from the kit. "Your poor hands." She healed his hand with a mini-scanner and worked on the other damaged palm.

"You learn to reduce its power over you, your emotions, and your actions. You take back your life." She glanced at him briefly. "But it's hard and you can't do it alone."

Head bent, he whispered, "I don't know if I can do it at all."

After healing his hand, she kissed his palm gently. "You can, Karid. But you can't do it all at once. It's a process."

"I'm ashamed you are seeing me like this."

"I understand feeling that way. Just know I am not judging you for what happened or what you're currently experiencing. You were a victim. You survived. You're surviving the aftereffects now. You just need to figure out how to do it without making it worse."

He shivered at her compassionate tone. "I don't deserve you."

"You're right." His head whipped up at her words. She grinned. "You deserve better."

He shook his head. "I doubt there is anyone better than you."

She patted his hands. "Flatterer." She stood and went back to the counter. "Today, you're going to try an Earth snack. Chips and salsa. For evening meal, we're having *clepella*. Talen told me it's your favorite. I hope I get it right."

"I'm sure whatever you make will taste wonderful, Ava."

He sat in silence as he watched her. His breathing sped up as he thought about her childhood. To keep his tail from flicking, he wrapped it around a chair leg. *She's the strongest person I know. Look at her—so beautiful, happy, and calm. What she went through would break most people.*

A tiny sliver of hope flickered in his heart. *Can I find peace like her? With her?*

"I'm going for a walk," Ava said as she washed her hands.

Karid frowned. "I'm not sure it's safe until we catch the traitors."

She smiled. "Then come with me."

He huffed. "I don't want to go anywhere."

"Then expect me in about an hour. I'll bake the chips and we can have our snack. The salsa needs some time to chill."

"Perhaps you should stay here." *Why am I being so stubborn?*

"Not happening, buddy. I need to work off some energy." Ava headed for the kitchen door. "And I want to see more of where we're staying."

Karid watched her leave. He stood abruptly and watched her through the window, debating with himself. As she entered the tree line, he growled. *She shouldn't be out of sight.* He ran to his bedroom and reached under the mattress. Pulling out his knife, he strapped the sheath to his leg. Rushing to catch up with Ava, he found her crouched near some yellow flowers under a tree. His anxiety lessened once he could see her. He rested his hand against his thundering heart. *Crek! That shouldn't have tired me.*

Consciously slowing his breathing, he approached. "Those are called *spirettas* because of how their petals spiral upward."

A shaft of sunlight highlighted her red hair as she turned to look at him. "They're beautiful. Do they always grow near the base of trees?"

"They prefer shade, so yes." He smiled at the lovely picture she made framed against the blue bark of the tree.

As she stood, she returned his smile. "The diversity of color in your flora is amazing. Tree barks on Earth tend to be brown, with a few exceptions. Lin would know more. But here..." she waved her hand, "blue, brown, green, orange, even yellow over there, and that's just in this one area."

"Costonia is a beautiful planet." His shoulders straightened with pride.

"It is. And I love how much Svesti integrate their dwellings with nature." She frowned slightly. "Getting humans to understand the importance of that has been an ongoing struggle. We're killing portions of our world without regard for the long-term effects."

Karid followed Ava as she explored the surrounding area, offering the names of the various plants and trees, and realizing he hadn't left the cabin since he arrived. He inhaled deeply, sorting the various scents of the earth and flowers. Ava's *wimma* sweet smell tickled his nose.

Her gasp made him stiffen, and he rushed to close the distance between them. The break in the forest opened up to a small lake at the bottom of a waterfall.

"Oh my god. This is absolutely gorgeous. Do you think it's safe to swim here?" Ava gushed.

"I would think so."

"Oh, I'm definitely coming back to spend more time here." She spun to face him with a wide grin. "Maybe we can have a picnic one day and swim."

"Picnic?" *I don't know if I want to swim with her. If I'm wet, she might notice.* He gnashed his teeth.

"You set up a blanket on the grass and bring food to eat. It's fun." Her excitement made him smile a little, despite his reservations.

"Perhaps we can do that."

Ava sat on the blue grass, leaned back on her elbows and crossed her ankles. Eyes closed, she tilted her head back to feel the sun on her face, her curly hair rustling in the breeze. *Goddess, she is so alluring. I've missed spending time with her, just looking at her. I could watch her all day.*

Karid eventually looked around. *She's right—it is beautiful here. I didn't even know this existed.* He shook his head, feeling his ponytail brush his shoulders. *I've had other things on my mind.*

Legs trembling, Karid swung them to sit sideways on the machine in the dimly lit, quiet training room on the lower level of the cabin. *It's embarrassing how out of shape I am.* He huffed. *I need to build my strength back so I can protect Ava while she's here. I can't force her to leave.*

While waiting for his muscles to stop spasming, he wiped the sweat from his face and body. He thought back on the evening with Ava. Before Ava baked the chips, she squeezed some *wimmas* and brushed the juice over them. She said the blue fruit was very similar to an Earth one called a lime. He enjoyed the chips and salsa, although he didn't entirely understand her mumblings about finding a better corn substitute. The House Glixon dish, *clepella*, tasted even better than the one his mother used to make. Ava said it seemed like an Earth's ratatouille.

They—well, primarily she—talked well past dark. Ava brought him up to date on the others. Lady Talia's plan to bring the truth to Earth worked. A Svesti-Zuvgran hybrid kidnapped Lady Natasha on Talonka Six to save other Zuvgran hybrids from a contagious disease. King Sovex and Vared's father were building an orphanage for them on Costonia called the Phoenix House. As shocking as all of that sounded, what really surprised Karid was the fact that human females were sparking fated mate bonds. Vared and Lady Talia, Devik and Lady Emmy, Ash'n and Lady Lin, and even Lady Natasha sparked a bond with the hybrid whose mother was a cousin to the Durek family. Fated mate bonds hadn't been seen by the Svesti in over a century.

When she told him other Svesti kept attempting to spend time with her and Lady Rachel, hoping for a bond, Karid growled at the thought of other males hounding them, especially Ava. *Before my mission, I hoped for a true mate bond with Ava when I returned, but now it will never happen. But I can't picture her with another male...ever.* His tail slapped at the floor. *They took so much from me. No, us.*

Legs fatigued but working, he walked to the sanitary facility for a quick shower. He hung his head under the stream of hot water. He hadn't realized it earlier, but today he allowed another's touch for the first time since he arrived at the cabin. Ava's small, but gentle, pats, and nudges throughout the day left trails of heat in his body. Nothing like the pain of his captivity but still emotionally painful when he thought of all they would never have. But he couldn't make himself tell her to stop. His skin, his body, his heart craved contact with hers.

His cock hardened. Tentatively, he reached down to fist it lightly. He grimaced and abruptly let it go. *There's no point. I won't enjoy it. Crek.* Silently, his tears mixed with the shower water and disappeared down the drain.

Chapter 16

DRESSED IN A light camisole and pajama shorts, Ava crawled into bed. She lay in the dark, replaying the day. *It went much better than I hoped. He cleaned, ate, and got out of the cabin. He was much quieter than he used to be, but I expected that. He didn't even fight me about the no alcohol rule.*

Although she was certain she would never tell him every sordid detail of her childhood, she surprised herself with how much she did share with him. It felt like a weight resting on her heart had lifted. *Maybe helping him is helping me in some way, too.*

She heard him come up from the training area and take a shower. *Exercise is good. Maybe it will get rid of some of those demons so he can sleep.* She rolled to her side and punched her pillow. *I miss his smile and humor. Too bad those bastards are dead. I'd like to kill them myself.*

A smug grin broke out on her face as she remembered him chasing after her in the forest. *I knew his protective instincts would override his desire to hide in the cabin and lick his wounds.* She never mentioned it, but she noticed his knife strapped to his leg when he caught up to her.

But she worried about all of the weight he'd lost. *I need to get him to eat regularly. And find him a project to keep him active and out of his head.* She wracked her brain but came up empty. Nothing seemed right. *Get some rest. You'll figure it out.*

Painful, agonizing screams jarred Ava awake and had her shooting out of bed. She rushed to Karid's bedroom and saw him thrashing in his bed, as if he were fighting against invisible restraints.

"No, I won't! Don't touch me. I might not be able to control myself." He mumbled more, but she couldn't understand his words.

Slowly, she approached his bed, debating the best way to rouse him from his nightmare. She gently touched his shoulder and found herself pulled under him. His hand encircled her throat and the pinch of his extended claws scratched against her neck. She concentrated on keeping her breathing calm and even.

"Karid, it's Ava. You're having a nightmare. It's time to wake up." She quietly repeated the same words as she reached up to cup his cheek with a hand. Her thumb gently stroked his face. Long minutes passed as she waited for her repetitive words to reach him.

She saw the moment he came back to himself. His gray eyes widened in horror and he scrambled backwards falling off the bed. Leaning back, he brought his knees up to his chest and wrapped his arms around them. Head down on his knees, tail wrapped around his calves, he began rocking.

"I'm so sorry, Ava. Please leave." His voice broke. "I can't bear to hurt you."

Witnessing his distress, her heart squeezed in her chest. Slowly and deliberately, she dropped from the bed to plant her butt on the floor next to him, close enough to feel his heat, but not touching. She raised her knees and dropped her head back against the side of the mattress.

"You didn't hurt me, Karid. You would never hurt me."

He glanced sideways at her, his face tortured. "I had my hand around your neck. I could've killed you."

She nodded. "Yes, but you didn't. Even in the grip of your nightmare, your honor would not allow you to do more without a direct threat."

"You don't know that," he argued.

Her lips rose in a sad smile. "Yes, I do. There are men—males—who enjoy killing or inflicting pain just to do so. It makes them feel strong and powerful. Unfortunately, I am intimately familiar with those types. You are nothing like them. You are an honorable warrior who will inflict no more pain than necessary and won't kill unless someone is in danger. You may not trust yourself and your training, but I do."

His long hair hid his face as he shook his head. His voice shook as he whispered, "It would have been better if they had killed me."

She frowned and took a deep breath. "I never told you how I got someone to help me all those years ago." She felt him stiffen beside her. "My father never sent me to school. Too many people I might have told the truth to. He hired tutors. There was a science lesson about Earth's animals, and my tutor arranged to take me to the zoo."

He stilled. *Good. He's listening.*

"The night before was one of the worst of my childhood. Three men at one time. They hurt me badly." She stared straight ahead into the dark of the room. She heard him hiss, then growl.

"I hid the evidence as best as I could, so my tutor wouldn't cancel the trip. My father sent two bodyguards along. I noticed a lot of school buses in the parking lot. I found an opportunity to get away from the adults and snuck onto a bus. It ended up going to an inner-city school about forty minutes away from the zoo."

Karid whispered, "What happened then?"

"A group of older girls found me, but I told them I needed to get to the police far away from the zoo. They hid me and told me how to get to a police station about two blocks from their school."

"And you went there?"

"Yes. I walked in, pulled out a box cutter I had hidden in my sock and started stabbing myself in the stomach, screaming 'Make it stop.'"

Karid turned to her, his gray eyes wide, blood leaving his face. "You tried to kill yourself?"

Ava turned toward him and tucked her knees under her. She raised her camisole to show him her abdomen. "This is the only scar Rivezt wasn't able to heal." She ran her fingers over her belly. "The smaller dots are the remnants from cigarette burns."

His tail unwrapped itself from his legs and cautiously touched her thighs, resting there lightly.

"A man grabbed the knife from me and pulled up the bottom of my shirt to figure out where to apply pressure to my wounds. He saw the bruising, cuts, and burns from the night before. I don't remember much after that—mostly fragments of the pain and chaos, although he told me later what happened."

"What did he say?"

"He said I smiled angelically as I grabbed his wrist with a bloody hand. I told him it was okay if I died, but I wanted him to know why I did it. Expecting I would bleed out, I gave him enough information for him to follow up on. I remember the relief I felt when he said, 'I believe you. Now your job is to survive. You're strong enough.' He was the first adult man who treated me with kindness and respect. Afterwards, they found the evidence in my home—videos and records." Her eyes filled with unshed tears. "Detective Daniel Taylor saved me in so many ways."

"Taylor?"

She smiled. "Yes. My birth name wasn't Ava Taylor. I changed it after I was safe and Dan adopted me." Her eyes met his. "Dan is everything a father should be."

"I think I will like him." Karid's lips tipped upward a fraction.

"You will. You two have a lot in common." She grinned. "I'll tell you a secret. We women were instructed by our governments not to tell anyone about the Svesti. I told Dan everything before I left. If I disappeared for a year and a half without any contact, he would burn down the universe to find me.

I'm glad we now have communications with Earth so I can talk to him regularly."

Karid's fangs gleamed in the small bit of moonlight from the window. "Now I know I will like him."

Fluidly, she rose to her feet. "You ready to be the little spoon?"

His brows drew together. "Little spoon?"

"Get in bed and lie on your side." Stiffly, he followed her instructions. She scooted up behind him, her breasts pressed into his back. "Lift your head." Sliding an arm under his ear, she wrapped her other arm over him and entwined her fingers with his. "I'm the big spoon in the drawer and you're the little one."

"I'm not sure about this, Ava. What if I have another nightmare? I might hurt you." Karid's voice was low and uncertain, but his tail wrapped around her ankle.

"Shh. It's fine. I'll tell you what Dan told me thousands of times." She paused. "Are you listening? It's important."

His hair tickled her arm as he nodded.

"You are not your trauma. You did nothing to cause it, and you did not deserve bad things happening to you. Right now is hard, but you *will* have a long, wonderful life. You deserve the best this world offers. While you might feel you are weak, you are not. In fact, you are stronger than you realize. For now, get through. Moment by moment. Hour by hour. Then day by day. I wish I had the power to ease your pain or fight your fight. All I can do is share it and walk side by side with you. My shoulder is always available when you want to talk, cry, rage, or just sit quietly. If you need it, I will push or lead you. But no matter what, you are *not* alone."

She felt his indrawn breath. Stroking as much of his hair and forehead as she could reach, she whispered. "I'll be here letting those nightmares know they are not welcome. Rest, sweetheart." Softly, she hummed lullabies. Eventually, his breathing evened out. Once she felt sure he was asleep, her quiet tears soaked her pillow and hair. *I hate that you hurt.* His musky, cinnamon and pepper-tinged scent filled her nose. She drifted off, keeping him cradled in her arms.

Chapter 17

KARID WOKE TO mid-morning sunlight on his face. His body felt relaxed and his mind clear. He inhaled, enjoying Ava's lingering scent on the sheets. The space next to him felt cool. *She must already be awake.*

Sitting up, he rolled his neck and stretched his arms, working out the kinks. *I haven't slept peacefully in months. What a difference it makes.*

Grabbing clean clothes from the refresher, he dressed before folding the rest and putting them away. *I don't deserve Ava's kindness, but I don't think I'm strong enough to send her away.* He glowered when he remembered his hand wrapped around her neck. *After everything she's been through, I don't understand why she wasn't afraid. I was. I need to get well enough so I don't risk hurting her.*

After brushing it, he bound his hair in a ponytail with a leather tie. Sniffing, he followed the smells wafting from the kitchen. His rumbling stomach took him by surprise. *I haven't felt hungry in months either.*

Hesitantly, he stopped at the door to the kitchen when he saw Ava dipping bread slices in a bowl before placing them into a pan. She looked up and smiled at him.

"Good morning. I started the French toast when I heard you moving about."

"I don't know what French toast is, but it smells wonderful."

"Could you get some juice out for us?"

"Of course."

As he was passing behind her, she flinched when a splatter from another pan spit hot grease. His tail caught her by the waist before she could back into his groin. He stepped away quickly once he felt certain she was steady on her feet. *That was too close. She might've noticed.*

His tail made short flicks. He froze when she grabbed it.

"Are you okay? You seem upset." Her eyes shone with concern.

Swallowing hard, he nodded. Wrinkles appeared on her forehead and she released his tail.

"Thanks for catching me before I barreled into you. It's a good thing you're a big, strong guy with quick reflexes." She winked.

His shoulders tightened and his tail wrapped around his ankle. Gruffly, he said, "Keeping you safe is my priority."

Frowning slightly, she turned back to finish making morning meal. After getting the juice and setting the table, Karid sat and watched her economical movements as she cooked and placed the food between them.

"I made a syrup or you might like jam or sugar on the French toast."

Karid watched as Ava put a slice of the golden brown bread on her plate with a fork. She waved the utensil at him.

"Eat. You lost too much weight."

Glancing down at his empty plate, he admitted, "Food hasn't tasted good in a long time."

"Mmm." She buttered her French toast and poured some syrup on it. "The alcohol probably messed up your taste buds."

His stomach growled loudly and she laughed.

"I think you need to fill that up before the rumbling brings down the roof." Her green eyes twinkled.

Sheepishly, he took some food and began eating. A slow smile spread across his face.

"This is really good, Ava." Enthusiastically, he ate and found room for a second helping. Resting his hands on his full belly, he sat back with a groan.

She bit her lower lip.

"Maybe you should have started slower if you haven't been eating well. I should have thought of that."

"I couldn't stop myself. It's been so long since I enjoyed food."

"I'm glad you liked it." She sighed, then squared her shoulders. "I want to tell you something, but I ask that you don't try to respond until I'm done. In fact, you don't have to respond at all. I just need to say it."

Karid stiffened, then relaxed. His tail wound around his chair leg.

"I'm listening."

She stared over his shoulder for a long moment before meeting his eyes.

"Ever since your rescue, I have been dealing with a lot of feelings. I can count on one hand the number of people I trust as much as I do you. When you refused to let me see or talk to you, I was angry and hurt. I felt like you ghosted me." *Crek.*

She shushed him when he opened his mouth.

"I'm not finished. I understand you pushed everyone away, not just me. I'm not saying this to make you feel guilty. I just don't want it to fester inside me." Her eyes filled with tears and her voice became quieter.

"I missed you, Karid. We were good friends who joked and flirted. When our relationship progressed, I began having feelings that I've never had. Not being able to just sit and hold your hand while you recovered crushed me." His tail flicked.

"I know you're dealing with a lot. I hope some day soon, you'll trust me enough to tell me why. I'm not angry or hurt anymore. I just wanted you to know."

He reached across the table and held her hand.

"I'm sorry, *raralumia.* I wasn't trying to hurt you. I was trying to protect you." Shamefaced, he glanced down at their hands before looking into her eyes. "Maybe I was protecting myself."

"I didn't tell you so you'd apologize, Karid. If someone wants to kill me or kidnap me, please protect me. However, you do not need to protect my feelings. You'll hurt me more by not respecting me." She paused. "Unless you decide you hate my cooking."

His tail wrapped around her ankle. He widened his eyes in mock horror.

"I could never hate your cooking."

He joined her when she laughed.

"This is why I missed you, you silly man." She squeezed his hand.

His lips thinned.

"I may never be ready to tell you my reasons for how I acted. Or even how I might act in the future. But please know my intent has never been nor will it ever be to hurt you."

"I've always known that, Karid."

"Let's eat outside tonight," Ava said.

"Whatever you wish." It took Karid a couple trips, but soon everything for the evening meal covered the table in the outdoor seating area.

Ava smiled as she lit a chunky candle. "Thanks for doing the heavy lifting."

"You cooked it. The least I can do is help set it up."

Comfortably silent, they ate their salads.

"Have you ever had spaghetti before?"

"No," said Karid.

"Let me show you how you 'properly' eat it." Ave held a large spoon in one hand, then used the tines of her fork to twist some pasta. She smiled encouragingly as he did the same.

"Now here's how a lot of people eat it." She twirled some pasta onto her fork, but a couple longer strands refused to stay. She lifted the fork high, ducked her head to put her open mouth with her tongue sticking out to catch the loose strands.

"Really?" His grin surprised him. Conflicting thoughts tumbled through his head. *I never expected to feel any happiness again.* He shook his head. *Don't question it. Just enjoy it for the gift it is. What was it she said last night? Get through moment to moment.* He ate peeking at Ava frequently. *I want more moments like this to remember after she leaves.*

"Really, Karid. It's more fun and messier this way." She took another bite, hollowed her cheeks, pursed her lips as she sucked in a dangling noodle. His cock hardened and he stood abruptly.

"I need more water." He rushed to the kitchen and grabbed the edges of the counter. Head hung low, his breath rasped in his chest. *Crek. I desire her and I can't have her. She won't want me when she knows the truth.*

When he calmed, he grabbed a water pouch and went back outside. Remaining on his feet, he took something from a basket and bit into it while keeping his back to her and looking out toward the forest. "What is this? It's very good."

"Garlic breadsticks." He stared unseeingly at one tree without answering her.

"Karid, please look at me." Slowly, he turned his head to meet her warm eyes. "It's okay if you have moments you need to yourself. You don't need to explain or worry about my reaction."

She glanced at the food in his hand. "Try dipping it into your sauce." She grabbed her own to demonstrate.

Inhaling deeply, he returned to the table to finish the meal. His anxiety calmed as she talked quietly about inconsequential things before falling silent to watch the last of the sunset behind the trees. He turned to look at her profile to see her brow wrinkling.

"What are you thinking?"

"Hmm," she said distractedly. "Oh, I was wondering if I should have Talia get me some kitchen appliances from Earth when she goes back. Making the spaghetti without a pasta maker was labor intensive." She looked at him. "Do you think someone could convert the machines to Svesti power sources?"

"I don't see why not," he said. "But I didn't know Talia was going back to Earth." He frowned. "That will make Vared very unhappy."

"Oh, you don't know." She gestured excitedly. "Traxen named Durek and Talia co-ambassadors to Earth. They're leaving soon to pick up some Earth diplomats and bring them here to negotiate treaties."

"Vared Durek as a diplomat?" Karid chuckled. "That's hilarious. We'll be lucky if he doesn't tear off someone's head."

Ava grinned at him. "I know, right? But Talia should be able to keep him calm." Her face turned thoughtful. "I'll have to make a list for her. Or maybe I'll go back with them."

His tail flicked. "You're thinking of leaving Costonia?"

She looked at him. "Just to get some things I'd like to have here and see Dan. I should probably find out what you use for currency in space and convert my accounts to that, so I'll have something to live on. I'm just not sure how to do that. It's not like Earth money has any value out here."

"Some items can be converted for credits," Karid said.

"Like what?"

"Some gemstones or valuable ores are the most common."

"Gemstones might work. I can trade my money for diamonds or whatever has value to convert to credits. If I give you a list of what's available on Earth, could you let me know what would work best?"

"Of course."

"If you travel to Earth, you will be gone for months." Karid frowned, and his tail moved restlessly. *I don't like that idea.*

Confused, she said, "Well, if you're going back on duty before then, you'd be with us. I'm not sure when they're leaving."

He stared at her and tried to slow his breathing and keep his heart from racing. Quietly, he said, "I'm not sure when or if I'll be ready to reinstate my warrior status."

She reached over to squeeze his hand. "Karid, whether or not you go back to work, you will always be a warrior at heart. They didn't take that from you."

Looking at her pale skin against his, he said, "I don't know if I believe you, but thank you."

An understanding smile crossed her lips. "You will believe it. Trust me."

I hope so. He kept her smaller hand in his, enjoying the warmth and smoothness of her skin.

Pointing with her free hand, she said, "We walked that way yesterday and over there today. Which way should we explore tomorrow?"

"Whichever you like."

"Okay." She paused for a moment. "I noticed there are no fireplaces or grills here."

He frowned. "Have you been cold? I can adjust the cabin temperature for you."

"Oh, no, that's unnecessary. I was thinking it would be nice to cook some grilled foods while the weather is still nice. A fire pit for evenings like this would be wonderful, too."

"It's not something I've seen on Costonia."

"If I give you some plans for them, do you think you could build them? I can ask Traxen if it's okay."

"Is it something you want?" *Anything you desire.*

She nodded, the waning sunlight highlighting her red curls. "Yes. I'd love to introduce you to barbecued food." She tilted her head as she glanced at him. "As in tune with nature as Svesti are, I'm surprised it's not something you have."

"If the King approves the additions, I'll do what I can."

She beamed at him, her face glowing with happiness. "Thank you, Karid."

When Karid awoke from a nightmare later, he closed his eyes in despair as he saw Ava under him again with his hand around her throat. Soothing motions of her thumb on his cheek had him resting his forehead on hers as he removed his hand and used his elbow to take his weight. Sharing his breath with hers, he murmured, "I can't stand waking up this way—worried I may have hurt you."

"You're not physically hurting me, Karid. I know you won't."

He shuddered, then flipped to his back. Resting his forearm over his eyes, he said, "You need to stop trying to wake me."

She rolled to wrap her arm around his waist. Snuggling with her head on his shoulder, she threw her leg over his. With a harsh indrawn breath, he shifted his hips away from her. *I crave her touch, but I'm afraid to let her know my shame.*

"Ava, you must leave."

She sat up and withdrew her hands from his body. Lifting them, she softly said, "I only want to hold you. Nothing more."

Staring into steady green eyes, he focused on calming himself, before opening his arms to her. Returning her head to his pecs, she laid next to him rather than on him. She drew lazy patterns on his chest with his unbound hair. Her scent and body heat surrounded him. *If only she were here because we were mates and not because she feels sorry for me. But that can never be.*

"I still think you should go back to your room."

"No, I will not leave you to suffer alone," she said in a firm voice that contrasted with her gentle touch.

"I don't want your pity," he growled.

Her body stiffened. "Good, because you don't have it, and I have none to give you."

Anger tinged her citrusy, sweet scent. *Goddess, she really means it.*

In an uncertain voice, he broke the tense silence. "You don't pity me?"

Ava lifted her head. "No. My heart hurts because you're suffering, and I'm livid at those who caused it. But pity implies you're broken beyond repair. And I don't believe that."

Turning his head to search her serious green eyes, he stared for a long moment. "I find you more amazing every day."

Cracking a grin, she said, "But, of course. I'm awesome."

Tentatively, he hugged her close as they laughed. Burying his face in her unruly hair, he said, "I don't deserve you."

"Enough of that, Karid." She giggled. "Stop it. That tickles."

He pulled his nose away from her neck. "Your laughter brightens my darkness. And I didn't think I would see or feel the light again."

She licked her lips. "Then stop trying to push me away. I'm not going anywhere."

He stared at her mouth, shimmering in the moonlight. *I want to kiss her.*

"Big spoon or little spoon tonight?" she asked.

His curtain of hair swung as he shook his head to clear it. "I'll be the little spoon again." *I don't want her to feel my erection.*

"Okay. Get into position."

She repeated Dan's words from the night before. Her humming and gentle caresses on his chest and abdomen soothed him. *If only I could keep her.*

Karid enjoyed the routine they fell into over the course of the next several days. He would awaken after at least six solid hours of sleep and share breakfast with Ava. They walked and explored the forest. She pointed out dead trees he could chop to use for firewood for her grill and fire pit. His strength began returning when he did his training forms after lunch and used the training area at night. Fortunately, most of the shakiness he felt from the lack of alcohol he hid from her and abated fairly quickly. *Thank the Goddess Ava made me promise to stop before I deteriorated more. Having her to help after the nightmares makes a huge difference. They don't linger as long.*

She fed him snacks throughout the day and, as always, her meals were delicious. His body felt healthier, and the fresh air and sunlight kept his mind mostly clear. *I wish we could stay like this forever.*

Chapter 18

AFTER SEARCHING EARTH'S internet that the *Invictus* had downloaded months ago, she found plans for the items she thought would go well at the back of the cabin, Ava comm'd Traxen.

"Ava. How are you?"

"I'm doing well. I have a request."

"What is it?"

"I'd like to have Karid build a fire pit and a grill at the cabin in the backyard."

"I'm not sure what a grill is, but what do you need to make that happen?"

"The grill is for cooking food outdoors. I can send you the plans and the supply list." Ava tapped her comm to send the information she gathered.

"I'll look it over and if I have any questions, I'll contact you. Otherwise, I'll arrange a delivery." Traxen paused. "How is he doing?"

Ava's lips turned up. "He's no longer drinking. He's eating regularly and walking outside with me." She wrinkled her nose. "He's having nightmares, but we're working through it. He hasn't told me what happened yet, but I didn't expect him to. I'm doing my best to create an emotionally safe environment to help. I just need him to keep busy first and out of his head."

"You are a wise female." Traxen's fangs gleamed. "I am glad he is making progress."

"Do you know if he has any hobbies? He and I never discussed that before he left on his mission."

"Sculpting. He's very talented."

"Like big statues?"

"Usually he makes smaller items. Wait. I'll show you." Traxen disappeared for a moment before returning. He held up a golden bronze-colored stone sculpture that was as tall as his head. A Svesti with broad shoulders stood gazing at something unknown. A crown topped his head and the detail on the face was incredibly lifelike. Ava looked at the sculpture and then at Traxen.

"Is that your father?"

Traxen nodded with a smile. "It's one of my most treasured possessions. Karid gifted it to me after my father's death three solars ago."

"You're right. He truly has a gift. Could you find out from his friends what tools and stone he prefers and send some of those as well? Maybe it will be another way to remind him of things that bring him joy."

"Absolutely. I will ensure he has the best of everything." Traxen looked at her solemnly. "Thank you, Ava, for insisting you could help Karid. You've done more in a few days than any of us has been able to achieve. You have our gratitude."

"Gratitude is unnecessary. I care about him, too. I'm just glad he has such good people who care about and support him. He's traveling a very rough road right now and will sometimes stumble in the future. We need to get him to where he's willing to lean on us when that happens."

"I must admit, you human females are extraordinary in your strength and intelligence."

Ava grinned. "Most of us have had to learn to be resilient. Better watch yourself or we'll end up taking over."

Traxen laughed. "That may not be a bad thing. Was there anything else?"

"No, that's it for now."

"You'll have what you requested soon."

Picking up a satchel, Ava went outside to find Karid. His muscles glistened with a light sheen of sweat as he hauled a large tree trunk to a pile of other dead wood to use for the fire pit. She licked her lips when he wiped his bare chest with a towel. *Yum. He hasn't regained his full weight yet, but he's already looking so much healthier.*

"Are you ready for a break?"

He glanced at her and tilted his head. "What do you have in mind?"

"A picnic." She patted the satchel. "I've got everything right here. I'm hoping for company. Picnics aren't as much fun alone."

He arched an eyebrow. "Should I comm the other females for you?"

"Not the kind of company I was hoping for." She tapped her lips with a finger. "I guess I could comm one of the males at court. I'm sure somebody would be willing to join me."

One moment he was ten feet away, the next he was standing right in front of her. She blinked at his crossed arms over naked pecs. *Shit. He's fast...and lickable.*

The low growl from his chest invited her to look up at him. Gray eyes narrowed.

"I am the only male who will accompany you."

"Oh?"

His arms fell and his tail wrapped around her waist pulling her flush against him. His unique scent surrounded her. Her tank top provided little protection from the heat of his hands where they rested on her back. Not that she wanted protection. Her head fell sideways when he nuzzled her neck. Goosebumps rose on her arms.

"I know you won't be with me forever, *raralumia*, but while you're here, please don't tease me about other males. Allow me the illusion of having you all to myself for a little longer. I can't bear to imagine otherwise just yet," he whispered shakily.

Ava raised her hand to his cheek and turned her head toward his ear. She spoke as quietly as he had. "You are the only male I want, Karid. I'm not going anywhere."

He shuddered and embraced her tightly. Releasing her, he said, "We'll see."

She opened her mouth to argue but remained silent when she saw the pain in his eyes. *I think my actions will speak louder than words. I won't let him chase me away. Two steps forward, one step back. Just keep making progress.*

He donned his shirt and held his hand out for the satchel. She handed it to him without a word. As they walked toward the lake, she searched for a topic to lighten the mood.

"Oh, I forwarded a list of gemstones to you. You'll have to let me know what might convert best to credits."

"You know I will." *Well, that went nowhere.*

When they reached a place with a good view of the waterfall and lake, she pointed to the satchel.

"There's a blanket in there we can use."

After he handed it to her, she shook it out and let it float onto the blue grass. She took off her shoes and socks before plopping her butt on the blanket. He sat beside her.

"Are you hungry now or would you like to wait a bit?"

"Whichever you prefer is fine."

Ava pulled out containers, as well as water pouches, and opened several. The meal consisted of sandwiches, *lobile* chips, and some fruit. She saved the pie for later.

"Did I tell you I talked to Dan last week? It was really good to see his face. I've missed him and Gram."

Karid leaned back on his elbows and glanced at her. "He must have been happy to hear from you."

"Yes. Unfortunately, Gram wasn't there when I called. Maybe next time." Ava scooted down on her side and rested her head on her hand.

"If you could have one superpower what would it be?"

Curiosity filled his face. "What do you mean?"

"On Earth, we have fictional heroes, some with unusual powers. It's fun to imagine what it would be like to have one."

"What types of powers?"

"Things like telepathy, teleportation, shooting lightning from your fingertips, flying, talking to animals, levitation, and stuff like that. We even have one who is a woman with a golden lasso that makes people tell the truth."

Amusement lit his eyes. "Humans like their stories."

"Uh, huh. So what would you choose?"

He chewed on a chip as he thought. "The ability to go back in time."

"It would be cool to see life was a thousand years ago." She purposely ignored what she thought he meant. "It's a toss-up for me whether I want to fly or breathe underwater. I think either would be amazing."

"You wouldn't want telepathy? There are some species that actually have that ability."

"No way. It's noisy enough in my own head without everyone else's thoughts bombarding me. It ruins the mystery of getting to know someone like we're doing now." She grinned. "Besides, you'd hate it. You'd know the punchline of every joke."

He rolled onto his side, tugged one of her curls, and chuckled. "Your views are illuminating."

"And insightful." She stuck her tongue out at him, then laid back shading her eyes with a hand. "I still find myself surprised to see a periwinkle sky. It's so pretty." He leaned over her. "You're blocking my view."

"Never change, Ava. Keep finding your delightful joy in the little things." Karid's gray eyes were solemn.

Her eyes met his. "Karid, everyone changes. Sometimes a little at a time, sometimes a lot. It's the nature of life. Remaining static is a death sentence to wonder, innovation, and dreams."

"You think you've changed since we met? I don't see it."

She bit her lip and her eyes darted to the side before returning to his. "Yes. Given my childhood, I keep my innermost feelings to myself. A lot. Part of the reason I enjoy cooking is I can connect with others without revealing anything truly personal about myself. But between meeting the other women and you, I'm finding it easier trust enough to let others in and know more of the real me. That's huge for me."

"Then you're changing for the better, whereas I am not." His gray eyes turned stormy.

"Hey." She reached up and stopped him with her forefinger on his lips. "We're all works in progress. Cut yourself some slack. You've recently experienced trauma. It takes time to adjust. I'm still adjusting to residual effects of my own trauma."

He wrinkled his nose. "You want me to cut my pants?" She watched the tempest calm.

"Huh?"

"You said to cut my slacks."

Her jaw fell open, then she giggled. "No, cut yourself some slack is slang for be kind to yourself and don't judge yourself so harshly."

"I love hearing you laugh." His lips formed a wide smile.

"Then it's a good thing you're a comedian." She tapped his chest. "Alright, handsome, let's pack up and head back. I need to figure out what we're having for evening meal and you have your training forms to do."

He pushed himself to his knees and held out his hand to help her rise. When they finished replacing everything in the satchel and stood, he wrapped his tail around her waist and said, "Thank you, Ava, for the picnic. We need to do this again sometime."

"I'd like that."

Chapter 19

EVERY NIGHT, KARID had a nightmare. To wake him, Ava started caressing his cheek instead of touching his shoulder. For some reason, it didn't trigger his instinct to immobilize a threat. Each time he woke from the terror to find her sitting by his side instead of underneath his body with him grasping her neck, he was relieved.

Traxen approved the outdoor projects and had supplies delivered. Karid smiled when he recalled the day he jokingly laid out the fire pit. Ava looked at the lopsided stone structure and said, "Please tell me that is not what it is going to look like. Did you even look at the directions I gave you?"

"I looked at the pictures," he said innocently.

Hands on her curvy hips, she snarled, "Goddamn males are the same throughout the universe. Read the fucking directions, Karid." She stomped back into the cabin.

He laughed so hard at her reaction that he fell to his knees, trying to catch his breath. A water pouch smacked the back of his head. She stood there, scowling at him, before she started laughing as well. He made a production out of reading the directions aloud, loving the irritated looks she gave him. In those moments, he forgot he was a disfigured warrior and felt more like himself than ever.

Ava came out often while he worked to build the fire pit the correct way. She said it was to ensure he followed the instructions, but he noticed her scent became heavier when he removed his shirt and wiped the perspiration from his chest. He found ways to tease her, just so he could smell her.

When the mortar finally cured, they started their first fire in the pit. The crackle and pop of burning wood broke the silence of the night. The smoke drifted upwards, creating patterns against the shadows of the trees and added a new calming odor to the forest. The firelight's glow highlighted Ava's beautiful features. Taking a deep breath, he looked away to stare into the fire.

"When the Zuvgran captured me, they tortured me," he said quietly.

He felt the weight of her eyes on him but couldn't look at her.

"I guessed as much from your scars," she said calmly.

"They wanted to know what the Svesti knew about the latest virus and their labs, especially the one we destroyed on XB9428B."

"But your nightmares aren't about that, are they?"

His tail flicked, and his shoulders tightened. "Why do you say that?"

"Because of what you say during your nightmares, Karid."

In shock, his head whipped in her direction. His worried eyes darted all around before he looked at her.

"You never told me I said anything."

She met his eyes. "You weren't ready to talk about it."

He muttered, "I'm still not ready." He returned his gaze to the fire finding it easier to talk while watching the colors play. "In between the beatings, stabbings, and everything else, I thought of you."

Her fingers clasped his. Quietly, he continued, "Before I left on the mission, I had hopes you might want to true mate with me when I came back. I relived every interaction with you. I imagined what our future would be." He glanced sideways at her. "I know it's not possible now, but I wanted you to know thoughts of you kept me alive."

"Why isn't it possible now, Karid?" Clutching his hand, she said, "Tell me what changed."

"You won't want me when you know all the truth," he mumbled.

Her voice firmed. "Let's get one thing straight, Karid Wurvez. Do not presume to tell me what I want or need. Do not make decisions for me. Even if we mated, that would not be your responsibility."

His hand trembled. "When my captors realized they weren't breaking me with physical pain, they tried emotional pain."

She sucked in a breath. "Can you tell me?"

"They said they would break my warrior's honor. They injected me with a sexual stimulant." His voice broke. "They brought in a young, terrified Jalaxian female in a sheer gown."

"What happened then?"

"I was hanging from manacles on the wall. They shoved her at me. I started screaming that I wouldn't rape her. I begged her to get as far away from me as possible."

"Did she?"

"Yes, she tucked herself in the furthest corner of my cell. When my captors realized I wasn't trying to reach her, they gave me more of the drug and released me from my manacles." Breathing heavily, he stopped talking.

"Karid?" Her voice sounded strained. "You need to finish telling me."

"I curled myself into a ball away from her and cried like a youngling. When the increased dosage started acting on my body, I punched the walls. I ended up breaking the bed apart and used one of the broken legs to stab myself, so I wouldn't touch her. Goddess, I even masturbated with my bloody hands to relieve the need." Tears ran down his face. "At some point, I heard her whisper, 'Whatever happens, it's okay. I know it isn't your choice.'"

He peeked sideways at her and saw firelight glinting off her tears.

"How long did it last?"

"I have no idea. They'd come in periodically to give me more of the drug. By the end of it, I was a bloody mess. But I never touched her."

"Why would you think I would have issues with this? It sounds like you did everything you could to keep from hurting the girl."

He shouted, "Goddess help me, there were moments I wanted to just to make it stop. And then I felt like I betrayed you, even if we weren't mates." Panting, he hung his head. "I am so ashamed."

Abruptly, she let go of his hand. Dejected, he squeezed his eyes shut. *I knew she'd leave. And I haven't even told her the worst of it.*

His head jerked up when he felt her hands on her shoulders. She maneuvered onto his lap facing him. Panicked, his eyes darted away. She cupped his face and said, "Look at me, Karid."

"Please get off my lap."

"Look at me, Karid."

"I can't. You can't be this close to me."

"You should go. Just leave and never come back. I will treasure my memories of you forever." He tried to scoot back a little away from her.

"Karid...Look. At. Me. Now."

Warily, his eyes met hers. She leaned her forehead on his. His body tensed impossibly more.

"You silly male. Even if you had given into the drug, you didn't betray me. Instead, you only proved what I already knew— you are an honorable warrior." Her lips lightly caressed his. "You inflicted pain on yourself to keep from hurting that poor woman. I am so proud of you."

Tremors wracked his body as he enveloped her in his arms. Tears soaked her hair and shoulder as he sobbed. "They damaged me more after, Ava. I'm no longer a male."

Wiggling on his lap, she said gently, "You certainly feel male to me."

He tensed again and moved her back slightly.

"I'm not sure I can tell you the rest, *raralumia*."

She hugged him tighter. "Is this the last of it? If so, let it out so you can move on. Please, sweetheart, you need to trust me."

He sat silent for a long time. Her palms rubbed hard against his back as if she were trying to absorb him into her. Beyond that, she waited patiently.

His voice muffled from his stuffy nose, he whispered, "They said since I wasn't male enough to take the female, then my body should reflect it." Inhaling deeply, then slowly letting it out, he continued, "They cut off my head nodes."

"Head nodes? What are those?"

"Svesti males have sensitive nodes on their cock. Three near the head and one near the base."

"Oh, sweetheart." Her hands gentled. "Do you still have sensation?"

"I don't know. I can barely touch my cock now," he admitted.

Her hands moved to his forearms where her thumbs drew gentle, calming circles.

"They also cut off my balls. I can no longer sire young."

"Those bastards. Tell me they're all dead."

Nodding, he said, "According to Vared, no one was left alive."

"Good. Saves me the trouble of killing them."

"You are a fierce female." He kissed her forehead. "So now you understand why I can't be with you. I can't be what you need. You can go. I don't blame you."

"For a smart male, sometimes you are incredibly stupid," she huffed indignantly.

Confused, he pulled back to look at her with red-rimmed eyes. "What do you mean?"

"Let's say none of this happened, and we mated. Now imagine you were in some kind of accident where you lost not only your balls but your cock, too. Would you expect me to walk away then?"

"It wouldn't be unreasonable to expect."

"Well, then, you know jack shit about human women. There are lots of ways to have a sexual relationship. When I make a commitment to someone, it will be forever, not just when it's easy." She crossed her arms. "If I were in an accident and my breasts were gone or I could no longer have children, would you leave me?"

"Of course not."

"Well?" She tilted her head and stared.

He stared back. "It really doesn't bother you?"

Sighing heavily, she caressed his cheek. "Karid, it only bothers me because it upsets you. Human males don't have nodes, so I can't miss them, but I really don't care one way or another. And your missing dangling bits?" She smirked. "So I won't have the experience of your balls slapping my ass. You'll just have to work harder to make sure I so good I don't even think about it."

"What about young?" *Does she really mean it?* He was afraid to hope.

"I'm not sure I want children. And if I do, then we can always adopt a Zuvgran hybrid or two. Those poor kids could use some love." Her eyebrows came together. "Did you freeze any of your sperm like Vared did? If so, that's another option available to us."

He slowly nodded. "Yes. I forgot about that."

"Well, since the latest virus killed Talia's eggs, her twin sister is donating some of hers to use with Vared's sperm. Talia will be inseminated with the embryos and carry the baby."

"I hadn't heard about that." *What else have I missed?*

"Don't worry about it. You've had other things to think about."

He kissed her forehead. "Will you sleep with me tonight?"

"I sleep with you every night."

"I mean before I have a nightmare. I just want to hold you close. Maybe even be the big spoon." He kissed her smile.

"No sexy stuff. We're not ready," she said earnestly.

"You're right; I'm not ready. But you'll join me?"

Nodding, she said, "Let's put out the fire and clean up. I think I'll take a quick shower to rid my hair of the smoky smell before we head to bed."

As he helped her put things to rights, his chest felt lighter. *Goddess, please let this damaged male be enough for her.*

Chapter 20

ONCE AVA WAS in the shower, her tears flowed unchecked. *He's been through so much.* Her heart thumped wildly as she reviewed their conversation. *I forgot to ask what happened to the woman. I hope they rescued her, too.*

Stepping into the drying tube, she worried about his statement that he could barely touch his cock. *I know I had difficulty looking at and touching at my scars for a long time. I don't know if my acceptance will make it easier for him.* She dressed in a tank top and pajama shorts, then brushed her hair and teeth. Looking at the covered mirror, she debated. She took down the cloth. *Let's see if he notices and covers it again.*

Staring at her reflection, she squared her shoulders. *He said he was thinking of asking me to true mate before all this. Am I ready for that commitment?* She nodded. *Yes, I think I am. I can't imagine my life without him. I trust him with all of me.*

"Now I need him to trust himself or it won't work."

Although Ava's footsteps padded noiselessly on the carpet, Karid's head turned from where he stared out a window into the dark night. She realized it was the first time since she arrived at the cabin he was wearing loose pajama pants instead of his daywear. He swiveled his body and held out his arms. She walked into his embrace and wrapped her arms around his bare torso.

His steady heartbeat sounded reassuringly in her ear and his musky scent enveloped her. Warmth emanated from his body as she rubbed her cheek against the soft suede-like texture of his flesh. The softness of his pants rubbed against her legs, and his tail wound around her ankle.

Unbound, his hair created a silky veil around them when he lowered his head to nestle his nose against her neck. Shivers ran down her spine when he softly kissed her pulse. He moved back slightly and rested his forehead on hers.

"How do you feel?" She reached up to cup his jaw gently.

"Emotionally ragged, but also my heart isn't as heavy."

"Good. Let those of us who care about you help carry the burden."

Bemused, he wondered, "It's strange. I told you my deepest shame and pain, but I feel freer."

"That's because you're taking back your power. Suppressing it all keeps you in a victimized state. By choosing to share in a safe environment, you regain control."

"I honestly believed you would not want a damaged male."

Her lips thinned. "Do you believe I'm a damaged female?"

"Absolutely not." His hair swayed around them and tickled her face.

"If you believe you are broken, then you will act that way." Blowing out a breath, she said, "A couple months of hellish experiences doesn't erase the forty plus years—solars—of you being you. Yes, it's going to leave some scars, physical and mental, but it happened *to* you. It isn't who you are."

Karid lips pressed against her forehead, then he released her. "Come to bed, *raralumia*. Let me hold you."

Ava slid under the covers he held up for her. Laying on her back, she watched him walk to the other side of the bed and slide in next to her. He mirrored her position. His tail found its familiar place around her ankle. *I never realized it before, but I think his biceps are as thick as my thighs. He's like a mountain beside me.*

His hand gently clasped hers. He raised it to his lips and kissed her knuckles. *He's so sweet.*

She tugged his corded arm behind her neck to use as a pillow and rolled toward his warmth. His claws on one hand played with her curls, while her fingers combed the ends of his hair. His free arm draped over her waist. His breath stirred her tresses.

"May I ask you a question? You don't have to answer."

"Of course."

"Given your childhood, how did you get from there to the passionate female you are now? I can't imagine you wanted any male to touch you ever again."

"For a long time, I didn't. It took years before I would allow Dan to even hug me." She drew in a deep breath. "He knew all the facts since he was part of the investigative team, but I couldn't make myself talk to him about any of it. The therapists—mind healers—I had helped me reach the point where I could trust his support. He's never given me any reason to doubt his good intentions."

Ava raised her head to look into his compassionate gray eyes. "When I began dating, if a man made me feel pressured in any way, I never saw him again. I had a lot of first or second dates, but that was about it."

She rested her chin on her folded hands. "Then I met Stefan when I studied in France several years ago. He was older and taught one of my culinary classes. He was sophisticated but not snobbish, handsome without a large ego, and patient. We'd meet at cafes or he'd show me the sights and he'd kiss my cheek or hand."

A half-smile of remembrance tipped her lips as she continued quietly. "One day he said only women who carried deeply wounded hearts had eyes like mine. For some reason, it made me want to extend a little more trust and take a chance. I told him about being sexually molested as a child but not by whom and never having consensual sex. I thought he'd move on."

"But he didn't, did he?"

Her curls brushed his chest and arms as she shook her head. "No. He said if I changed my mind, he would be honored to be my first real partner. The thing that struck me most, though—he didn't offer platitudes or pity, just empathy."

She licked her lips. "Are you sure you want to hear the rest?"

His chest rose high as he deeply inhaled. "Hearing about you with another male isn't easy, *raralumia*, but if you're willing to share, I think I need to hear what you have to say."

Pressing a soft kiss over his heart, she said, "We took things very slowly. If I became the slightest bit uncomfortable or unsure, he stopped. If I wanted to be held, he held me. If I wanted space, he gave me space. It took months, but little by little, he helped me learn my body and my earlier experiences hadn't killed my capacity for pleasure. I am grateful beyond measure I had that time with him."

"Why are you not still together?" His hooded gray eyes were unreadable.

"Stefan's choice. He said he knew he didn't inspire fire in my soul and we both deserved to be with someone who did that for us. I admit I felt hurt, but we parted amicably. I went home to Canada. The last thing he asked of me was to be open to the possibility of a love that would burn so brightly it would keep the shadows small."

"Very poetic." Karid sighed. "I am glad he treated you well."

"He did." She nibbled on her lower lip. "Do you remember when you asked about me holding myself back?"

He hummed his agreement and it reverberated through-out her body. *Mmm, I liked that.*

"I think that's what Stefan meant. The thoughts start in my head and I analyze or worry and it takes part of me away from the moment."

"Understandable."

"Before you left on your mission, I wasn't having those thoughts."

His lips turned up. "I noticed the difference. You were magnificent."

Heart thumping wildly in her chest, she said, "I think maybe you have the ability to keep my shadows small. I hope I end up doing the same for you."

Moonlight highlighted the sheen in his eyes before he gathered her close and hugged her.

"You already do, Ava. More than you know." Tenderly, he kissed her lips. "It's late and it's been an emotional day for both of us. You need your rest."

She lowered her head and slowed her breathing to match his. His scent wafted in her nostrils filling her with comfort. *No spoons tonight, I guess. That's okay. I like this, too.*

Chapter 21

THE NIGHTMARE CAME several hours later, but this time Karid awoke on his own. Heart racing, sweat beading on his upper lip, and harsh breaths left him momentarily frozen in the still darkness. Eyes panicked, his muscles relaxed a fraction when he realized Ava continued to sleep deeply in his arms. Gazing at her pale, slack face against the darkness of his skin, he slowed his breathing to match hers. The feel of her trusting body and her scent strong in his nose slowly brought him back to the present.

He maneuvered cautiously to slide out of the bed and not interrupt her slumber. Drawing the covers she'd kicked off over her to keep her warm, he resisted the urge to kiss her. *She's woken up with me every night since she arrived. Tonight, I want to handle it without her.*

Soundlessly, he walked to the sanitary facility, closed the door, and relieved himself. The darkness hid his cock from his view. He hesitated, then turned on the light. Forcing himself to really look for the first time, he realized he couldn't tell he once had head nodes. The area was clear of scars. *Ash'n did a good job, but it still doesn't seem like it's mine. I can't have more with Ava if I can't come to terms with the changes in my body. I want more. I want it all...with her.*

Gingerly, he stroked his length from the base to just short of his missing nodes. It felt odd not to brush his knuckles against his balls. Using his thumb, he rubbed the healed area gently, then harder to determine how much sensation he'd lost. *It's different, but I can feel it. Should I try?*

Undecided, he turned toward the sink, startled by his reflection in the mirror. While not yet back at the weight and fitness from before the mission, he looked healthy. He met his own eyes and stared. *I see the shadows resting there.* He thought of Ava. His eyes seemed to lighten and his cock bobbed. Hesitantly, he looked down and squared his shoulders.

Soaping his hand, he grasped his shaft and imagined tonguing Ava's core. He licked his lips as he recalled her taste, her gasps and moans, her scent becoming richer and heavier, and how she rode his face enthusiastically. He closed his eyes and fisted himself tighter as he imagined what it would feel like to sheathe himself in her wetness. His cock swelled and his fingers gripped tighter as his hand moved faster.

He took his fantasy further and envisioned his fangs elongating and her begging him to true mate. She would hold him tightly to her everywhere—with her arms, legs, and cunt. He bit his tongue to keep from calling her name as he came in jerky streams in the sink. He bowed his head and tried to catch his breath. When he looked at himself in the mirror, his eyes were silver and his face flushed. A big smile spread across his face. He cleaned the evidence of his orgasm from the sink and his body and just took a moment to look at himself. Really look, before he headed back to bed. Back to Ava.

Well, my cock still appears to work. I just have to get to the point where I can let her see everything without feeling shame.

One step at a time. This was a huge step for me.

Soft tickling sensations roused Karid from the depths of a dreamless sleep. Light beyond his eyelids brightened and darkened. Inhaling, Ava's scent swirled heavily around him and he opened his eyes. She was on her knees and had her hands planted on either side of his head.

The tickling sensations was her hair brushing against his skin as she bestowed light kisses on his face. When she changed positions, her head blocked the morning sunlight. Her nipples rubbed against his bare chest as she bowed her body in a *rulah*-like stretch. When she noticed he was awake, she murmured a husky "Good morning."

His hands clasped her waist and pulled her to straddle him.

"How can it be anything but a good morning when I find you bestowing such affection on me even before I arise?"

"Pretty words." She pressed herself harder against him. "Do you have any pretty kisses to go with them?" She licked his chin.

"Bring that hot little mouth closer, and I believe I can accommodate you." His tail smoothed the back of her leg from ankle to thigh.

"Mmm." Her hands moved to grip his shoulders and she shimmied higher. "Like this?" she said against his lips.

He burrowed one hand in her hair while the other rested on the small of her back. His tongue traced her open mouth. Playful green eyes met his at the same time the tip of her tongue touched his. They teased each other before he sealed his mouth over hers and deepened their kiss. His fingers squeezed in reaction to her moan. His cock hardened. He tugged her nightgown over her head to find her naked, bared to him. He sucked in a breath at her nudity.

Karid's fingers lightly trailed from her hair to the front of her neck and downward. Circling her plump breast, he started at the outermost softness and decreased the circles drawing closer to his destination. Extending a claw, he rubbed the smooth curved side of the nail underneath her peaked nipple. She gasped and thrust her chest closer to him. His mouth left hers.

"I have to taste," he murmured against her skin. His lips followed the path of his fingers. He extended another claw and lightly held her nipple hostage until he enclosed it with his mouth. He smiled against her flesh when she cried out his name and bucked.

His hand at her back moved to her waist as he suckled deeply before tasting his way to her other nipple. Her fingernails dug into his skin. He loved the idea of her marking him. He released her nipple with a loud pop.

"Ride my face, Ava. Let me taste that beautiful cunt of yours." He frowned and looked at her when she stiffened slightly. "What's wrong, *raralumia*?"

"Nothing."

"Please don't lie to me. Something just happened."

She bit her lip. "It's that word. Cunt. Sometimes on Earth it's used as an insult or a way to demean a woman. I don't like it much."

"I find it to be one of the most wondrous parts of a female's body." He tilted his head. "What word would you prefer I use?"

"You can use it. I know you don't mean anything bad when you do. I'll adjust."

He emphatically shook his head. "No. I want you comfortable. What should I say instead?"

"You don't mind?"

Grinning, he said, "I'll be happy to say anything that makes you want to ride my face, Ava."

She giggled. "I prefer pussy."

He wrinkled his nose. "Like the slang for cat? Do humans use the word like that?"

"Yes, I don't know the origins, but that's how I think of my parts in my own mind."

"Well, then, would you please bring that gorgeous pussy closer so I can make us both feel good? It's been far too long."

She sat up and grasped the headboard to pull herself as she walked on her knees.

"Here, kitty, kitty. Karid wants to taste you." He waggled his eyebrows at her and was rewarded with her smile.

"You are such a character." Straddling his face, she pursed her kiss-swollen lips. "Like this?"

His eyes closed partway as he inhaled her aroused scent. "Lower yourself. I want you to take your pleasure." His hands squeezed her ass and pulled her closer. The dark pink of her sex drew his eyes and he licked his lips in anticipation. He glanced up and saw the undersides of her breasts curved up to her dusky pink nipples. *Sweet Goddess, she's so crekkin' beautiful.*

He moved his hands and used his thumbs to spread her wider. Flattening his tongue, he licked her from the bottom of her opening to her clit. His eyes rolled back in his head. *Nirvana.*

Pushing his tongue inside her core, he explored her and lapped voraciously. Her hips undulated, but she didn't lower herself further. Her breathing quickened and she mewled and whimpered as her excitement grew. His cock leaked dampening his lounge pants. He withdrew his tongue and replaced it with his tail. His lips pulled gently on her clit.

"Oh my God. Is that your tail?"

Humming around her nub, he nodded. She moaned and jerked seating his tail deeper inside her. He moved his tail slowly mimicking what he'd love to do with his cock. His tongue licked circles around her clit. When he used the tip just underneath the swollen pearl in gentle steady motions, she sank down on his face and pressed hard.

"Right there. Oh my. Karid, don't stop. It feels so good." Her head fell back and she began riding him harder and faster. He could barely breathe, but he didn't care so long as he could stay buried between her soft fleshy thighs. Her passion rose higher and higher and she grunted with her exertions. He glanced up to see her breasts bouncing. He moved his hands to her ass again and clenched her cheeks hard pricking her skin with his claws.

Her thighs tightened and her pussy squeezed his tail so hard he thought he lost blood flow. Her body spasmed and she screamed his name. When her movements slowed, he removed his tail and used his tongue to lap her flowing juices. Aftershocks shook her intermittently. She lifted her body off his head and he growled.

A tired laugh met his ears. "Too sensitive, sweetheart." She flopped onto his chest. "Damn, you're really good at that."

A grin broke out on his wet face. "I could do that all day, every day, *raralumia*."

She glanced down to where his cock tented his damp pants. Her hand traced his lower abdomen above his waistband. "I could take care of that for you."

He clasped her wandering hand. "No. I'm not ready yet. I'm happy."

"Are you sure? It looks uncomfortable."

"I'll live." He pushed her hair back behind her ear. "Do you know how much pleasure I get from making you feel good?"

"I hope as much as you give me."

"Are you ready for another orgasm? I'm happy to pet and lick your pussy some more."

Smiling, she said, "Maybe later. Let's get dressed and have breakfast."

Chapter 22

A VA'S PARTS STILL tingled while she took her shower. She washed quickly and jumped into the drying tube. She brushed her teeth and hair. In the mirror, she looked at her flushed skin and bright eyes. *I look happy. I should be after Karid eating me like a starving man. I can't believe I fucked his tail. Hell, I want to do it again.*

Realizing she forgot to bring clothes with her, she walked naked into Karid's bedroom. She turned to see Karid watching her. Even better, it looked like he was gripping his cock through his pants.

She slowly slid her hands from her waist upward to lift her breasts.

"Like what you see?"

"Always. You are a vision."

She smiled licentiously. "Bathroom is all yours. I need to put some clothes on." She turned and deliberately swayed her hips as she left.

"You are a tease, Ava." His voice was gruff but amused.

"You love it. See you in the kitchen," she called out cheerily.

Ava sang and swayed as she beat eggs in a bowl. Turning, she shrieked when she noticed Karid standing against the door jamb.

"You startled me!"

Grinning widely, he said, "I was enjoying the view."

Sticking her tongue out, she blew a raspberry at him, then laughed.

Casually, he walked up to her. "I can think of more adult things to do with that tongue."

Her pussy clenched at his words. He bent forward, his nose brushing her hair and grabbed something from the counter. Stepping back, he plopped a piece of breakfast meat into her mouth.

"There. Much better." He smirked.

Ava narrowed her eyes. He watched her mouth move as she chewed. When she licked her lips, he groaned. A wicked smile lit her face.

"Are you ready to...eat?"

Looking into her eyes, his tongue passed over his own lips. "I find myself very...hungry," he said.

"Mmm. So am I." She raised herself up on her toes to whisper in his ear. "Western omelets coming right up." She giggled and spun to pour contents from the bowl into a hot pan.

Surprised laughter burst from him, the sound mingling with the sizzling from the stove. *Teasing each other feels good.*

The back door chimed. She answered it and one of the kitchen males stood there.

"Delivery from the king, Lady Ava," he said as he handed her a package. He pointed to a small crate on the ground. "This is also part of the delivery, but it is very heavy. Would you like me to bring it in for you?"

"That won't be necessary," Karid said from behind her.

Ava smiled. "Thank you for bringing this to me. I appreciate it."

The male smiled shyly. "I'm happy to be of service."

"Was there anything else? If not, you should be on your way." The heat of Karid's body seared her back, yet shivers raced down her spine.

"Good day to you both." The male hurried to the flitter.

Ava turned and slapped Karid's chest. "That was rude."

"You shouldn't have opened the door."

"I recognized him from the palace, and I was expecting something specific."

"What?"

"I'm not sure I want to tell you now. It was going to be a surprise." She walked back, placed the package on the counter, and finished plating the food. "Let's eat."

As they ate, Karid said, "I hope you're not upset with me. Your safety is important to me."

"I didn't like you being mean to someone just doing his job."

He grunted. "I didn't like the way he looked at you."

"Seriously? You're jealous? After this morning?"

"Females are rare on Costonia."

"Karid, I'm not going anywhere. No other male interests me."

"But you interest them."

She tilted her head. "How about if I need help showing my disinterest, I will ask you for it?" *I admit I like the alpha attitude sometimes, but I don't think I can handle it all the time. Gotta set some boundaries if we're going to make it.*

"I'll do my best to not upset you, but I feel very protective." He widened his eyes like a mischievous child. "May I have my surprise now?"

"You may." She didn't bother trying to hide her amusement. *I just can't stay irritated with him.*

He reached out and grabbed the package. When he found a leather pouch inside, he opened it and stared at the sculpting tools. Silently, he picked up each item and examined it closely, testing its weight and fit in his hand before replacing it in the pouch. He raised his eyes and smiled.

"Thank you. These are perfect."

"The crate outside should have various types of stone for you to choose from. If none of it will work for you, we can get something else."

He bounded up from his seat to the crate with his tail swaying in excitement. Standing in the doorway, she bit back a moan when he squatted in front of the metal box. *Damn, those pants do a great job outlining his muscles. Is it hot out?*

Gently he picked up stones one at time turning them one way, then another before holding his hand closed around each one. Some he placed to one side in a large pile, while only a few made it into a smaller pile. When he stopped about halfway through the crate, he gently returned the large pile to the box and resealed it. The others he gathered carefully and brought them in and placed them on the table.

Curious, she watched him program the synthesizer. When it finished, he pulled out several soft cloths and wrapped the stones in them.

"What made you choose those?"

"They spoke to me about what they were hiding underneath the surface." His gray eyes gleamed with emotion. "I hope I can still find the joy in sculpting that I did before."

Her face softened and she said quietly, "I think you already have."

"Perhaps you are correct. I will begin one later."

"Do you have everything you need?"

"For now. When one is closer to being finished, I will require some additional tools and supplies. I have some stored in my quarters on the *Invictus.*"

His thick arms surrounded her and he rested his forehead on hers. His tail curled around her ankle.

"Thank you, *raralumia.* Each day with you reminds me that I have more to be thankful for than I remembered on my own."

She blinked back tears and tilted her head back to give him a light peck on the lips.

"Every day is a gift, Karid. Our experiences have proven that to us. It's just hard to remember sometimes."

His callused thumb wiped a lone tear from her face.

"Wisdom and beauty. An intoxicating combination."

She snuggled into his chest inhaling his scent. *Damn, I think I'm falling in love with him.*

After some debate about how high the surface of the grill should be, Ava left Karid outside to start the construction and spent some time in the kitchen making large batches of cookies. She wanted to send some to Phoenix House even if she couldn't go herself. Humming as she worked, she decided her next project would be making a barbecue sauce. *I think he'll enjoy the new flavors once the grill we can grill.*

Finished with the baking, she packed up the cookies leaving a couple dozen aside to keep at the cabin. She placed several on a plate and went to check on Karid's progress. She sucked in a breath at the sight of him bent over lifting a stone. His firm ass strained the seams of his pants. Shirtless, a light sheen of sweat glistened on the corded muscles of his back and arms and her panties dampened.

His head lifted and turned toward her. The flare of his nostrils let her know he smelled her arousal. His eyes glinted as he grinned in her direction.

"I think someone likes what she sees."

"Mmm." She licked her lips and said innocently, "The grill looks great."

He straightened and dropped the stone in its proper place. Dusting off his hands on his pants, he said, "Just the grill?"

"My cookies look good, too. I brought you some." She tossed her hair and winked.

He rubbed his taut stomach with its eight-pack abs drawing her gaze to the light dusting of brown hair of his happy trail. Seeing the bulge in his pants, she squirmed. *From here, you can't tell he's missing his balls. Damn, I want to lick the muscles walking this way.*

"Ava?"

"Hmm?"

"Are you going to share?"

"Share what?"

Amusement laced his voice. "The cookies." He stepped closer and took the plate from her.

"Oh, yeah. Sorry, I got distracted."

His lips curled upward. "I noticed." A cookie disappeared into his mouth. She sighed.

"Karid?"

"Yes?"

"I need to tell you something."

A few loose strands of his hair danced around his face in the breeze.

"What is it?"

"I'm not trying to put any pressure on you, but as soon as you think you might be ready for more, I want you to know I'm ready, too."

He sucked in a breath and his eyes melted into the silver color that she loved.

"What are you saying, *raralumia*?"

"I'm saying I want to explore all of you, touch you everywhere, and give you pleasure. I want to feel you inside me, filling me."

"Sweet Goddess," he whispered as he cupped her cheek with a trembling hand. "You slay me with your courage and honesty."

Watching his eyes as she spoke, she caressed his face. Her heart raced in her chest.

"I trust you with all of me. I hope someday, sooner rather than later, you can trust me the same way."

His eyes watered slightly even as they searched hers. His lips quivered.

"I'm afraid, Ava."

"Of what?"

"That you'll turn away when you see me and all of this will be gone. I think that's a big part of what broke me to begin with—the thought of losing what we have."

"I would never walk away because of circumstances beyond your control, Karid. How you treat me and how you make me feel are the most important things." She smiled tenderly. "Like I said—no pressure. I just wanted to let you know where I stand."

"I want to be ready. But I'm not yet."

"Then you're already halfway there, sweetheart." She patted his cheek. "Now get back to work on that grill. I'm going to see if I can come up with a good recipe for our first meal on it later this week."

She felt his gaze on her as she walked back into the cabin. *He's closer than he thinks. I hope.*

Chapter 23

KARID TOOK HIS time laying out Ava's grill. He wanted it to be perfect for her. She deserved it. Her patience and understanding warmed him but also terrified him. *Goddess knows I want her in every way possible. But what if she's wrong and the changes in my body do make a difference to her? I don't know if I could survive losing her now.*

Another internal voice warred with the first. *What if she's right? She's never seen my cock. It works just fine. I wasn't afraid to take risks before this all happened. She's stood by me, pulled me up when I needed it, and remained steadfast throughout. Why won't I trust her?*

Costonia's hot yellow sun beat down on him as he mixed some mortar to set the first few levels of stone. The repetitive motions of hand stirring soothed him and quieted the voices for a little while. When the mixture was ready, he picked up the trowel and began spreading it, stacking stone around the metal rods he had placed in the ground for additional structural integrity, and wiping down the excess mortar.

He decided to quit for the day with the grill halfway finished. He cleaned his tools and walked around checking his work. Satisfaction filled him. *The foundation is good and strong.*

Karid stilled, then sat down heavily in a chair as his thoughts repeated in his mind. *It's not her I don't trust. It's me. I have to trust that I am strong enough to handle the worst if it happens. I have to trust that I will reach out for help if I need it. I have to trust that the foundation of my healing is good and strong and will weather any storm. How do I do that?*

Staring at the trees, he pondered the question. Absently, he grabbed a water pouch from the small cooling unit Ava left out on the table. Rehydrating, he turned over options in his brain. When he settled on one, he took a deep breath. *Can I do it?*

Nodding to himself, he picked up his comm.

"Karid. It's good to see you. How are you?" Traxen's lavender eyes were surprised, but happy.

"I'm doing much better. I still have some more healing to do, but I feel better overall."

"That's wonderful news. We've been concerned about you."

"I know. I have a request."

"Name it, my friend."

"I would like to invite you, Vared, Devik, and Ash'n to a late evening meal here at the cabin sometime in the next couple days, if possible. I think I might be ready to talk, but I don't think I can tell the story multiple times just yet."

Traxen sat back and steepled his fingers.

"Did Ava give her approval?"

"Why would I need Ava's approval?"

"One of her conditions when she went to be with you was no visitors without her prior approval. She's very protective of you."

Karid smiled. "I'm sure she will be pleased at the prospect of the four of you coming to visit."

"Unfortunately, I can't do tonight, but the rest of the week I can make happen."

"Could you coordinate with the others, choose an evening, and let us know?"

"Of course." Traxen's fangs were bright against his huge grin. "I can't tell you how pleased I am to see you looking and sounding so much better."

"Thank you." Karid smiled and mock shuddered. "I guess I need to go tell Ava now."

"One of us will let you know what evening we can get together."

Karid took a moment after disconnecting the comm. He wasn't crazy about sharing his ordeal again, but felt he needed to do it before he could go further with Ava.

Inhaling deeply, he stood and went to find her. She was mixing something in a bowl that smelled tangy and tart while listening to her Earth music player. Her foot tapped and her hips swayed along with the beat.

He snuck up behind her, wrapped his arms around her waist, and moved in time with her. After ceasing for a startled moment, she continued. He leaned down to speak in her ear.

"I have a confession to make."

"What's that?"

"I've asked my best friends and the king to come to a late evening meal here sometime soon."

She put down everything and spun to face him.

"You did?"

Nodding, he said, "I was told I need your approval."

She laughed softly. "You must've spoken with Traxen."

"Yes. Do I have your approval?"

"Of course." She searched his eyes. "Is this a social visit or something else?"

"A little of both. I was thinking we could all eat together, then I could speak with the males by the firepit like I did with you."

"Do you want me there for support or do you want me to find somewhere else to be?"

"Would your feelings be hurt if I asked it just be us males?"

"Of course not. Whatever you think is best is good with me."

"Could I request that you occupy yourself in the living area so you're close if I do need extra support?"

"I'm happy to do whatever you need." Her finger gently rubbed where his brows came together. "I'm proud of you. I know this is difficult."

"I know I need to take this step."

"You do, but it doesn't have to be so soon if you're not ready."

He squared his shoulders. "I've avoided it long enough. I felt much better after I told you." She hugged him tightly. He bent his head to whisper, "Dance with me."

Later that night, Karid suggested they watch another of Earth's movies. They cuddled closely on the couch and laughed at the comedy. When the front door chimed, they looked at each other. Then a loud knocking started with a voice yelling, "Karid. I know you're in there. Open up now."

Karid stiffened. Ava sat straight and asked, "Who the hell is that?"

"My father. Did you invite him?"

"I wouldn't do that without talking to you about it first. Did you tell him you were staying here?"

"No." The banging and shouting continued. Karid frowned. "I'm going to have to let him in. Otherwise he'll just keep doing what's he's doing."

"Okay." Ava grabbed her comm. "I'm going to let Traxen know and ask him how your father found you."

Karid stood and reluctantly opened the door. He dodged the fist that was bearing down for another round of banging. He heard Ava talking with Traxen.

"What is it, Father?"

The angry male pushed into the cabin.

"Why do I have to find out that you were captured by the Zuvgran from other people and not you?" his father blustered.

"I've been recuperating and frankly, I did not feel it necessary to inform you any more than I did the other times I was captured. How did you know where to find me?"

Drikon raked his eyes over Karid's bare torso noting the newest scars.

"I have my ways. This warrior nonsense needs to stop. I've been patient long enough. You'll pack up, come home, and learn the business."

Karid felt his temper rising as it always did when his father tried to control his life.

"That is not going to happen. Ever. I have no desire to be a merchant. Never have. Never will."

"You will continue my legacy and life's work. That is your duty."

The gentle touch of Ava's small hand on Karid's forearm lowered his ire slightly.

"Introduce us, please."

"Ava, this is my father, Drikon Wurvez. Father, please meet Ava Taylor." Karid's jaw was tight.

"Leave us, female."

Ava's eyes narrowed and her fingers clenched on his flesh.

"No, I don't think I will." She glanced up at Karid. "Unless you ask me to."

"Please stay." His lips curled upward as her eyes softened.

"This is family business, and I do not want a foolish female involved."

"I consider Ava *my* family and she is anything but foolish." Karid's tail flicked in short movements. Crossing his arms, he growled. *How dare he insult her?*

Drikon bared his fangs angrily and his tail slapped the floor.

"You dare defy me?"

"Perhaps you could calm down and start over," Ava suggested.

Drikon clenched his fist and it rose. Karid pushed Ava aside and stepped forward.

"Do not even think of harming her." Karid glowered at his father.

"Then she should keep her mouth shut."

Ava hissed, then inhaled deeply. Anger tinged her *wimma* sugar scent. *She rarely becomes incensed, but when she does, it's amazing to watch.*

"Who the fuck do you think you are?" Ava said so coldly it could splinter glass. "You beat down the door. You yell and threaten us. You tell me to shut up in my own home. Yet somehow you're the one insulted?" *She could give Lady Talia lessons in eviscerating someone with words.* His cock stiffened.

"I wouldn't expect a female to understand."

Ava looked at Karid. "How on earth did you turn out as well as you did with him as a father?"

Karid bit the inside of his cheek to keep from grinning at Ava's comment.

"I had other influences in my life."

"Good thing you did." She turned hard green eyes back to Drikon. "Karid is not an extension of you. He does not need to follow in your footsteps. A good father would want him to find his own happiness. A good father would have first asked him if he was okay and if he needed anything."

Drikon's reddish bronze face darkened and his muscles tightened.

"How dare you, female? You should learn your place."

"What a misogynistic asshole you are." When Drikon stomped toward the door, she said, "I'm not done with you yet." Drikon whirled back to face them.

"Your legacy is not your life's work, it is your son. Somehow, against the odds with you as his pitiful example, Karid managed to become a good, strong, caring male, and honorable warrior. He is an adult and has been for decades. Either recognize and respect that or get the fuck out of our home."

Drikon raked his eyes over Karid with disgust.

"He's obviously worthless as a warrior if he keeps getting captured." Karid's head snapped back in shock.

Ava stalked forward and spit out. "You show your ignorance, not only of your son's character, but of the courage it takes for a warrior to volunteer for missions that are dangerous and live with the consequences." She poked a finger in his chest. "You, sir, are a *naroon* and unworthy of being a Svesti."

His father raised an open palm as if to slap Ava. A large hand grasped his wrist from behind.

"Lady Ava, are you well?"

"Royal Guard Previv, thank you for coming." Ava smiled and stepped back. "You have impeccable timing." Drikon struggled against being restrained. The other warrior with Previv silently secured Drikon's hands behind his back. Drikon muttered insults and threats until the guard smacked the back of his head.

"King Sovex wishes to speak with Drikon Wurvez about security matters. Do I have your leave to escort him from the premises?"

"I think that would be best for all concerned." Ava nodded regally.

"Lieutenant Wurvez, did you have anything else to say before your father speaks with the king?

"Yes." He glared at his father. "You are now dead to me. Never contact me again. Find another heir. I've put up with your unrelenting selfishness and attitude all my life, but no more. You not only insulted and threatened a female, you raised your hand in anger to her twice. The fact that it was a female that I care about only makes your actions worse. The only reason I have not ripped out your throat is I did not want to clean your blood from my residence. Had we been outside, you would already be facing judgment from the Goddess." He nodded at the guards. "You may take him now."

"Wait," said Ava. She rushed to the kitchen and came back with a container. She handed it to Previv and grinned. "Be sure to share."

Previv chuckled. "As you wish, Lady Ava." He dipped his chin. "We'll be on our way."

Chapter 24

AVA'S MUSCLES LOOSENED as she leaned against Karid's body. His hands rested on her abdomen, hugging her from behind. Small shivers racked her frame as her anger subsided. His unique scent filled her nostrils and she sighed as her world righted itself. He bent and nuzzled her hair.

"You were magnificent, *raralumia*. But you shouldn't have approached him."

"I knew the guards were behind him." She entwined her fingers in his.

"Even so, you put yourself in danger of being hurt."

She bit her lip. "Okay, I admit I was too pissed off at how he spoke to you and about you to worry too much about it."

"I'm used to it." *Oh, sweetheart.*

"You shouldn't have to be. I know you alluded to how bad your relationship was, but I had no idea how much toxicity you dealt with. No offense, but he's a total asshole."

His soft laugh stirred her hair and sent tingles down her neck.

"Yes, he is. He was completely unprepared for you. No one has ever stood up for me with him with such ferocity like you just did. I'm in awe of you." His fingers caressed her stomach and his tail stroked her leg.

"How did you turn out so well?"

"My mother blunted the worst before she died, plus I was young then. He changed, not for the better, when the virus took her from us. He traveled so much, my mother's father—a teacher—pretty much raised me. You'll like him. He's the one who encouraged me to follow my own path."

"I hate to ask, but did your father hurt your mother?"

He shook his head. "I don't think so. Today was the first time I ever saw him raise his hand to a female or treat one so callously. It surprised me." He paused. "I think my memories of how he used to be before she died are why I kept giving him chances to mend our relationship. But not after today."

She turned to look up at him. Solemn gray eyes gazed back at her.

"I'm sorry."

He wrinkled his nose.

"For what?"

"That he's unable to see and appreciate the good male you are."

"Thank you." Karid kissed the tip of her nose. "I think we missed the end of the movie."

"We can watch it another time. Why don't we clean up and go to bed early? It's been a long day."

Spooning together a short while later with Karid as the big spoon, she snuggled up close to him. His semi-erect cock pressed against her ass and his knees tucked up close to hers. He curled his upper body so his chin rested on the top of her head. Her fingers played with his in random patterns.

"Ava?"

"Hmm?"

"There's something I haven't told you." She concentrated on keeping her body relaxed.

"What is it?"

"Remember how you told me how you first met Dan?"

"Yes."

"I had a moment like that before you showed up." His breathing accelerated and her hair puffed across her cheek in time with his exhalations. She squeezed his hands and held tight.

"Did you hurt yourself?" *Stay calm. Don't cry. Don't cry.*

"I had one of my knives to my throat," he admitted in low voice.

"What made you stop?"

He took a long, deep breath but didn't answer.

"Can you tell me what you were thinking?" Her eyes focused on the moonlit trees outside the window while she waited for him to answer. It seemed like forever before he spoke.

"I wanted the voices in my head to stop."

"Voices?"

Even more softly, he said, "I could hear the Zuvgran saying I wasn't a warrior or male. My father telling me I was worthless. You stating you wanted nothing to do with me. The voices kept getting louder and jumbled and I couldn't make it stop."

"Oh, Karid, I hate that you suffered so much. What changed?"

"I saw your face along with my friends' faces filled with heartbreak and tears. I couldn't do it."

She rolled over to hug him, then cupped his cheeks in her hands.

"Promise me something."

"What?"

"That if you ever feel that way again, you will talk to one of your friends or me, or anybody who will listen. Never try to go it alone again."

They stared at each other, voicelessly speaking volumes. He clasped her to him tightly.

"I promise, *raralumia*."

"Thank you." She sniffed trying to hold back her tears at the thought of Karid no longer being in the world.

"Can you do something for me?"

"Of course."

"Could you tell me Dan's words again?" Her lips curved against his chest. Repeating the words before humming lullabies, she drifted off enveloped in his scent and arms.

The next morning, the only mention of Karid's nighttime confession was Ava thanking him for trusting her enough to tell her. After that, they both kept their interactions lighthearted and flirty. Ava was determined to keep him in a relaxed headspace, especially after Devik comm'd to confirm the males would be coming by that evening. *Tonight is going to be difficult for him.*

Ava spent much of the early hours in the kitchen prepping what she could in advance for the meal. Periodically, she would head outside to bring Karid a snack and check on the progress of the grill. When she went to tell him lunch was ready, she squealed when she realized the project was complete.

"It looks great, Karid."

"Thank you. Too bad we have to wait for the mortar to cure before you can use it." He finished cleaning his tools.

"That's okay. I'm just glad it's finished." She hugged him and pulled his head down for a kiss.

"I'm sweaty and dirty." His hands rested on the small of her back, while his tail teased her ankle.

"I don't care. You deserve some positive reinforcement for making me happy." She winked at him.

"I like how you think." He brushed her curls from her face and mock leered at her. "I can make you even happier and it would be positive reinforcement at the same time."

Her cheeks pinkened and she giggled.

"Maybe later," she teased.

He stepped back and dramatically put a hand over his heart.

"You wound me with the wait. However will I survive?"

"Good things come to those who are patient. Come on and wash up so we can eat midday meal."

While they ate, Ava mused that they would need additional chairs by the firepit.

"I found more in the shed. I'll bring them out and clean them."

"That's great. You should probably have the pit ready to light beforehand, too."

"I can do that."

When he left to take care of the chores, she cleaned up and began making the dessert for later. *I like how easy it is with him. Both of us working together at whatever needs done.*

Sometime later, after putting the dessert in the large cooling unit, Karid came in looking damp.

"Did you jump in the lake?" She tossed him a hand towel.

"No, I washed up outside after I finished." He dried his face and chest, then tossed the towel aside. He stalked close to her, picked her up, and sat her on the counter. Stepping between her thighs, he arched an eyebrow.

"I was a good male. I think I need some positive reinforcement."

"Oh, you do, do you? Like what? Some kisses?" *Damn, I love when he's playful.*

"That's a good start." He leaned down and their mouths met. As their tongues danced and hands roamed, her nipples hardened. She wriggled against his bare chest seeking more. His tail caressed her calves with a light shivery touch.

His hands snuck under her tank top and cupped her breasts. She moaned into his mouth when he rolled her nipples between his fingertips. *How does he make me feel so good so fast?*

When his tongue licked lower to her neck, she tilted her head to give him better access.

"I want to feel you come on my fingers, *raralumia*." A fang nipped her earlobe.

She whimpered and dropped her hands to the waistband of her shorts. Shimmying, she pushed them down to her hips. She lifted her ass so he could remove them altogether. *I never felt this needy or wanton with Stefan.*

One of his hands slid down her stomach in a light caress that made her clit throb. When he reached lower, he stopped and squeezed her pussy in his large, hot hand. Mewling, she spread her legs wider for him.

"You're so *crekkin'* responsive, Ava. What a passionate female you are." His thumb stroked soft circles around her swollen nub.

"Need more," she gasped. One long, thick finger slowly pushed inside her wet core and her pussy clenched onto it. His thumb never stopped moving even as he began pumping in a steady rhythm. Ava could smell herself as the wet sucking sounds grew louder. She tried to lift her hips to meet him, but his tail wound over her leg and held her firmly.

"No, let me do all the work. Just enjoy." He added a second finger and pinched her nipple with his other hand. Her head swung from side to side and she moaned.

"Fill me, Karid. Make me come, please."

Simultaneously, a third finger stretched her wide, a fang scraped along her neck, and he groaned, "Anything for you."

Her body wanted to twist and buck as he increased the rhythm, but she couldn't move. His thumb ceased its circles and instead, stroked just underneath her clit where she was most sensitive, occasionally brushing her nub.

"One day soon, *raralumia*, I will fill you with my cock and I'll *crek* you into next week." He sucked on her neck hard. "Your pussy is so wet and needy." He thrust faster.

Moaning, gasping, and mumbling nonsense words, Ava soaked up his dirty talk. A ball of desire spread throughout her body shooting electricity through her veins. Her pussy wanted him deeper and harder. She whimpered in need. His hand practically lifted her off the counter with each thrust in response.

"So close."

Quivering, her pussy spasmed and rippled, clenching on his fingers. Her head thrashed, her fingers dug into his skin, and she wailed his name as his tail loosened and her entire body shook with the force of her orgasm.

"Sweet Goddess, you are glorious," he said reverently as he gentled his movements until her body calmed. He withdrew his fingers and sucked them clean. Sated and boneless she couldn't muster the energy to be embarrassed at how wet the counter was beneath her.

Ava curled into his chest and inhaled his wonderful scent when he carried her to their bedroom. He sat on the bed, leaning on the headboard, and kept her on his lap as he gently caressed her and the claws of one hand combed her hair. Encased in his arms and care, she fell asleep.

Chapter 25

KARID SAVORED THE weight of Ava's soft body against his. He licked his lips—her scent enveloped him. Everything about her called to his heart—her trust, her openness, her passion—not just for him, but for everything and everyone she cared about, her humor, and so much more. *She really is a gift from the Goddess. I want to true mate with her.*

His jaw hardened. *I can't lose her because I am worried about her seeing me completely naked. The risk is worth the reward. I have to remember that and use my love for her as the basis of my strength to do the difficult things.*

Tenderness filled him as he gazed upon her face. The excited flush of her skin waned. Her lashes hid her beautiful eyes and rested delicately on her face. Realizing he left her pants in the kitchen, he pulled the covers over her. She breathed his name in her sleep and his heart hitched in his throat. He leaned back and closed his eyes with a contented smile.

"Sir, we found him. He's in a cabin in the King's Forest."

The Svesti noble smiled. "Good. Make a plan to retrieve him."

"It may take some time, sir. The route Drikon Wurvez used to circumvent the guards is most likely unusable."

"Why is that?"

"The Royal Guards took from the cabin. I'm certain they will have interrogated him and learned how he avoided security. They will close those gaps."

The noble frowned. *I need to know what Wurvez has told Sovex.*

"I want him under my control as quickly as possible."

"Understood, sir." The warrior left the room.

Staring into his glass, the noble swirled the expensive liquor and watched the striations of color merge into a new one. *Not much longer now until Sovex will be dead and I can take the throne.*

Karid knew Ava and his friends deliberately kept the atmosphere lighthearted at evening meal. He noted the relief on their faces when they first saw him. *I wasn't the only one suffering in some way.*

Traxen and Devik informed Ava of the progress at Phoenix House which was almost completed. Devik agreed to deliver the cookies Ava had baked for the younglings.

"Devik, I made a batch of cookies for the younglings. Would you take them to them?"

"I'll be happy to deliver them for you, Ava." Devik smiled. "The construction of Phoenix House is almost complete."

"The furniture is being synthesized now," added Traxen. "We're also gathering the initial supplies so everyone can move in as soon as the building is finished."

"I'm really happy to hear that." Ava's brows knitted. "I hope we thought of everything. Those kids deserve a real home."

"Ronan and Largon expressed their pleasure at the progress and the support they've been receiving on Costonia," Vared said. "They visited my family's estate yesterday and my father accepted both of them into our family and the Ruxila House."

Ash'n looked at Karid. "You'll like both males. They are honorable warriors who care greatly for the younglings." Everyone nodded.

Vared's facial scar whitened. "My father needed to hear what they knew about his cousin, Ronan's mother. He was pleased that Jorn, Ronan's father, did love her and treat her well."

"When you're feeling ready, my grandmother wants to have a party to celebrate our fated mate bond," Ash'n said. "Lin asked her to wait until both of you could attend. She said it didn't feel right not to have all of the family present."

Karid's lips tipped up. "Lady Lin is a caring female. You are very lucky, my friend." He glanced at Vared and Devik. "As are you two. I hope I will be ready soon. But my feelings would not be hurt if the celebration happened without me." Everyone shook their heads.

"We'll wait for you," Ash'n said firmly.

After dessert, Ava pulled out two bottles of Estalan liquor and handed them to Karid. He looked at the bottles and then at her.

"Are you certain about this?"

She smiled and caressed his face.

"I trust you to be moderate with your consumption. And if you don't want any, I'm sure your friends will be happy to drink your portion. I'll be in the living area if you need me." She kissed his cheek and motioned for him to go outside.

Squatting in front of the firepit, Vared lit the kindling.

"Traxen said you built this."

"Yes. Also the grill." Karid handed the bottles to Devik as he sat in the chair next to him.

"You did a good job. They look solid." The growing fire cast an orange glow and flickering shadows on everyone's faces. Vared rose and took his seat.

"Glasses or straight from the bottle?" Devik asked.

"I never want to drink straight from a bottle again." Karid shuddered.

"Glasses, it is." Devik poured and handed out the drinks.

"I like this. It's relaxing to sit out by a fire," Traxen said, and everyone nodded.

Ash'n took a sip, then asked quietly, "Do you need more time?"

Karid shook his head before he stared into the flames. He spoke as if he were giving a report and refused to look at his friends until he finished. He told them why he and Jevax were on Millus to begin with and how he ordered the other male to the ship.

He repeated everything he had told Ava, though he was able to get through the story this time without sobbing. His voice choked several times, but he went into more detail of his captivity with the males than he had with Ava. His tail alternated between drooping and hard flicking. Ashamed, but honest, he spoke to them of his time at the cabin before Ava arrived.

He fell silent. He closed his eyes, afraid to look at his friends and see pity. The only sounds were his harsh breaths, the crackling of the fire, and the usual forest noises.

"So you're the one I need to bill for repairs to the walls. Good to know," Traxen said, breaking the quietude and the other males chuckled.

There was a long silence, then Vared said, "Look at us, Karid."

Hesitantly, Karid lifted his eyelids and saw they were on their knees surrounding him. He saw tears and understanding but no pity. He blew out a breath.

Vared clasped the back of his neck and rested his forehead on Karid's.

"I told you before and I will repeat it as many times as needed to pound it into your hard skull—you are our brother. There is nothing that would make us turn away from you or your pain. Do you understand?"

Karid choked back a sob as he nodded. Vared released him with a clap to the shoulder and Devik took his place.

"You survived something horrific. I'm beyond grateful to the Goddess you are choosing to live again." Devik's deep voice cracked. He gave Karid a bone-crushing hug. "We've missed you."

Ash'n was next. He stared into Karid's eyes.

"While we understand why you pushed us away, you need to know you hurt us deeply. Our brotherhood has always been honest with each other and shared our burdens." Karid turned his head away in shame. Ash'n gently grasped his chin to force him to meet his gaze. "You also need to know we forgive you." Karid buried his face on his friend's shoulder and cried.

When he could finally see through his tears, Traxen was waiting for his turn.

"I know I haven't shared the same depth of friendship with you as the others. But as your friend, fellow warrior, and your king, I have to tell you how proud I am of you. You are an honorable warrior. You stumbled and fell into a deep, dark existence because you temporarily forgot to lean on your brothers. The measure of a male's character is who he becomes after a heartbreaking, soul-crushing experience. You could have given up, but you didn't."

Karid whispered, "If Ava hadn't shown up, I might have never crawled out of the despair and shame."

"We know. She has a special place in our hearts for reminding you of who you really are and returning you to us," said Ash'n. His friends returned to their chairs.

"I want to ask her to true mate."

"What's stopping you?" asked Devik.

Karid waved a hand at his groin.

"I'm worried about her reaction to my missing parts. We haven't gotten that far yet."

Ash'n said, "You wouldn't allow me to talk to you before, but I wanted to tell you some medical facts."

"I'm listening now."

"You are still producing seed, but in much smaller quantities since your body has nowhere to store the excess. I implanted a time-released hormone so you should have no issues with sexual arousal or function. You'll have to have a new implant every solar."

"I understand."

"You've told her what your captors did?" Vared asked.

"Yes."

"How did she react?"

"She told me it only bothered her because it upset me."

"Has she ever lied to you?" Traxen said.

"No."

"Then trust her to know her own mind," said Devik, his teal eyes reflecting the fire's glow. "These human females are steadfast and loyal, even if they can sometimes be maddening." They all smiled.

"Talia told me some human mating, no, wedding, vows include the phrase 'for better or worse' when talking about the couple's commitment to each other. I think Ava has conclusively demonstrated her ability to stick by you during hard times," Vared said with a grin.

"True. She's amazing."

"Madix Previv told me what she said to your father last night," Traxen said with a smile. "I was quite impressed."

"What did she say?" asked Devik.

Karid told them of his father's visit and Ava's reaction.

"You have to be a strong warrior to withstand a human female's anger." Vared chuckled.

"You should know," said Karid. "You irritate Talia often enough."

"But the makeup sex is worth it."

Devik and Ash'n both nodded enthusiastically. Traxen looked thoughtful.

"You said you ordered Jevax back to the ship. Why?"

Karid frowned. "Didn't he tell you?"

His friends glanced at each other.

"What do I not know?"

"Jevax is still missing. We found the debris from the *Tenacity* in the asteroid field, but no evidence of biological matter. We were hoping you knew what happened. We didn't push you for information because you were already dealing with too much."

Karid fell back in his chair, stunned.

"*Crekkin'* Zuvgran was telling the truth when he said they destroyed a ship." He sucked in a breath. "I ordered Jevax to get word to either of you," he nodded at Vared and Traxen, "about the Svesti noble who met with the Zuvgran, then return for me."

His friends leaned forward eagerly.

"You know who the noble is?" Traxen said.

Karid said the name and they all growled. Tails flicked and snapped.

"He's the one who clawed my jaw. He said he was going to be king."

"Over my dead body," Traxen bit out.

"I think that's probably his plan," Karid said with a straight face.

There was a moment of shocked silence before they all laughed.

Devik said, "It's good to have you back, you *naroon*."

Karid grinned. Then his face fell.

"Are we still scanning for Jevax's tracker?"

Everyone nodded.

Karid said, "He's a dedicated warrior. If he's alive, he'll be trying to complete the mission." He paused. "Did you ever receive our transmissions about the labs? There were solar flares in the Lestanus system and we didn't know if they went through."

"No."

"I'll try to recall everything and send it to you tomorrow. The coordinates may not be entirely correct."

"We'll expect it."

They sat quietly enjoying the fire and being together. Karid squared his shoulders.

"I haven't said it and I should have. I apologize for pushing all of you away. You've always been true friends, but I let my shame consume me instead of asking for help. I won't do it again."

Vared raised his glass.

"We won't let you do it again. We've learned our lesson, too."

Karid settled back in his chair, sipping his drink as the conversation moved to less serious matters. *I should have done this much sooner.* He glanced at his friends. *I forgot how lucky I really am.*

Chapter 26

WHILE GETTING A drink from the cooling unit, Ava looked out the kitchen door to see Karid and his friends talking and laughing. *It looks like it went well. I'm glad. He's reaching out to his support system. They're good men.*

Ash'n came into the cabin.

"I need to use the sanitary facility," he admitted, his blue eyes smiling.

She gave him directions. Tilting her head when he hesitated, she said, "Was there something else?"

"Yes." He swallowed hard. "While we knew the results of his physical torture, we did not know all the circumstances of his ordeal. It's understandable why he pushed us all away. At one time or another over the years, Karid's humor and support have pulled all of us out of our own miseries. Now he's finally letting us do the same for him. We want to express our gratitude for everything you've done. You gave him back to us. The progress he's made in a relatively short time is amazing."

"You don't have to thank me. I care for him, too. I'm glad I've been able to help."

"You are the one who he allowed to meet him where he was at, reach him, and encourage him to move forward with his healing. Something none of us were able to do."

His face wavered as she blinked back tears. She inhaled slowly.

"Can I ask a question?"

"Of course."

"The Jalaxian female. Was she rescued? Is she safe?"

His smile encompassed his whole face.

"Yes. Young Molla has already returned home to her colony. She suffered only minimal injuries. Her concern was for Karid. She wouldn't tell us much, just that Karid was an honorable male and did not deserve what happened to him. She insisted it was his story to tell or not, not hers. Now we know why."

"I'm happy she's okay. I figured Karid didn't know, but I wasn't sure. And if I was wrong, I was afraid to ask him in case something worse had happened to her. I didn't want there to be a setback while in the early stages of his recovery."

"If there is ever anything you need, just ask. We are in your debt."

Her curls whipped across her face when she shook her head.

"No debt. Just friends who care, Ash'n."

He dipped his chin.

"As you wish."

During the remainder of the evening, Karid's other friends all found an opportunity to thank her privately. As the males left, each rested his forehead on Karid's. *It's obviously the Svesti equivalent of a man-hug, although Karid does it with me also. A gesture of deep emotion?*

Ava and Karid watched the males board the large flitter in the front yard. Karid's tail wound around her ankle and he had an arm around her back. She leaned into him as the ship rose and disappeared into the night sky.

"How are you?"

"Mentally exhausted and my emotions feel close to the surface. I was foolish not to talk to them sooner."

She smacked his abdomen with the back of an open hand. "Do not berate yourself for what's done. You were in survival mode and your mind tried to protect itself until you were ready."

"Whatever you say, *raralumia*. Let's go to bed."

The next morning, bright sunlight pierced Ava's eyelids. The space next to her was warm, but Karid was nowhere in sight. *Probably going to the bathroom.*

Still tired, she snuggled into her pillow. They had stayed up late talking about his conversations with his friends and his feelings. *He truly needed their brotherly love and understanding.*

Hearing Karid, she sleepily opened her eyes, then they widened. *Holy shit, he's even sexier without clothes.*

Her entire body throbbed with desire. Looking nervous, he froze. She sat up and motioned with her hand for him to turn around. *Damn, he looks edible from all angles.*

Ava lifted the covers. "Come to back to bed, Karid."

Without a word, he slid in beside her. She dropped the covers and her thumbs stroked his cheeks.

"I want to touch you, Karid. Do you want that? Are you ready to let me explore?"

He cleared his throat and nodded. His hand burrowed into her hair when she kissed him lightly. His tail caressed her back.

"Just lay back and let me take my time." She grinned happily. "I'm looking forward to this."

His eyes softened and he held his arms out.

"Be kind, Ava."

"Sweetheart, kindness isn't what I want to make you feel. If you want to stop at any time, just tell me and I will. I won't be upset and you won't hurt my feelings." She pursed her lips and whispered, "Thank you for trusting me."

Ava peppered light kisses on his face, occasionally licking. Then her lips and tongue moved to his neck while her fingers traced the muscles of his upper arms. He groaned when she tongued his ear. Bit by bit, she felt the tension leave his body. *Time to move on.*

She kneaded and pet his arms and upper torso. Nibbling and licking along his skin, she marveled how his flesh looked like fur, but wasn't. She tongued the outline of his clan marking. Breasts full and tight, she rubbed her needy nipples over his warm, suede-like skin. Abruptly sitting up and throwing off the covers, she tore off her camisole, then returned to squirm along his body. *Oh, much better.*

"You smell and taste wonderful, Karid."

Finding her way to his small, hard nipples, she lapped at one before circling it with the tip of her tongue. He grunted when she bit it, then sucked it. Taking one of his hands, she alternated between teasing his nipple and sucking a finger. His chest rumbled, and she smiled against his flesh when his first hand clenched in her hair. His hard cock left pre-cum on her belly as she shimmied her way downward.

Ava's fingernails lightly scratched the sides of his torso in long thin lines. His stomach tightened in response. Lovingly, she kissed the healing scars before she licked her way along one side of his Adonis belt. She left a damp trail from one side to the other, moving lower and lower, the distance shortening as she got closer to his cock. He held his breath when her breasts and throat rubbed against his erection.

She looked up Karid's body to check the expression on his taut face. Molten silver peered at her and his nostrils flared wide.

Licking her lips, she asked, "Moment of truth, sweetheart. May I continue or should I stop?"

"I don't have the strength to stop you." He exhaled on a long breath.

She shook her head, his cock pulsing hot against her skin.

"Not good enough, Karid. If you don't feel ready, I can move back up and we try again another time. If you feel ready, I'll move lower and get up close and personal. But I need you to give me permission. And you can tell me to stop at any time." Her fingertips traced the lower lines of his abdominal muscles as if reading braille while she continued to hold his gaze. "As much as

I love what I'm doing, I don't want to push you if you need more time."

"Do you have any idea how excited I am right now, *raralumia*? Finally, my bare cock is touching your skin. It's been weeping and marking you, even as you mark me. I want you to make me yours in any way you feel comfortable. I'll face any fear if it means I can feel you handling me with those soft hands of yours, even if it's only this one time. I'll tell you to stop if it's necessary." He groaned deeply. "Touch me, please."

Keeping her eyes on his, she sat back on her heels between his thick thighs. His cock bobbed up against his stomach without her body in the way.

"You like marking me?" She rubbed his pre-cum into her skin and cupped her breasts. She lifted a finger and sucked it. *Oh, he tastes like he smells. Nothing like a human man.*

"Yes, it's *crekkin'* beautiful," he whispered.

She dropped her hands to his legs and caressed him, needing a moment to figure out how she felt. She had no painful memories to ruin her receiving oral since none of her abusers ever did that. But giving oral had too many awful incidents associated with it. Even with Stefan, she only gave him a blowjob twice, but she never enjoyed it.

But looking at Karid's gorgeous, swollen cock with its veins throbbing all because of her, she really wanted to try again. Tasting his pre-cum excited her and she wanted to give him as much pleasure as he routinely gave her.

He shifted underneath her hands and she looked back at his face. Discomfort grew in his eyes.

"My lack of balls disturbs you. We can stop now." *Fuck. I was in my head too long and hurt him.*

"Honestly, I haven't even looked there yet. I was admiring your cock and trying to figure out what I wanted to do first."

Karid stilled.

"Truth?"

"Always, Karid." She chewed on her lower lip. "I have many bad memories being forced to use my mouth on a man's cock."

He growled and his tail slapped on the mattress.

"Then don't use your mouth. Do not do anything that makes you uncomfortable."

She smiled at his reaction. *And that is why I'm going to give it a try.*

"That's the thing, Karid. I find myself wanting to make you feel good with my mouth and it took me by surprise."

He inhaled deeply, then grinned.

"We agree neither of us will do anything that takes away from our enjoyment of times like these."

"I think that's reasonable."

Relaxing again, he said, "Then I will concentrate on how you arouse me so easily."

"You are such a sweet talker." Running a finger along the top length of his erection, she said, "You feel like suede over steel."

She continued her gentle exploratory touch, tracing the head of his cock, swiping the drop of pre-cum, and licking it off her finger. His low, continuous growl caused her pussy to clench.

When she drew a line on the underside of his cock to where his balls should have been, he shivered. She added a second finger and rubbed harder in the newly healed area.

"Sensitive?"

"Dear Goddess yes. I had no idea." His legs moved restlessly.

"Good?"

Moaning, he nodded quickly.

She leaned down and replaced her fingers with her tongue. Moving her hand further back, she explored and found a bump in the area where a human man would have a prostate gland. She massaged it as she licked harder.

"Ava," he shouted. "That feels incredible." He panted and moaned.

Keeping one hand pressing on the gland, she licked the underside of his erection. *His scent is so strong here. I think I could come from the smell alone.*

She used the tip of her tongue to circle the head of his cock. Seeing his base node, she used her other hand to play with it. He clutched the sheets and his hips bucked. *I did that. I made this huge warrior lose himself in the pleasure of my touch.*

Feeling powerful and sexy, she moved a hand to caress his tail where it met his back. He shivered the harder she squeezed. Her panties went from damp to full on wet and she stopped playing with his tail to shove her hand into her panties and rub her clit.

Jaw opening wide, she encased the head of his cock in her mouth. With the hand not fingering herself, she gripped the base of his erection. Flattening her tongue, she took more of him into her and hummed. The taste of him made her smile around his thick length. Fingers tunneled into her hair and held on lightly.

Starting with a slow in and out rhythm, she moved her hands in time with her mouth. She experimented with her tongue to see what made him crazy with want. On one downstroke, she let the tip of his member hit her throat. She swallowed around him and his hand clenched in her hair. She looked up at him to see his jaw tight with arousal and his eyes glittering.

"Do you know how many times I imagined your mouth on my cock? The reality is so much more arousing than anything I dreamed. I can smell how much you are enjoying it and watching you pleasure yourself is too much for me right now. I don't want to come in your mouth. I want you to ride me."

His words caused her to moan around his cock. She pulled back and tugged her panties off. Crawling up his body, she maneuvered herself over his hard shaft. Slowly lowering herself onto him, she used her hands on his pecs to support herself.

Ava moaned as he stretched her wide. Her thighs trembled. *Oh my god, he feels so good.*

"Your pussy is so wet and tight, *raralumia*. I'm not going to last long."

When she was fully seated on his cock, his hands clasped her waist to hold her in place as he shifted to a partially reclined position. She gasped as his base node connected with her clit. He extended his claws and moved his hands to her ass.

"Now, Ava. Take me, use me, *crekkin' crek* me."

He leaned forward to suck a hard nipple. His claws pricked her lightly as she began to rise and fall on his cock. She moaned each time her clit met his base node. He bit her nipple just hard enough to make her groan and more wetness flooded his thighs. Finding her rhythm, she ground herself against him. She tossed her head back and tried to go faster, but his torso was so high and wide she couldn't get him deep enough.

"Help me, Karid," she whimpered. "I need you harder and faster."

"As you wish." He retracted his claws and held onto her while he thrust upward.

"Yes. More like that." Mewling at the fullness and heat of him, she writhed looking for more.

His tail slid into the wetness dripping from her core, then gently poked her ass. She shivered.

"May I?"

She dropped her head forward and nodded.

"Slowly, just in case."

On her downstroke, his tail slipped past the tight ring of muscle in her ass. Her eyes widened and she gasped. Watching her eyes, he pumped his tail in small, increasing increments.

"So full, Karid. Feels so good."

Breathing heavily, they moved in unison faster and faster. Her climax cascaded throughout her body and his name erupted from the depths of her lungs. Waves of delight flowed through every nerve and muscle. Her pussy clamped hard on his cock and rippled, milking him. He grunted her name as he threw his head back and rode out his own orgasm, pumping into her several more times before he stilled. Spent, she collapsed forward onto him.

Karid wrapped his arms around her and gently removed his tail. His cock twitched inside her when her pussy occasionally trembled. He pushed her sweaty curls from her eyes. Then he threaded his fingers in her hair and kissed her forehead. She opened her eyes and smiled.

"How do you feel, sweetheart? Still worried about my reaction to any missing parts? Because I'm not sure I would've survived much more."

His chuckle sent tremors through her, especially her pussy where his cock started to harden again.

"I think I can put that particular concern to rest. You were quite persuasive in your arguments." *God, I love when he's all snarky.*

"Good. We'll have to do this again sometime."

"Most definitely."

Chapter 27

KARID HELD AVA nestled in his arms, their combined scent filling him with contentment. Her soft snores puffed against his chest. His softened cock slipped from her body. Tears formed in his eyes at how lucky he was. *Goddess, she's so loving, honest, loyal, and passionate. She gave me back a part of myself I thought the Zuvgran ruined forever.*

Her *wimma* and sugar scent proclaimed her arousal loud and clear. She didn't find him lacking. In fact, she found ways to excite him that he wasn't expecting. The feel of her hot, wet pussy squeezing his cock exhilarated him and was unlike any other previous sexual experience. No other female existed for him now. He buried his face in her curls. *If I could, I would never leave her side for a moment.*

All his friends, even Traxen, approved of him asking her to true mate. He thought of the Earth movies they had watched. Males asked females to share their lives in so many different ways—some elaborate, some small. *How long should I wait before asking? How should I ask to make it special for her? Where should I do it? What would she like best? Will she say yes? Please, Goddess, let her say yes.*

When Ava woke after her nap, Karid pulled her into the shower with him. He worshiped her body with soapy hands, then his tongue. When she started panting and dripping from her core, he lifted her and took her hard against the wall with her moaning his name and kicking his ass with her heels. Sated and clean, they stumbled into the drying tube and kissed. She laughingly pushed him away as she was dressing, saying he had more hands than an octopus.

Karid enjoyed the midday meal immensely, especially since they never had morning meal. He'd never admit it, but he felt like a giddy youngling. When she took out ingredients to make more snacks for Phoenix House, he unwrapped one of the stones and his sculpting tools and began a project at the kitchen table. *It feels good having her nearby.*

Several hours passed with the two of them working at their separate pursuits. She occasionally brushed his shoulders with a hand as she walked by. He lightly kissed the back of her neck when he stood to stretch and get a water pouch. She turned on her music player and sang along softly. He hummed in time but quieted when he heard a noise outside.

Ava screamed when the kitchen door burst open and three Svesti males he didn't recognize entered. The baking pan in her hands dropped with a clang and uncooked food scattered everywhere. Extending his claws and baring his fangs, Karid stood with a chisel in his hand and his tail whipping angrily. He launched himself at the nearest male who raised a blaster.

"No." Ava shouted and threw herself in front of Karid. The pulse of the blaster grazed her shoulder before hitting Karid with the bulk of the blow. They both dropped to the floor stunned. *Dear Goddess, don't let her be hurt.*

"*Crek.* He was supposed to be alone and drunk out his mind."

"I don't like that we hurt a female, even if she is human."

"Would you two be quiet? Restrain them before he recovers."

"What about the female? We only brought one set."

"Find something to use. Gag them both."

"Are we leaving her?"

"No, she's seen us and his scent is all over her. She'll be good leverage. We'll let our leader decide her fate. Now hurry up and let's get out of here."

The males cuffed Karid with his hands behind his back. They found some twine in one of the drawers and used that to bind Ava's hands in front of her. Shredded strips of the curtain covered their mouths and blindfolded for Ava. A dark cloth bag reduced Karid's sight to small bits of light through the weave and shadows.

Karid's chest rumbled as the males dragged him outside. He heard a thud before being thrown into a small transport. He landed across Ava's legs. She shifted slightly. *Good, the stun didn't last long for her. I bet it still crekkin' hurts, though.*

"Come on. It will be a couple hours before we arrive."

Karid heard the males walk to the front of the ship and the whoosh of a door closing. He hated that she was a captive. *I didn't keep her safe.* Before his thoughts spiraled, her bound hands moved and her fingers tugged gently at the bag over his head. Sneaking her hands underneath, she worked at loosening his gag. When the tension released, he spit out the curtain remnant and tried to generate some saliva.

Whispering, he asked, "Are you okay?"

She put her fingers under his chin and attempted to move his head in a nod. *Smart female.*

Tingling in his body indicated he now had limited movement.

"I'm going to extend my claws. See if you can use them to free your hands."

Her fingers traced along his arms and when she reached hands, she carefully felt for his claws. Maneuvering cautiously, she hooked the twine on one claw and began a sawing motion.

"I'm going to retract my other claws so you won't cut yourself."

She sawed faster. The twine snapped and her hands moved away. Rustling sounds let him know she was taking off her gag and blindfold. She lifted his head and pulled the bag off.

"Are you okay? You took most of the blast." She leaned over and kissed his cheek. He nodded against her thighs.

"I'm starting to get feeling back. As much as I like where my head is, we should probably figure out how to get these restraints off."

"You can't help yourself, can you?"

"Not when it comes to you."

She bent over him sideways.

"I don't know how to release the cuffs. I don't see a keyhole or anything."

"What type of material are they?"

"Uh, alien girl here. Spices and food I might recognize, metals not so much."

"What color are they?"

"A shiny silver."

"*Crek.* Probably valadium with an electronic lock. Can you help me sit up?"

Soft grunts escaped Ava's mouth as she slid out from under him and pushed him up. His face ended up buried in her breasts until she got him upright.

"Wipe that grin off your face." She shook her head. "How can you make me want to laugh when we've been kidnapped?"

"Talent, I guess." Karid reluctantly took his eyes from her face to look around the space. He grinned. "Do you think you can walk yet?"

"Yes."

"That compartment under the seat…" He jerked his head to the opposite side. "It should have a medkit in it. Bring it here, please."

Instead of walking, she crawled to retrieve what he wanted. *Crek. Her ass. Focus, you naroon. Now's not the time.*

"Find the healing wand."

"What am I doing with this?" She held it up.

"You're going to make an electronic key." He talked her through opening the innards, making adjustments, and changing frequencies until they finally heard the snick of the restraints opening.

Karid hugged her close and ran gentle hands over her body once they were free. He cupped her face and kissed her.

"No injuries?"

Her curls bounced when she shook her head.

"Maybe a couple bruises, but nothing major. I promise. I'm more worried about you."

"I'm fine and in the mood for a little payback. We need to escape before we reach their destination."

"They have blasters, remember."

He bared his fangs in an evil grin as he picked up the restraints and tucked them in his pocket with the modified wand. "There's something you should know about blasters on a stun setting."

"What's that?"

"The pulse ricochets off metal reflective surfaces. Kill setting won't, but stun will."

Her face took on a thoughtful expression as she looked at the shiny metal walls around them.

"So we could make shields?"

"Just one for me. I want you out of the line of fire."

She pouted. "I want to help."

"You'll help me more if I know you're safe, Ava. I will be able to concentrate on doing what I need to do."

She searched his eyes, then huffed.

"Fine. I don't like it, but I'll do it."

"Thank you, *raralumia*." Clasping her hand, Karid tugged her to the rear of the space. He bent and retrieved a tool kit from a compartment and began unfastening a large panel from the wall. When it was loose, he grasped the two handles that were on the back side of the panel. At her questioning look, he said, "Most large ship panels have a way to easily lift them for maintenance."

"So what's the plan?"

"I take the ship and get us home."

She tilted her head.

"Okay. Where do you want me?"

He lifted an eyebrow. "Everywhere and anywhere. I thought you knew that."

She giggled. "Seriously?"

Nodding solemnly, he said, "I'm very serious. But for now I have an escape to effect, so no distracting me with your charms. Sit your beautiful self down." He led her to a seat. "And strap in. The ride might get rough." Quickly, he unfastened a smaller panel from a compartment. "If the fight moves back here, shield yourself as best you can."

"Be careful." At her words, he bent and kissed her.

"We'll be home soon."

Karid picked up his shield and halted by the door. Listening, he determined all three were seated and sounded like they weren't paying much attention. *I have one shot to make this work.*

He opened the door and swiped with his claws to take out the throat of the warrior closest to him. Blaster fire sounded and he steeled his arm against the impact. He heard grunts, sizzles, clanks, and thuds. Cautiously peering around the panel, he saw the other two Svesti on the floor stunned and the control panel damaged. The transport dipped its nose. *Crek!*

Hurriedly, he clapped the restraints on the leader and searched his pockets for the electronic lock. He kicked the other warrior in the head knocking him out. As he turned back to the console, he hesitated, then kicked the leader as well. *No sense leaving them conscious and behind me.*

Sitting at the console, Karid attempted to correct their flight path. He was unable to regain altitude, although he was able to turn the transport back the way they came. He yelled for Ava to stay strapped in. He tried to send a comm, but the circuits were fried.

Despite all Karid's efforts, the nose dipped lower increasing their rate of descent. He swiveled when he heard a noise.

"I told you to stay strapped in."

"I'm strapping in next to you." She held onto anything she could find as she made her way to the seat next to him. Her determined face turned to him once she fastened the safety belts. "Is there anything I can do to help?"

"No." Wayward strands of hair that had escaped his ponytail blew across his face. "You would have been safer in the rear."

She reached out and squeezed his arm.

"I go where you go. We face shit together, remember." Her expression softened. "I haven't said it in words yet, Karid, but I love you. If our time is up, I wanted you to know."

Joy and pain pierced his heart. Joy because she loved him. Pain because they may die soon.

"I love you, Ava. And our time is not up. It can't be. We have too much left to experience together."

"Then let's land this sucker and start working on that, sweetheart."

Karid attempted to keep them at an angle that would minimize injuries. When the ship started skimming trees, he told her to brace for impact even though he knew she saw what he saw.

The last thing he heard was Ava's scream. *I'm sorry, raralumia.*

Chapter 28

"AVA? CAN YOU hear me?"

She winced at the sound of Natasha's voice. Her whole body felt like one huge bruise. *Did I get poisoned with berries again?*

"Squeeze my hand if you can hear me."

Her trembling fingers clenched as much as she could manage. Her forehead wrinkled as she tried to figure out why everything hurt so much.

"Oh, good. You're coming out of it." Natasha's voice sounded relieved.

A gentle finger pried open an eyelid. Ava made a pained noise at the light.

"I know you feel like shit and we'll give you something for it soon, but we really need to know what happened."

Groaning, Ava tried to sit up. A warm hand pressed her shoulder against the pillow.

"No, don't strain yourself. I'll adjust the med bed for you," said Ash'n. The surface below her moved her to a more upright position.

"Where?" she mumbled through dry lips. *Damn, my head hurts and I'm so thirsty.*

"Here." A straw touched her mouth and she drank greedily. "Not so fast. You don't want to upset your stomach," Natasha said.

"Where am I?"

"Palace med bay."

She groaned when she tried to open her eyes. *What am I doing in the palace?*

"Ava," Vared's voice boomed in her head.

"Not so loud."

"The kitchen delivery males discovered evidence of a struggle at the cabin and notified security. We found you via your tracker. You and Karid had crashed a transport. What we don't know is what happened."

"Karid. How is he? Is he alright?" Ava's panic made her voice shrill. "Where is he?"

"He's in a med bed. He had more extensive injuries than yours. He didn't have safety restraints on," Ash'n said.

"Need to be with him." *You're not keeping me away this time.*

"If you open your eyes, you can see him next to you," Natasha said.

Forcing her eyelids to move, she squinted and turned her head slowly. She ignored everyone standing near her and searched for Karid. He was enclosed in a med bed to her right. Her lips trembled and she exhaled harshly when she saw his chest rise and fall. *He's alive.*

She looked back at everyone who'd spoken. Devik and Traxen also stood there with concerned expressions, and Traxen's jaw flexed. *He looks pissed.*

Memories surfaced slowly and she raised a hand to her temple.

"Can I get something for this headache?"

Ash'n injected her with something and the pain ebbed enough so she could think.

Hesitantly, she relayed everything that had happened. Tails flicked and growls rumbled in the air.

"There were three of them. I know Karid killed one when he took the ship. The last I knew, the other two were only unconscious."

Devik spoke for the first time. "None of them survived the crash."

"Do you know where they were taking you or why?" Vared asked.

"No. But they wanted Karid. One of them said they thought he was supposed to alone and drunk. I was a complication. I think the plan was to use me to coerce Karid in some fashion."

"Is there anything else? If not, I'd like to give her something stronger for the pain so she can rest comfortably," said Natasha.

"Ava, I apologize that this happened while you were under our protection," Traxen said.

She waved a hand halfheartedly. "Not your fault, Traxen." She looked at Ash'n. "How bad are Karid's injuries? How long before he'll wake up?"

"He had some broken bones and deep lacerations, but he'll be fine in a day or so. Like you, he needs some uninterrupted healing rest."

She chewed her lower lip. "Can you move my bed closer to his? Please?" They all smiled.

"Of course," Ash'n said.

After they pushed her closer to Karid and gave her some meds, Ava gingerly turned her head to the side to observe him. She reached out to rest her hand on his bed. Her breathing slowed to match his and her eyes drifted shut. *I'm here, sweetheart. I'm not leaving.*

The next day, Ava heard hushed voices. Mentally checking her body, she realized she felt much better. A little sore around her ribs and head, but she no longer felt like she'd been rattled hard. She opened her eyes and saw Karid still unconscious.

"Hey, girl, how are you feeling?" Emmy said.

"Better."

"We were worried about you," said Lin softly. "Talia and Rachel just left. We've been taking turns sitting with you."

"That's sweet. Thank you." Ava wiggled trying to sit up. "Karid hasn't woken yet?"

"No. Ash'n said maybe later today."

"I know the guys were really happy to see how well he was doing the other night. Devik said it got really emotional, but they had their brother back." Emmy's foot tapped. *The woman can never sit still.*

"Karid felt better after talking with them. They all needed to talk."

Emmy and Lin brought Ava up to date on the progress of Phoenix House, which was almost complete. They said the younglings missed Ava visiting regularly but understood that she was helping a friend in need.

Ava's stomach growled loudly.

"I think we need to go get you some food," said Emmy with a grin. "I'm sure Previv will have something for you."

"I'd appreciate that. Anything is fine, but I am hungry, so bring lots of it."

"Will do." Natasha and Ash'n came in once Emmy and Lin left.

"Any pain, dizziness, or nausea?" Natasha asked as she examined her.

"Nope. Just a little soreness here and there."

Ash'n checked the med bed stats. "I think food and rest are all you need. But you need to take it easy for a few days." He tilted his head toward Karid. "He'll probably need the same and will need someone to remind him regularly. He's not as bad as Vared as a patient, but he has his moments."

"I'll make sure he follows doctor's orders."

Emmy and Lin returned with food and visited while Ava ate herself into a food coma. When she yawned for the third time, Lin said, "I think you need some sleep. Do you want us to stay?"

Shaking her head, Ava said, "I'm okay. You guys can head out."

"Alright. We'll come back and check on you later." They were almost at the door when Emmy added, "Oh, by the way, there's some huge dinner next week that we're all supposed to attend."

Ava wrinkled her nose. "Dressy?"

"Yep. Command performance."

"Remind me later so I can forget again," Ava said with a shudder.

Later that evening, Ava pulled a chair up to Karid's bed and held his hand. His warmth reassured her. *Looks like he'll have another scar on his forehead.* She fell asleep in the barely lit room.

"Ava," he shouted. Startled awake, she looked in alarm at him as he abruptly sat up, muscles tense.

"I'm here. I'm alright." She placed a hand on his face. He turned into her palm and inhaled deeply, then relaxed.

"I'm sorry I didn't protect you." His tail rose, then drooped to the bed never touching her.

"What are you talking about? We're safe."

"At the cabin. They stunned you and kidnapped you."

"I know. I was there."

"I should be a better male."

She pressed her hands on his cheeks and squeezed hard. "Look at me, you *naroon*. Sometimes bad shit happens and there's nothing anyone can do about it except get through it. There was nothing either of us could've done to prevent this. Stop blaming yourself. We're alive. They're not."

She held his gaze as he searched her face.

"You're not upset with me."

"I will be if you keep this up." Ava blew out a breath. "Karid, you can't protect me from everything. Knowing you'll do your best is more than enough for me. *Your* best is good enough."

His thumb stroked her cheek. "You mean that."

"Of course I do." She turned and kissed his thumb.

"What did I do to deserve you, *raralumia*?" he breathed softly.

"You are just you. That's all I need." She leaned forward and pressed her lips to his. His arms and tail snaked around her pulling her closer until their torsos touched. She drew back to rest their foreheads together.

"When we're released from med bay, I want to take you to the lake. Maybe another picnic and swim."

"You want to go back to the cabin?" she asked.

"I can have Devik upgrade the security before we go. I'm sure Traxen won't mind. My best memories are there and I don't want what happened to be our last memory of the cabin." His earnest face melted her heart.

"Okay."

Two days later, Karid flew them in a small flitter to the cabin. When they entered, they found someone cleaned up the mess left after the kidnapping. Even the holes in the walls had been fixed. Karid's sculpting tools and stone sat on the counter.

"It's nice we don't have to clean up," Ava said. "I wasn't looking forward to that."

"Let's change and go to the lake. I had Lady Reesa pack us a lunch."

"Are we going to swim?"

"I'd like to check out the waterfall."

She grinned happily. "Me, too."

Changing quickly into a swimsuit under a T-shirt and shorts, Ava grabbed some towels, then joined Karid to walk to the lake. When they left the forest, the sun warmed her skin and the breeze lifted her hair.

"It's such a beautiful day. Not a cloud in the sky." Ava tilted her head back and shaded her eyes. Her lips curved up when she saw a small flock of birds fly across the periwinkle background. *This really is a beautiful planet.*

Karid spread out their blanket and left the satchel on a corner.

"Would you mind if we swam and went to the waterfall before we ate?"

"Sounds like a plan to me." She dropped the towels and stripped out of her clothes. Karid's low rumble made her turn. He stood frozen, his pants at his ankles and something like board shorts covering his goods. His eyes were silver and his tail swayed.

"I'm glad no one else is around," he growled. "You look edible."

She glanced down at her tankini which covered most of her. The built-in support pushed her cleavage up slightly and a sliver of skin peeked out between her top and the boy shorts that hugged her hips. Her pale skin flushed. *Wow. I love how he thinks I'm the sexiest thing alive.*

Kicking free of his pants, he stalked toward her and lifted her for a kiss. Her arms wound around his neck and her legs found their way around his waist. She wiggled against his waist as their tongues danced their familiar, exciting moves. Reluctantly, he drew back.

Breathing heavily, he said, "I need cold water now."

"Or we can just get naked."

He shook his head. "No, waterfall first."

"You seem awfully obsessed with this waterfall."

"Trust me, *raralumia*."

She dropped her legs and she slid down his body.

"Alright, let's go."

Holding hands, they walked barefoot across the deep blue grass. Fine pink sand interspersed with larger pebbles edged the lake. Dipping her toes in the mint green water, Ava shivered. The water was cool, but not cold.

Comfortably chatting, Karid led her along the sand until they were closer to the waterfall. The exercise heated her body so the water felt refreshing when they finally entered it. Leisurely, they played and swam.

The water churned white and crashing sounds filled her ears the closer they got to their destination. Beads of water sprayed them as they climbed onto a large flat rock near the falls. Sitting on the sun-warmed stone, Ava leaned back with her arms supporting her. Karid pulled himself up, his biceps bulging. He swung a leg up and got his foot under him to stand. *Oh my. I want to lick the water running down his body.*

Closing her eyes, the light mist dusted her face and rivulets of water flowed down her back. Karid plopped next to her, his skin cool from the lake.

"Let's rest a bit, then we can explore." When he shook his head, his hair spread droplets on her. Goosebumps rippled down her arm.

"Hey, knock that off." She bumped shoulders with him.

"You're already wet." He bent and kissed her. "I like making you wetter."

She laughed. "Okay, that's enough. Let's go see this waterfall up close and personal."

Chapter 29

AT HER WORDS, Karid stood and held out a hand to help her rise. Unable to resist, he ran his claws through her wet curls.

"You look beautiful."

"I'm glad you think so." She shifted on her feet.

"I know so. Your beauty shines from within." Kissing the tip of her nose, he led her toward the waterfall. "Come."

The roaring became louder as they got closer. She suddenly darted ahead of him and ran under the falling water. Tilting her head back with her arms spread wide, she twirled underneath uninhibited joy lighting her face. *Goddess, she's amazing.*

Karid rushed to join her. Picking her up, he spun her around, both of them laughing as the falls drenched them. Speaking loudly in her ear so she could hear him over the water, he said, "I found this."

He tugged her through the falls to a cavern hidden underneath. Large enough for them to stand and deep enough to step away from the continual splashing, bioluminescent lichen kept it dimly lit. Bits of shiny ore sparkled in the light.

"How did you know this was here?" Ava's jaw dropped open as she hovered her fingers over one wall.

"I came down here this morning to investigate." His tail wrapped around her waist and pulled her closer. "I wanted to find something to surprise you."

Placing her palms on his chest, she said, "You succeeded. It's magical." She stood on her toes to peck his lips. "Thank you."

He bent for a deeper kiss. Need coursed through his body. Her scent deepened as his hands caressed her back. His tail meandered up her leg in random patterns. Her fingernails scraped his nape lightly.

"I need you," he rasped. Her nipples pebbled against his chest.

A claw traced the top of her swimsuit. Shivers turned to a moan when he pulled her top down and plumped a naked breast in his hand. His fingers played with her tight bud as he licked his way downward. The tip of his tongue wet her nipple. He pursed his lips and blew a warm breath over her flesh. It puckered even more. His mouth closed over her and he sucked hard. She arched her back and clasped him to her. Running a fang sideways over the erect nipple, his lips curved against her soft flesh when she groaned.

He turned his attention to her other breast, lavishing it with similar attention. His tail reached between her legs and rubbed her clit through her bathing suit. Gasping, her breathing quickened. Her hand drifted lower to close over his erection. Groaning, he tucked his fingers into her waistband and pulled down her bottoms. Her scent bloomed around him mixing with the smells of the earth, lichen, and water unleashing his primal instincts.

His swimsuit hit the dirt. He spun her so her back was to his front. Bending his knees, he rubbed his cock against her cheeks, while his fingers found her clit. Circling the hot, swollen pearl, he rocked against her.

"Does this pussy need filling, *raralumia*?" Karid's voice was guttural around his elongated fangs. "Is it dripping for me?"

Ava's head tossed side to side and she moaned. "Yes. Only for you. Fuck me." She tried to move her hips, but he kept her body secure as he played between her legs. His tail teased a nipple.

Releasing her, he said, "Hands on the wall and spread those luscious thighs."

She whimpered and did as he commanded. Slowly, he ran a hand down her spine and pressed her shoulders down.

"I love your ass. Soft and plump. Just the right size to fill my hands." Karid squeezed her cheeks. Uncaring of the stone beneath him, he knelt and licked her pussy from behind taking care to avoid scratching her with his fangs. *Crek. Her taste. I'll never get enough of it.*

He worshipped her pussy until her body shook with her first orgasm. Licking his lips, he stood and grasped her hips.

"I'm going to *crek* you hard. Are you ready?"

"Please, Karid. I want you inside me." She wiggled her ass.

Giving her a light slap on one cheek, he said, "Be still. I don't want to hurt you." She moaned. Bending his knees, he fed his engorged cock into her wet heat. When he was fully seated, he straightened and her feet left the ground. His tail circled her waist to support her.

"Oh."

"Let me do all the work. Just enjoy the ride."

She mewled and her channel sucked around his length as he withdrew then slammed back into her.

"Your ass and breasts jiggle so erotically, *raralumia*."

Panting, she said, "Less talk. More action."

Chuckling darkly, he said, "As you wish."

He moved his arms to wrap around her thighs, spreading her wider. In and out, he varied his thrusts, his base node hitting her rosebud. Her moans and his grunts echoed in the cavern. Arms bracing on the rock, her head hung down. Her wet curls bounced as much as her breasts. She began to spasm around his cock and she threw her head back screaming his name. Pumping through her climax, he gritted his teeth trying to last longer. He lost the battle as her orgasm milked him so tightly his breath stopped momentarily.

He shouted, "Mine."

Moving erratically, white heat shot through his spine. Every cell in his body exploded with pleasure as he filled her with his seed. He locked his knees so he wouldn't drop her. Breathing heavily, he curled his torso over her back.

"I love you, Ava," he said in her ear.

Turning her head, she kissed him languidly. "I love you, too."

When he felt steadier, he pulled out his cock. They both moaned. He lowered her to her feet and turned her to face him.

After gently kissing each nipple, he reluctantly pulled her top back over her breasts. He held out her bottoms for her to step into and froze. His nostrils flared.

Placing a hand on his shoulder, she asked, "What's wrong?"

"Nothing. The sight of my seed running down your thighs is incredibly arousing."

He dressed after her, then knelt on one knee.

"I hadn't planned on making love to you in here, but I couldn't help myself."

She grinned. "I'm not complaining."

"No. What I mean is I planned to offer you this ring and ask you to true mate with me. I would be honored to spend the rest of our lives together." Karid held up a valadium band with green stones embedded into it.

Her eyes filled with tears. His heart thundered in his chest. Sweat formed on his back.

"You're proposing?"

"Isn't this an Earth custom?" His tail swayed faster. She grabbed and stroked it.

"I'm touched you wanted to ask me this way."

"You would be leaving your life on Earth, but I want to give you as many of the traditions of your home world as I can."

"You're so sweet." She knelt in front of him.

"Does that mean your answer is yes?"

The curls he loved so much bounced and her green eyes shone.

"Yes, Karid, I would love to true mate with you."

Excitedly, he hugged her to him and they kissed. She held out her hand and he slid the ring on her finger.

"Is there a special ceremony we have to plan or anything like that?"

"No. True mating is a treasured, private moment for a couple."

She squirmed. "It involves biting, doesn't it?"

"Yes. We bite each other here." He pointed to her shoulder. "When we make love."

"I'll be honest. That weirds me out a little."

"From what I understand, there is a short moment of pain, then incredible pleasure."

Her stomach growled loudly. They both laughed.

"Sorry. It has its own mind."

"Let's go back to our picnic."

Sitting on the blanket later with Ava tucked between his thighs, Karid fed her bits of food. It satisfied something deep inside him to provide for her needs. He snuck kisses when he could and licked anything that spilled over from her mouth.

When his comm chimed, he wanted to ignore it. However, Ava saw that it was Vared and prompted him to find out what he wanted.

"Feel like hunting?" Vared said.

"Hunting what?" Karid played with one of Ava's curls.

"Devik and Emmy were able to recreate some of the crashed flyer's database. Including the last coordinates entered into the autopilot. The traitors are probably long gone, but we might find something worth knowing."

Karid sat straight. "Where?"

"A remote area a couple hours away."

"I won't leave Ava alone at the cabin, even with the increased security. Not after what happened." Karid's tail flicked. Ava grasped it.

"Bring her back to the palace. She can visit with the other females while we're gone."

Karid looked at Ava. She nodded.

"That will work. We'll get to the palace as soon as we can. We're not at the cabin right now and have to walk back."

"We'll see you when you get here." Vared disconnected the comm.

"You don't mind?" Karid asked her.

"No. Do what you need to but come back safe." Ava tossed on her T-shirt and shorts. "Let's pack up and get back."

He stopped her and rested his forehead on hers. "Thank you for understanding." He kissed her reverently.

"You're welcome. Now let's move it. Vared's not the most patient person."

Grinning, he agreed.

Karid took in the assembled Svesti selecting weapons from the palace armory. Vared, of course, would be leading the group. Devik and two members of one of his *Invictus* security teams, Krivez Tesix and Slaiv'n Westov, stuffed their weapons harnesses with knives and plasma grenades.

"Ash'n, what are doing here? You usually don't go on missions like these?" Karid arched an eyebrow.

"They took my family. I'm going," Ash'n growled. *Crek. I have good friends.*

Traxen and his admin, Xeliv, watched the males. The king's tail flicked.

Xeliv said, "It's best you don't go, sire."

"I should be gearing up with them." Traxen crossed his arms and his jaw tightened.

Vared slapped Traxen on the shoulder.

"I know you want blood, cousin, but your place is here."

"I'm going." They all turned to see Rachel dressed in black from head to toe, the daggers she purchased on Theron strapped to her thighs.

"You are not," Traxen said.

"I am tired of these traitors messing with us. I have a right to go."

"Female, cease this nonsense." Traxen's tail slapped the floor. *That sounded like it hurt.*

Rachel narrowed her blue eyes and glared at Traxen.

"I think she should go," Karid said quietly. Everyone turned to him. "She's correct, she has a right to go, but more importantly Rachel is a warrior that those that don't know her will underestimate. I've sparred with her many times and I can attest to her skills." A steady rumble emanated from Traxen's chest.

Karid looked at Rachel. "You do realize that we do not expect to find anyone at the location? They must know by now their warriors crashed and have gone to ground."

Rachel nodded. "I understand. No offense meant, but I have different training than all of you and I might see something you miss."

Devik said, "None taken." He glanced at Traxen. "My experience is the human females are well aware of their own capabilities. If she believes she will be an asset, I am inclined to believe her."

"I forbid it."

Rachel stalked up to Traxen and poked his chest with a single finger. "Never try to tell me what to do, Your Majesty."

To Karid's surprise, Vared was the one who deescalated the tension.

"Rachel, if you go, you must promise to follow my orders."

"So long as those orders don't include me babysitting the shuttle, I'm fine with that."

"Does anyone on the team believe Lady Rachel will hinder our efforts or put any of us in peril?"

All the males shook their heads.

"I don't like it," said Traxen. His lavender eyes darkened to amethyst.

Rachel started to speak, but stopped when Vared shook his head at her.

"My hand-picked warriors feel confident in Rachel's skills. I am also certain that my team will not put anyone in unnecessary danger, especially a female. Rachel will follow orders that will not include babysitting the shuttle. She goes." Vared dipped his chin at her as he uttered his last statements.

"Watching the shuttle is my job," said Tesix with little expression, but his eyes twinkled.

Traxen stared at his cousin before nodding curtly. "Very well. I'll hold you responsible, Commander."

Vared said, "Everyone finish gearing up. We leave in ten minutes."

Chapter 30

A T THE PALACE, Ava let Karid get ready first. When he left after a panty-dampening kiss, she showered quickly, then dressed to meet the women in the quarters Talia and Vared shared. She actually wanted him to go on this mission but hoped all would be well. *He'll be with his best friends. They'll keep an eye on him. Maybe today will quell his doubts about remaining a warrior.*

"Where's Rachel?" she asked as she entered. The other women all had snacks and drinks. *Oh, please not another drunken evening. I don't think I can handle that right now.*

"Probably pissing off the king," Emmy said mischievously.

"How do you mean?"

Talia popped a *leringa* berry in her mouth and chewed before answering. "You haven't been around, but Traxen has been treating Rachel as a fragile female and she's had enough. She wants to go on the mission."

Ava poured herself a drink. "Why would he think she's fragile? She's the most badass of all of us." She took a sip. "Will Vared let her go?"

Talia shrugged. "Maybe? I don't know."

"Are you worried about Karid going so soon in his recovery?" asked Natasha.

"A little. But I think he needs to do it."

"When are you going to take him to Phoenix House?" Talia grabbed a handful of green crackers.

"I'm not sure. I haven't talked to him yet. I don't know how he'll react to Largon and Ronan. I know he understands they're not like his captors, but I'm afraid to set his progress back if he has a flashback." Biting her lip, she continued, "I don't want him to lose it at all, but I definitely don't want him to be around the kids if he does."

"Maybe introduce them here with his friends around," said Talia. "You know they'd be willing."

"That might be the best way." Ava stared into her glass.

"Is that a ring?" Lin hopped off the couch to take a closer look. "Oh, look. The stones match your eyes."

Ava grinned. "Karid gave it to me when he asked me to true mate." Laughing at the other women surreptitiously looking for a scar on her shoulder, she pulled on her collar to show her unmarred skin. "We haven't true mated yet."

"So did he propose?" Emmy tossed a berry up and caught it in her mouth.

"Down on one knee and everything in a cool cavern behind a waterfall." Ava suppressed a grin. *Not gonna tell them what we did beforehand.*

"That's so romantic." Lin sighed. "None of our males gave us rings."

"Ronan gives me everything I need," Natasha said with a satisfied expression. "A ring isn't necessary for me."

"He said he wanted me to have as many traditions from Earth as I could since I would be giving up my home planet."

"Are you going to have a wedding?"

Ava chewed her lip. "I don't know. We never got that far in the discussion."

"Do you want one?" Talia asked.

"I never expected to find anyone, so I've never thought about it."

"Maybe you should now." Natasha poured more wine for herself.

"I think if my dad and grandmother could be there, I'd like to do it for them."

"Maybe a small ceremony on Earth. You could come with us when we go to pick up the diplomats," said Talia.

"That depends on whether or not he's ready to go back to work. Hopefully, today will help him clarify what he wants to do."

"I'm not sure Ronan would want to spend four or five months on the *Invictus* and leave Phoenix House." Natasha frowned. "That means I couldn't attend."

"Two small ceremonies, maybe? One on each planet," Lin suggested.

"How did we go from I never thought about it to two ceremonies? If having one here means I have to invite his father, it's not happening." Ava shuddered.

"Oh, you don't know yet," said Natasha.

"Know what?"

"When Traxen was interrogating him about how he found out about Karid and bypassed royal security, Karid's father collapsed. The healers found evidence of a neurological disease. They're trying to treat him now."

"Would that explain his aggressive behavior?"

Natasha nodded. "It's not uncommon to see behavioral changes."

"Well, shit. I'm not sure how Karid is going to deal with this info." Ava tapped a fingernail on her glass. "He basically told Drikon he wanted nothing more to do with him."

"You have to trust it will work out," said Talia.

They were silent, each in their own head.

Then Emmy said, "Okay, there's nothing we can do about that right now. Can we discuss what we're going to wear for that dinner next week?"

Astonished, the women gaped at her.

"You want to talk about clothes?" said Natasha. "That's unusual."

Emmy's face flushed. "I really disliked having to wear a traditional gown. I didn't feel like me. I'd like another option. I need you all to help."

"I'm with Emmy on this one," agreed Ava. "I don't mind the one-shouldered thing, but the long skirt felt restrictive. Not comfortable at all."

"Would adding side slits help?" asked Lin.

Emmy huffed. "I'd rather wear pants."

Talia pursed her lips. "You know, maybe something like palazzo pants might work, especially with extra fabric that makes them look like a long skirt."

"Hmm, that's a good idea," said Natasha.

"Let me guess," said Emmy. "You wrote a book once."

Talia nodded sheepishly. "The character was a fashion designer."

Everyone laughed. *I missed this.*

Ava decided to go to the kitchen before heading back to her quarters to wait for Karid. *I'm sure he'll be hungry when he gets back and I could use some real food in my belly. We missed evening meal. I'm glad I stopped at two glasses of wine.*

She was surprised to see Traxen sitting at a table eating pie.

"Ava, would you like to join me?" *He looks tense.*

"Sure. Let me grab something for myself." She went to the large cooling unit and found *maxiem* sandwiches in plasfilm. Taking one, a water pouch, and a piece of pie, she sat across from him. "So why are you sitting by yourself?"

"I needed some time alone to think."

"Oh, I can just pack up and leave you to it."

"No. Please don't. Until you showed up, I didn't realize that I wanted company I could relax with."

"Are you sure?"

"Absolutely."

Ava unwrapped her sandwich and took a bite. After she swallowed it down with some water, she asked, "Do you want to talk about it?"

"About what?"

"About whatever is bothering you."

"Not particularly."

"Okay." She ate a few more bites. "Did Rachel go on the mission?"

"Yes." His tail began to flick.

"You're worried about her. She can take care of herself."

"I know she's competent, but I can't help feeling it was wrong to let her go."

Ava pointed a forefinger at him.

"I'm surprised you haven't learned yet that telling a human woman what she can or cannot do is a one-way ticket to pissing her off." She shook her head and teased, "And I thought you were an intelligent male."

A reluctant laugh left his chest. "It's ingrained in our DNA to protect females."

"There's a difference between protecting and controlling. It can be a fine line, Traxen. Sometimes trusting we know our limitations and just being there if we stumble is the best course of action."

"You're very wise for someone so young." His tail slowed.

"Yeah, well, life's kicked me in the teeth more than once."

"I did not mean to bring up unhappy memories."

She waved her hand. "No worries, Traxen. I don't need to be treated with kid gloves."

His brows closed over his lavender eyes.

"Kid gloves?"

"The phrase is slang for fragile or prone to break at the slightest stress."

"Your language can be confusing."

Her lips turned up. "For us, too."

"Do you believe Karid was ready for this mission?"

She sighed. "I hope so. If he hadn't spoken with all of you, I'd be extremely concerned. The fact that they're looking for clues as to who kidnapped us will probably keep him focused."

"You don't mind if he continues as a warrior? He could sculpt full-time here on Costonia and provide well for you. He wouldn't be putting himself in danger."

She shook her head. "I want him to be happy. If he chooses to leave the military because he wants to, that's fine with me. If he chooses to leave because he doesn't trust himself, I'm against it. Besides, are you telling me you would not allow me to travel with him and cook for the warriors?"

"You're not a warrior."

"Nope." She emphasized the p. "I wouldn't be going on missions unless they were humanitarian ones like Talonka Six."

"So you're staying with Karid?"

"We plan to true mate. He even gave me a ring today when he asked." She held up her hand to show him.

"Congratulations. I can think of no one better suited to be his mate."

"Thanks."

"Will you miss your life on Earth?"

"I'll miss my dad and grandmother, but between trips to Earth and comms, it won't be as bad."

"What does your father do?"

"He's a detective." At Traxen's quizzical look, she expounded, "Law officer who investigates crimes."

"Something similar to our peacekeepers, then."

"Probably." Finishing her sandwich, she pulled her pie closer and cut into it. "So how long have you been king?"

"Three solars. My father died unexpectedly."

"I'm sorry for your loss."

"Thank you." He glanced away, then back. "I'm constantly surrounded by people, but few understand the complexities of ruling."

"Alone in a crowd," she murmured.

"Exactly. That's why I sent my guards away, although knowing them, they're not far. But then you came in and I wanted company. Strange, isn't it?"

"Perhaps you need to spend more time with people who want to interact with Traxen, not those who want the king's ear."

Barking out a laugh, his eyes twinkled. "I think you may be correct."

"Of course I am." She arched a brow. "How could you doubt me?"

He shook his head, his thick braid moving slowly across his shoulder. "Yes, Karid chose well. You even share his sense of humor."

Ava became serious. "I just heard about his father being ill. Do you know the prognosis?"

"Not good. The healers can slow the progression, but not cure it. One moment, he is lucid and reasonable, then switches to aggressive and violent. He will get worse over time."

"I'm not sure how Karid react when we tell him."

"It doesn't seem fair, does it? He has so much to contend with all at once."

She pointed her fork at him. "That's why he has us."

Chapter 31

O N THE SHUTTLE, Karid sat in the back with his friends and Rachel. In the cockpit, Tesix piloted with Westov as backup.

Devik bumped shoulders with Karid. "I'm glad you decided to join us."

"You couldn't keep me away. I want the ones who put Ava in danger dead," Karid growled. "I need a better insult than *naroons*. The word doesn't convey my anger enough." His tail slapped the metal floor.

"Emmy has been teaching me more Earth slang. Assholes, shitheads, and dickheads are a few that might work for you." Devik's fangs shone white against his caramel bronze skin in the dim light.

Ash'n said, "I've heard Lin say bitch and prick."

"Talia uses asshole a lot," Vared said with a smile.

"Is that her pet name for you?" Karid teased.

Vared faked a slap to the back of Karid's head. "No respect. We need a sparring match so I can remind you who is in command."

Rachel piped up from where she had her head leaned back and legs stretched out. Eyes closed, she said, "I personally prefer wankers, bastards, fuckers, motherfuckers, and cocksuckers. Adding a goddamn in front of any of them provides more emphasis."

They all looked up when they heard Westov's voice over the speaker. "I'm taking notes. This is good stuff. Did you notice almost all of them use body parts?"

They heard a slap and grunt. Then Tesix said, "Apologies, Commander. We had you on speaker in case you discussed the plan."

Karid let out a belly laugh. "Instead you received a mini-lesson on Earth insults." Everyone shared his amusement.

"What is the plan?" asked Rachel. "What do we know about where we're headed?"

Vared nodded at Devik who tapped his tablet. A holographic image of a long, rectangular building with small, high windows in a huge clearing appeared.

"No cover to approach," noted Rachel with a frown.

"We've been monitoring the location via satellite since we discovered it. There's been no activity," said Devik.

"Where is it located?" asked Karid.

"Between Nuxar and Srotix territories," Vared said.

"The two Houses that believe in racial purity. Not surprising." Karid's shoulders bunched.

"What was the building's original purpose? It looks to be too large to have been a home," Ash'n asked.

"Interestingly, we have found no record of this building being erected." Devik's tail flicked a couple times before it stilled.

"So we have no idea of its interior layout." Rachel's eyes narrowed.

"Correct." Vared nodded his approval at Rachel's observation. "We will arrive after dusk. Tesix will hover over the roof while cloaked. Instead of using the ramp, we'll use that hatch and rope down." He pointed, then looked at Rachel. "Will that be an issue?"

"Not a problem for me."

"Good. Rachel and Westov will position themselves at the center of the long sides, while the rest of us will take a corner. We'll rappel down from our positions and attempt a look in the windows. On the ground, we'll quietly take out any guards we might find. We enter simultaneously on my command. Any questions?"

"I'm assuming we'll have comms and grappling hooks." Rachel said.

"Yes. We'll don the rappelling gear and each take our own equipment."

"What's the objective once inside?" asked Westov from the cockpit.

"We take out any opposition, preferably without killing them, and look for information to identify more traitors. Depending on how many, if any, we find, we may need to call in more help to transport. If I know Traxen, he's got a team following us, just in case."

Karid joked and laughed with everyone after Vared completed the briefing, but he was impatient to get inside the building. He mentally cataloged his physical state and he felt healthy. When Tesix informed them they were fifteen minutes from their target, Rachel pulled out a jar of a cream and rubbed it on her face darkening her pale skin. She put on a black cap and tucked her blond hair inside, then black leather gloves encased her hands. *Smart female. She'll blend into the shadows.*

Devik handed out the comms and Karid showed Rachel how they worked. After testing them, Westov joined them and they all began gearing up for the insertion.

Vared tested the rope secured to the floor of the shuttle and opened the hatch that was just large enough for a Svesti male to fit his shoulders through. When they were over the structure, he tossed the rope down. Westov went first, then Rachel.

Karid went next. The cool night air tickled his skin as he used his feet to control his descent. Fortunately, there was very little wind to contend with. He landed lightly and took off silently toward his corner. Once there, he found a good spot to attach his grappling hook and waited for Vared's command to descend.

On the move again, he slowed next to one of the high windows and peered in. He didn't see much of anything, but open space, not multiple small rooms. He continued downward, scanning for movement. Devik reported an office of some sort on his corner. On the ground, Karid left the rope in place and found the nearest door. Testing it, he found it locked. He listened intently but heard nothing to indicate anyone near him. Using his tools, he picked the lock, but waited to open the door.

Vared gave the order to breach. Karid silently cracked the door open and slid inside with a knife in his hand. Moving slowly along the wall, he waited for his eyes to adjust to the reduced light of the space before taking any significant action. He scanned the darkness—left, right, in front of him, as well as up to the ceiling. He could see Vared to his left who gestured for them to move forward.

Karid found nothing noteworthy. Some chairs stacked, a few carpets on the floor, not even security cameras. *What the crek is this place?*

The group met by the room Devik saw which took up a large portion of that corner of the building. When they entered, the males growled when they saw half the room was actually a cell. Dried blood stained the floor and the cot, but no one was there.

Westov rushed to a workstation across the room. He began typing and downloading information. Smiling, he said, "I don't know what's here, but I will get everything copied."

Rachel pursed her lips.

"This building doesn't make sense." She walked back to the main open area and walked down the center of the room.

Karid and Vared followed her.

"What are you thinking?" asked Vared.

"One cell in this huge space. No quarters for guards. Not even a food synthesizer. Just chairs and rugs." She kicked the edge of one of the carpets. "They're not even dusty. Why aren't they rolled up and stored like the chairs?"

Karid thought Rachel was onto something. He crouched and lifted a rug. A huge grin spread across his face.

"Probably to hide something like this." He pointed to a hatch in the floor.

Vared comm'd for the others to help. They found twelve hatches. Surrounding one with weapons drawn, Vared nodded for Karid to open it. Devik illuminated the darkness with a portable light. All they could see was a ladder. Vared gestured for Devik and Ash'n to go down.

Karid focused on keeping his breathing calm as they waited in silence. The males returned.

"It appears to be a tunnel leading north," said Devik quietly. "Evidence of recent activity. No security cameras in the section we traveled."

Karid closed the hatch. Vared motioned for them to move to another. They discovered the four center hatches held supplies, including weapons. The outermost hatches were tunnels leading in eight different directions.

After they investigated the last floor opening, Vared ordered them to replace the carpets and ensure there was no evidence they had been there.

"Get your grappling gear and meet in the clearing to the south. Tesix, land there and pick us up in five minutes," Vared said.

Everyone hustled silently to follow his commands. On the shuttle, Westov handed the data disk he copied to Vared as they stripped out of their gear.

"Devik, ensure we continue to monitor this building. I will brief the king in person. I will strongly suggest multiple teams to simultaneously explore the tunnels and see where they lead."

Vared speared each of them with a hard glance. "No one speaks of what we discovered."

Did we just find where the traitors meet?

On the shuttle, Ash'n pulled Karid aside and informed him of his father's neurological disease. Karid wasn't sure how he felt about it. It was good to have an explanation for the highly uncharacteristic behavior toward females, but his father's words still stung.

After they docked at the palace, Karid's need to see Ava overrode his stomach's hunger. He walked swiftly to their quarters. On the table sat thermal and cooling units that contained food for him. His heart swelled when he saw her asleep on the couch in the living area, her head at an awkward angle. *She tried to wait up for me.*

He took the tablet from her hand and gently adjusted her position to make her more comfortable. Glancing at the display, it looked like she was recording recipes. He covered her with a small blanket and sat in a chair to eat. His eyes roamed affectionately over her slumbering form, her hair awry and soft snuffles breaking the quiet of the night. Peace settled into his bones just being near her.

When he finished eating and cleaning up after himself, he removed his boots and weapons harness. Not wanting to disturb her, he left her on the couch and took a quick shower. Naked, he drew back the covers of the bed before he went to tenderly pick her up. She snuggled into his chest without waking as he carried her to bed. He slid in next to her and ensured she would be warm enough. Wrapping his arms and tail around her soft body, he fell into a dreamless sleep.

Chapter 32

KARID'S MUSKY CINNAMON and pepper scent filled Ava's nostrils and his warmth surrounded her. His hand pressed hot on her spine and his chest rose and fell beneath her cheek. *I like waking up this way.*

She lay there enjoying the sleepy comfort and safety of his body holding her close. Not wanting to move and disrupt the bliss, she blew out a silent breath when her bladder started making itself known. *Damn, I have to get up.*

Not wanting to wake him, she tried unsuccessfully to slip out from under his heavy arms.

"Don't leave yet."

"I have to pee. I'll be right back."

Ava protested when he hugged her. "Hey, no squeezing right now."

His sleepy chuckle rumbled under her ear, and he let her go.

After taking care of her most urgent need, Ava washed her hands and brushed her teeth. After a quick swipe of a comb through her bedhead hair, she went back to the bedroom and felt her heart trip over itself. On his back, Karid's hands were behind his head and his beefy arms dominated the pillow. The covers slipped down to his hips. His eyes turned molten silver as he watched her every movement making her pussy throb. *Damn, he's sexy.*

She crawled into bed and cuddled up to him. He rolled onto his side and embraced her. The fingers of one hand combed through her hair. *I love it when he does that.*

"How did the mission go?

"There was no one there, but we found enough for further investigation. I can't say more. I'm sure Traxen and Vared are organizing something now."

"Good. How do you feel?"

His hips pushed against her and his hard length poked her thigh.

"Aroused."

Laughing softly, she said, "I meant about going on the mission. I know you were concerned about remaining a warrior. I just wondered if last night made a difference."

His eyes became unfocused as his thoughts turned inward. Her hands caressed his chest as she waited.

"I didn't realize it until now, but I never even worried about whether I was fit to go on the mission. I just focused on finding the males who took us and put you in danger." He grinned. "It gave me hope that I can continue as a warrior." Pausing, he said, "Unless you don't want me to."

"I would never expect you to give up a big part of yourself, Karid. I like that you're a warrior. I'll like if you're not, so long as you do it for the right reasons, not because of self-doubt or fear."

Taking his time, he kissed her until she was breathless, then he pulled back slightly.

"I am the luckiest male in the universe."

Her hand burrowed under the covers and grasped his cock. Stroking it, she smiled lasciviously.

"I predict you're about to get even luckier."

After she brought him to the point of growls and hips twitching, he disengaged himself from her fist and licked his way down her body. Spreading her thighs wide, he used his lips and fingers to give her two rousing orgasms, then speared with his cock. She moaned and became incoherent when he proceeded to pound her into delicious oblivion.

Sated, she savored the press of his weight above her as he rested on his elbows and kissed her. A surprised "Oh" left her lips when he rolled onto his back taking her with him.

"What should we do today, *raralumia*?"

"I'd like to go back to the cabin at some point, unless you'd rather stay at the palace."

"We can do that." His tail pet her ass and the small of her spine.

"I'd like to stop by Phoenix House for a visit first. I can go alone if you prefer."

"Why wouldn't I go with you?"

She lifted her head to watch his expression.

"I'm not sure how you feel about being around Zuvgran hybrids or Largon."

Wrinkling his brow, he said, "I know they had nothing to do with my captivity. Most of them are younglings."

"If you're comfortable with it, I'd love to introduce you to them. I think you'll like them and be impressed with the setup."

"Phoenix House, then cabin. We have a plan." Smiling, his tail tickled her waist.

She shrieked, "Stop that." Playfully, she slapped his chest. "Food first."

"As you command."

Younglings swarmed Ava and Karid when they arrived at Phoenix House. Ava handed off some containers to Herrah after introducing Karid to the female. Most of the younglings followed Herrah hoping for treats.

"Karid, I'd like you to meet Teeka and Crutaw. They were both on Straxis before coming here. This is Lieutenant Karid Wurvez." The teenagers greeted him with smiles, Teeka's noticeably more hesitant. "I want to give him a tour of the new building."

Crutaw, a Romittel-Zuvgran hybrid with brown skin and a high, narrow forehead topped by baldness, said, "We should be able to move in soon."

The four of them walked toward the large structure appeared to have large trees growing up out of the center.

Ava pointed. "Those trees are actually in a courtyard and playground surrounded by the building. There will be additional plants added to the facade to incorporate more of the natural habitat."

Karid scanned and noted the security features. "How many younglings will be living here?"

"Over five hundred. The rest are adults who have been caring for them all these years."

"This is a huge undertaking."

"Well worth it, I think."

Teeka whispered to Ava, "Is this the friend you've been helping?" Ava nodded.

"He's a large, strong warrior. I doubt he needs much help," said Crutaw.

Karid looked at the youngling and said quietly, "Everyone needs help sometimes, Crutaw. It's not always easy for those who are used to protecting others to admit they require assistance for themselves." He paused. "You have the look of a youngling who has been training as a warrior."

Crutaw puffed up his chest proudly. "Ronan and Largon have been teaching me."

"Good. If you learn nothing else from me, young warrior, learn this. No matter how strong you become, do not hesitate to ask for help from those who care about you most. There is no room for shame amongst those who love each other." *Oh. My. God. I think I'm going to cry.*

The teenager appeared thoughtful. "I will remember your words."

Karid dipped his chin and clapped the youngling on his shoulder. "Now show me where you will be living."

Ava let the teenagers do most of the talking during the tour. She watched Karid interact with other younglings and loved how comfortable he was with all of them. He expressed genuine interest in each child. When he picked up one of the toddlers and made them laugh, she thought her ovaries were going to burst. *He would be such a good dad. We're not ready for that yet—if ever—but I have no doubts about his abilities.*

When they reached the rear of the building, a large transport landed in the clearing. Surprised, Ava hurried out to see what was going on. Karid followed quickly behind.

A ramp opened up. Talia, Emmy, Ronan, and Largon stepped out. Warriors began filing out carrying headboards and mattress frames. Talia looked at each, called out a name, and Emmy told the warriors which room to deliver it to.

Ava said, "Hey, guys, what's with all this?"

"Emmy had a great idea. We allowed each of the kids to choose their own beds from a selection available. Traxen secured the use of an industrial synthesizer and these guys are helping set them up," Talia said. "We even let them pick out their own bedding."

Emmy shifted on her feet. "I just wanted them to have something they chose right from the start. It can be demoralizing in a group home if you're not treated as an individual."

Ava hugged her friend. "It's a fantastic idea. I'm glad you thought of it."

She introduced Karid to Ronan and Largon. They sized each other up, then Karid offered his arm for a warrior's clasp to each.

"I understand the two of you have been rescuing younglings and keeping them safe for a long time. A worthy occupation," Karid said.

"Largon rescued me, then when I was old enough, I began to help."

"You're a cousin to Vared, correct?"

"Yes."

"Well, nobody's perfect." Everyone laughed.

Largon spoke, "I heard you were a recent guest in a Zuvgran facility. Please know I am sorry for whatever treatment you received there."

Karid's tail flicked once. "I do not hold all Zuvgran responsible, Largon. Just the ones directly involved and any that may have ordered it."

"Your friends have missed you," the older male said. "You are fortunate to have so many who worry about your well-being."

"I know. You have many as well." Karid gestured to the building of younglings.

Largon smiled. "Thank you."

"Is there anything I can do to help?" Karid looked at the mountain of deliveries.

Ava conversed with the women in between their directing warriors to the proper rooms, while Karid helped carry items, too. He worked with Ronan and Largon and more than once she heard him laugh. Once the beds were set up, the warriors set up an assembly line like they did on Talonka Six and the mattresses and sheets moved indoors. By then, the younglings waited in their rooms, excited to help make their beds.

Happy chatter filled Phoenix House. Ava couldn't help but smile each time one of the children wanted to show off their new bed. *They've been through so much, yet there's such joy in them.*

Ava and Karid returned to the flitter to fly to the cabin. He started the engines but didn't take off. Ava glanced at him staring at Phoenix House with glassy eyes.

"Karid? Is everything okay?" Concerned, she reached for his hand.

"So many younglings that would have been enslaved or died, just for existing. One of them, a Pellotian-Zuvgran hybrid, told me how happy he was when our healers fixed his wings so his shoulders no longer ached. His whole life, Ava, the poor youngling lived in unnecessary physical pain because of the cruelty surrounding him." She squeezed his hand.

"Oh, sweetheart. I know it's heartbreaking, but look at them now. They have people who love them and care for them. They have a community of people who have been protecting them and that community keeps expanding."

"Largon says he's been rescuing hybrids for forty solars. Those colonies he's hiding—most of them started from the first younglings he rescued when they became adults."

"He's a good male."

"He is."

"Nothing like the ones who held me captive."

"No. He's a protector, just like you."

Karid lifted their clasped hands to his lips and kissed her fingers.

"I needed to meet everyone here today. Thank you."

"Let's go to the cabin, Karid."

Karid insisted on helping Ava make evening meal. They put on some music and worked easily together. Occasionally, he would surprise her by hugging her from behind, singing lyrics in her ear, and spinning her around.

As they ate, Karid said, "I planned a romantic evening for us before we true mated to make it special. But I don't want to wait." His hopeful face made her melt. *He's such a romantic.*

"It will be special because we're making a commitment to each other. I don't need all the trappings."

"I did make you this, though." He handed her a box wrapped in gold cloth.

Carefully unwrapping it, she opened the present and gasped. Her eyes burned.

"You made this? It's beautiful."

Lifting the stone sculpture gently, she turned it to view his creation from every angle. "It looks like a single rose. The detail is amazing, Karid. I love it." She leaned over and kissed him.

"I found the red stone in the crate and remembered reading how roses are a symbol of love on Earth. I wanted something that would last as a token of my eternal devotion to you." *Oh, shit. I'm going to cry.*

"I'll treasure it always," she said through the thickness in her throat. She carefully placed the rose on the table and sat on his lap. Placing her palms on his cheeks, she kissed him, then gazed into his eyes.

"Take me to bed and true mate with me, Karid." She giggled at how fast he stood and carried her to the bedroom.

Chapter 33

TAKING CARE WITH the precious cargo in his arms, Karid hurried to the bedroom when Ava commanded him to true mate with her in that sweet voice. He didn't want to rush their mating. In fact, he planned to make love to her slowly and worship every part of her beautiful body.

Once he reached their destination, he gently sat her on the bed. Kneeling, he took off her shoes and socks. Her hands rested on his shoulders. He massaged her small feet and tiny toes. She groaned as the tension left her soles. Her head fell forward and they touched foreheads.

Sharing her breath, he said, "Allow me to undress you and treat you as the gift you are, *raralumia*."

"As you wish, Karid." Her green eyes twinkled in the dwindling light of the day.

Sliding under the hem of her T-shirt, his callused fingers smoothed a path upward baring her pale skin to his eager eyes. Small gasps fell from her full, pink lips and goosebumps rose on her arms. Pulling the fabric over her head, he tossed it aside and touched her unruly hair.

"I love how silky and springy your curls are. They tempt me to play with them constantly."

She reached behind his nape and released his leather hair tie.

"I like when you comb my hair. Take off your shirt. I want to touch you."

Reaching behind him, he tugged off his too and sent it in the same direction as hers. Tenderly, he pressed his lips to her face in barely-there kisses. Her forehead, brows, eyes, cheeks, and jaw all received his patient attention. With slow movements, his hands stroked her arms and his tail caressed her calves. Sighs left her mouth and her fingernails lightly scratched his skin. Her scent perfumed the air.

"Twenty-seven," he whispered before skimming her lips with his.

"Twenty-seven?"

"Sun-kissed dots on this gorgeous face."

"You counted my freckles?"

"Only the ones on your cheeks and nose so far. When I wake before you, I memorize your features while you slumber. It soothes me."

"If I didn't love you so much, I might find that creepy. But since I've watched you sleep as well, I understand." Her pink tongue wet her lips. "Kiss me some more."

Their mouths met and their tongues languidly connected in a slow dance. Minutes passed before he moved to her neck and shoulders. Alternating between the flat and the tip of his tongue, he licked a sensuous path over her satiny flesh. His fingers unhooked her bra and he tugged it from her arms without ceasing his explorations. Her hands clenched in his unbound hair when the hard points of her nipples brushed his chest.

His hands burrowed under her shorts and panties to squeeze her ass. When he tugged on her clothes, she lifted her hips to make it easier for him to slide them down her legs.

"Lay down on your stomach, Ava."

She scrunched her nose but arranged herself as he instructed. Resting her head on her raised arms, she turned it sideways to watch him strip off the rest of his clothes. He sat on the bed, his hip touching hers, and began massaging her shoulders and back.

"Oh, that feels wonderful."

Her body relaxed further as he gently rubbed her. He moved to straddle her hips, his erection resting in the crease of her ass. Interspersing kisses and licks with his strokes, he lavished attention on her bare flesh. Scooting down, he changed his target areas.

Time stood still as he used his hands, lips, and tongue on her calves, knees, thighs, and her gorgeous ass. He kneaded the plump mounds, lightly pricking them with his claws, then mouthed gently with tiny licks, occasionally nipping with his fangs. Her legs shifted restlessly allowing him small teasing peeks at her glistening pussy. The aroma of *wimma* and sugar grew thicker around them.

Sitting back on his heels at her feet, his erection throbbed. A contented rumbling emanated from his chest. *I love touching her.*

"Turn over, my love," he rasped. Lazily, she rolled her body to rest on her back.

His cock twitched when she lay before him, her eyes glazed with pleasure. The dips and valleys of her satiny flesh drew his gaze in so many directions. Red curls framed her softened face and the shock of color against the gray sheets brought to mind thoughts of a sunburst.

He began his ministrations at her ankles working his way up her body, his tail leading the way with tender strokes. As he caressed, licked, kissed, and nipped over each of her body parts, he began speaking.

"When I began calling you *raralumia*, I had no idea how accurate the endearment was, Ava. Your strength." Kiss. "Your compassion." Lick. "Your loving heart." Stroke. "Your wisdom." Nip. "Your calm." Suck. "Your fiery anger." Caress. "Your beauty." Peck. "Your passion." He bypassed her core and moved to her stomach. "Your humor." Knead. "Your optimism." Fondle. "Your never-ending support." Nibble.

"I love everything about you. You have brought love and laughter into this poor male's life in a way I never dreamed." She moaned and clasped his head when he licked and suckled her erect nipples. He rubbed his cheeks against her breasts, then gently bit her nubs. Her head fell back when his tail stroked her neck.

Working his way back to where her scent originated, he continued.

"When I need you, you are there with an open heart and loving arms. You lift me up when I am down and lift me higher when I'm not." Lifting her legs over his shoulders, he inhaled deeply. He licked the wetness from the bottom of her opening to her clit and stopped. Looking up, he waited until she glanced at him.

"You see me. All of me." The love in her eyes softened further.

"I do see you, Karid, and you are worth seeing and loving."

Her words settled into his heart, warming him with her truth. Watching her watch him, he used the tip of his tongue to lick small circles around her clit. Taking his time, he steadily built her pleasure. Her gasps and moans delighted him. Her hips chasing his mouth and her hands clenching his hair thrilled him. When he closed his lips and slid his fang over her engorged clit, her orgasm elated him.

As she shook, writhed, and trembled, he licked lower where her juices flowed freely. His tongue entered her and explored. Her pussy rippled and squeezed.

He licked and sucked and fingered her while she wailed his name in between commands of "More" and "Right there." Two climaxes later, face wet with her pleasure, he nuzzled her inner thighs and placed gentle kisses on her sensitive flesh.

Rising, he settled between her legs and placed his weeping cock at her core. Entering her swollen pussy slowly, he buried himself deep within her and halted. *Crek. So hot and tight.*

"I want to be the one who chases any shadows from your eyes allowing your light to shine brightly. I want to be the shoulder you cry on when you're sad. I want to be the male who keeps you safe when you feel fear. I want to have the privilege of giving you all my love and laughter, my joy and pain, and receiving all of yours. I want to support your dreams and help you fulfill them. My deepest desire is that you wake each day and rest each night secure in my everlasting devotion to you. Will you allow that, Ava, and true mate with me now?"

Silent tears slid from her eyes, but her expression showed her joy and contentment. His heart thundered in his chest and his breath caught in his lungs while his cock throbbed inside her while he anxiously awaited her answer.

"Karid." She placed her small hand over his heart. "You are a grizzly of a male with a teddy bear heart. No one else can chase away the shadows with me better than you. You have a true warrior's heart—protective and caring. All that you say you want and desire with me, I want to be for you. From now until the end of time. True mate with me, sweetheart. Make me yours in all ways and I'll make you mine."

His breath released on a long exhale and his heart pounded harder in his chest. Fang elongating, he reached for her hands and entwined his fingers in hers resting them alongside her head. His eyes never left her gaze as hips began to move and his tail played with her nipples.

Slowly, inexorably, their rhythm grew faster and their desire burned brightly in the night. He ground his hips on his downstrokes and rubbed his base node against her clit as her hips rose to meet his. Their combined scents made him dizzy with hunger. Moans, gasps, groans, and grunts echoed around them. She began rippling around his cock and her back arched.

"Yes, Karid. Oh my god, yes."

He bent to lick her shoulder. When her pussy squeezed him tightly, he bit her with his fangs and she screamed. When she bit his shoulder, his ass clenched further and his cock vibrated. He pumped faster, the constriction of her around him sending him over the edge into an abyss of rapture. Ava's eyes widened as another climax hit her right on the heels of the first. He came even longer with colored lights blurring the edges of his vision. *Sweet Goddess. What was that?*

Panting, he rested his weight on his elbows before rolling them to their sides. His cock remained nestled in its favorite place. Brushing her damp hair from her glowing face, he reverently kissed her lips.

Her chest rose and fell quickly with her gasps for breath. Her soft hands caressed his face and chest.

"Karid, have you been holding out on me?"

"What do you mean?"

"I'm pretty sure your cock just vibrated."

"I thought I imagined that."

"Nope." She popped the p. "Definitely vibrated."

Chuckling, he pulled her even closer. "Must be the true mating, although I've never heard of it happening."

She grasped a handful of his hair and used it to trace his clan marking.

"Uh, Karid."

"Yes, my love."

"Your clan marking just turned to gold."

"What?" He looked down in amazement. Then he brushed her curls from her shoulders and froze. He closed his eyes and took a slow, deep breath before his fingers traced the clan marking now visible on her skin. She looked down, tears falling, and placed her fingers beneath his chin forcing him to look at her.

"We're fated mates?" Wonder filled her voice.

Tears filled his eyes as he hugged her tightly. "The Goddess has blessed our mating, *raralumia*." *Thank you, Goddess. I will do my best to be worthy of this glorious female.*

"I'm speechless."

He drew back and lifted an eyebrow. "Hardly, you just spoke."

Giggling, she shook her head. Then her expression turned serious and her hand rested on his face.

"I love you, Karid Wurvez, with all that I am and all that I will ever be."

Humor forgotten, he raised his hand to cover hers.

"Ava Taylor, I love you and I will spend my life ensuring your trust in my love never wavers."

They lazily kissed and their hands caressed each other with tender touches. His tail wound around her ankle and lifted her leg over his.

"Want to see if my cock will vibrate again?" He smirked.

"Fuck, yes." *Goddess, she's perfect for me.*

Recap

Races thus far

Human - Enough said.

Svesti - Warrior Race. About seven feet tall, skin in various shades of bronze, semi-retractable fangs, tails, and retractable claws. Ruled by a King. Honorable race protecting many regions of space from the Zuvgran, including near Earth. Most Svesti females died or were rendered infertile thirty Earth years prior due to a virus released by the Zuvgran. Plural is Svesti.

Crestillian - Reptilian Race.

Durelian - Mercenary Race. About seven feet tall, orange skin, three bulbous black eyes.

Ermipa - Mining Race. About four feet tall, furry, round head, oval eyes.

Estalan - Sybaritic Race. Known for its quality liquors and drugs.

Frezzian - Mercenary Race. Adverse to personal risk. Considered dishonorable.

Jalaxian - Warrior Race. About seven feet tall, blue skin, fangs, retractable claws, and tail. Considered honorable. Many work as mercenaries after the Zuvgran decimated their world fifty Earth years ago.

Mostiffian - Mammalian Race.

Nulorian - Mammalian Race.

Pellotian - Avian Race. Green skin and wings.

Praxite - Mammalian Race. Lavender skin and tails. Females have three breasts.

Romittel - Mammalian Race.

Straxian - Mammalian Race. Brown skin

Wrestikan - Mammalian Race. Four arms and red skin. Home planet was Himita Prime.

Zuvgran - Warrior Race. About seven feet tall, gray skin, fangs, claws, and horns. Ruled by an Emperor. Dishonorable race that invades planets to strip them of their resources and take the inhabitants as slaves. Considered violent. Plural is Zuvgran.

Planets and Space Stations thus far

Earth - Really not the center of the universe as humans might believe.

Costonia - Svesti Home World.

Crestillia - Crestillian Home World. Zuvgran-controlled.

Himita Prime - Wrestikan Home World. Zuvgran-controlled.

Millus - Unoccupied planet outside of Costonian galaxy.

Nulorn - Trading planet halfway between Pellotia and Talonka Six.

Pellotia - Pellotian Home World. Zuvgran-controlled.

Praxis - Zuvgran-controlled.

Romitte - Zuvgran-controlled. Closest planet to Lestanus system.

Straxis - Agricultural and trading world. Sixth planet in the Lestanus system.

Talonka Six - Mining world closer to Costonia than Earth. Fourth planet in the Lestanus system.

Theron - Space Station approximately one quarter of the distance from Earth to Costonia.

XB9428B - Uninhabited planet, home to a Zuvgran lab.

Svesti Houses

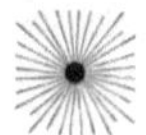 **Davelk** - Ruling House of Costonia.

 **Binova** - Primarily merchants.

 **Fresida** - Primarily educators and scientists.

 **Glixon** - Primarily merchants.

 **Kreliz** - Primarily scientists.

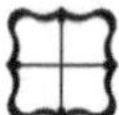 **Midnar** - Primarily agriculture.

 **Nuxar** - One of the two Houses that strictly adhere to the old ways of worship.

 **Ruxila** - Primarily agriculture.

 **Srotix** - One of the two Houses that strictly adhere to the old ways of worship.

 **Troliv** - Primarily merchants.

 **Vramel** - Primarily warriors and educators.

 **Yula** - Many Svesti healers come from House Yula.

 **Terran** - New human clan marking.

Characters

Humans

Ava Taylor - Canadian, chef.

Lin Chang - Chinese, botanist.

Rachel Llewellyn - British, MI-6.

Emmy Norton - Australian, hacker.

Natasha Petrov - Russian, medical doctor.

Talia Sullivan - American, U.S. Ambassador of Interplanetary Relations.

Daniel Taylor - Canadian, detective, Ava's adoptive father.

Svesti

King Traxen Sovex of House Davelk - King of the Svesti.

Lieutenant Karid Wurvez of House Binova - Head tactical officer on the *Invictus,* second in command of the space cruiser.

Lieutenant Triv'n Brauvix of House Kreliz - Communications officer on the *Invictus.*

Lieutenant Hozan Crulex of House Yula - Science office on the *Invictus.*

Commander Vared Durek of House Ruxila - Commander of the space cruiser, *Invictus,* the flagship of the Svesti military. First cousin to the king.

Merix Hunnek of House Nuxar - Head of aquiponics area on the *Invictus.* Rank - Major.

Grulen Jevax of House Midnar - Warrior.

Gal'n Kalix of House Binova - Security officer.

Rexus Markham of House Yula - Healer on the *Invictus*. Rank - Captain.

Nerid Mantoor of House Glixon - Warrior.

Reesa Naturu – Head cook at the palace.

Talen Previv of House Fresida - Warrior. Head Cook on the *Invictus*.

Ash'n Rivezt of House Yula - Head healer on the *Invictus*. Rank - Captain.

Narilla Rivezt of House Yula - Council member, Main Medical Advisor, Master Healer, Ash'n's grandmother.

Klero Rovex of House Glixon - Warrior.

Nerob Sinoaz of House Troliv - Healer on the *Invictus*. Rank - Captain.

Lerix Sproid of House Kreliz - Warrior.

Lieutenant Devik Tolvex of House Vramel - Head security officer on the *Invictus*.

Pex Tolvex of House Vramel - One of Devik's older brothers.

Rassix Tolvex of House Vramel - One of Devik's older brothers.

Solen Tolvex of House Vramel - One of Devik's older brothers.

Clen'n Vepiv of House Nuxar - Warrior and medic.

Lieutenant Leriv Volax of House Kreliz - Supply Master on the *Invictus*.

Lieutenant Gat'n Wrox of House Fresida - Head engineer on *Invictus*.

Drikon Wurvez – Merchant, Karid's father.
Brestov Xoriv of House Fresida - Security officer.

Zuvgran

Largon d'Ayen - Jorn d'Olorg's best friend and surrogate father to Ronan.

Other

Ronan d'Olorg -Svesti-Zuvgran hybrid. Son of Jorn and Saletta.
Crutaw - Romittel-Zuvgran hybrid.
Herrah - Wrestikan-Zuvgran hybrid.
Molla - Jalaxian female.
Talos - Pellotian teacher.
Yostal - Mostiffian-Zuvgran hybrid.

Svesti Words thus far

Bataavi - Cherished one.
Bloniv - Spice similar to Earth's turmeric, but grows in tube-like clusters.
Brellia - Small, rumik-filled pastry.
Caliana - Beautiful female.
Cold season - Comparable to Earth's winter in the northern hemisphere.
Crek - Fuck.

Drelix - Spice similar to Earth's ginger, but grows in tube-like clusters.

Estrecaro - Beloved grandson.

Forliza - Flower similar to Earth's jasmine, but with purple petals.

Harvest season - Comparable to Earth's autumn/fall in the northern hemisphere.

Hot season - Comparable to Earth's summer in the northern hemisphere.

Kirani - Female feline found in the wild. Similar to Earth's lioness.

Leringa - Fruit that has a hint of spice when ingested.

Lobile - Purple tuber, cross between Earth's potato and sweet potato.

Lunar - Month.

Maxiem - A large animal that resembles a hybrid between Earth's ox and cow. Used as a source of meat, milk and beasts of burden.

Mentok - Similar to Earth's myna bird, but larger and with plumage reminiscent of an Earth's peacock. Chatters incessantly.

Milara - Small brown bird with periwinkle/white chest and underside of wings. Known for its cunning.

Naroon - Large furry animal, similar to Earth's ape, with blue fur. Gregarious and known to be silly in their family groups.

Pertiza - Creamy yellow sweet yogurt made from maxiem milk.

Picana - Little one.

Plostiv - Meat similar to Earth's chicken.

Raralumia - Rare light.

Renewal season - Comparable to Earth's spring in the northern hemisphere.

Ristern - Ermipa organ that filters dangerous gases.

Rulah - Small, furry animal similar to Earth's cat.

Rumik - Meat similar to Earth's ground beef. Comes from maxiem.

Sedapi - Vegetable similar to Earth's celery, but white.

Shurlix - Similar to Earth's tomato, but yellow.

Sibella – Vegetable similar to Earth's onion, but tubular in shape.

Solar - Year.

Tempika - Green berries that taste tart, but also sweet.

Trezoura - Capital city of Costonia.

Trulet - Similar to Earth's oak tree, but with dark blue leaves and orange bark.

Valadium - Steel-like ore when tempered is one of the hardest substances known in the universe.

Wimma - Blue citrus fruit similar to Earth's lime.

Woolah - Red flower that blooms on Costonia during Harvest season.

Yeddom - Orange bean-like vegetable that tastes like Earth's asparagus.

Young – Baby/infant.

Youngling – Child.

Yuffa - Plant similar to Earth's aloe, but with orange ball-like leaves.

Other
Ermipa

Ristern - Extra organ that filters out air impurities.

Pellotian

Annum - Year.

Zuvgran

Grak - Fuck.

Author's Note

Wow. For those of you who are newsletter subscribers, you probably already know that I tend to start with a loose outline and then let the characters tell me their stories. I have to admit Karid and Ava surprised me.

My original outline did have Karid with an overbearing father and enduring captivity at the hands of the Zuvgran. However, he would joke his way through the ordeal and deny bouts of PTSD afterwards. Ava's backstory included being an orphan after her parents died in a crash that she survived. Obviously, my plan did not come to fruition as I expected.

When I was writing *Devik*, writer's block stalled me partway through the process. The scenes in this book—from Ava meeting with Traxen until she cried in the shower after Karid told her of his captivity—demanded to be written. Ten thousand words changed everything and my outline for *Karid* went into the trash. *Devik* flowed easily after that.

I sat there stunned. Not because my writer's block disappeared, but because of the depth of depravity both Karid and Ava suffered and triumphed over. It may sound strange to some, but I'm honored they chose me to tell their tale. It's also the reason the prologue refrained from my usual snarky author comments—it felt disrespectful to go that route with their story.

I know some readers may feel frustrated having so much of previous books show up again in the early portions of *Karid*. Ava needed that time to slowly build her trust and willingness to truly share her early history with Karid. I did my best to tell the worst of the worst after the fact, rather than experiencing it in the moment to keep the focus on their relationship, not their trauma.

Karid is my favorite book in the Svesti Fated Mates series thus far. The amount of strength it takes to trust someone with your deepest, most shame-inducing pain is courageous and creates a solid basis to work through it together and everything that comes after. I foresee a wonderful future for them.

- Wavy

Thank you for reading Karid and Ava's story. If you enjoyed this book, please leave an online review where you purchased it. This lets other readers know whether they might enjoy it, too!

If you'd like to hear about Wavy's other books, you can sign up for her newsletter or find her social media links at wavymartin.com.